ABOUT THE AUTHOR

Janet Gover grew up in outback Australia, surrounded by wide open spaces, horses ... and many, many books.

When her cat lets her actually sit in her chair, she writes stories of strong women, rural communities and falling in love. Her novel *The Library at Wagtail Ridge* won the 2023 Romance Writers of Australia Romantic Book of the Year Award in the romantic elements category. Janet's books have also won the Epic Romantic Novel of the Year Award presented by the Romantic Novelists' Association in the UK, and several chapter awards from the Romance Writers of America.

As Juliet Bell, in collaboration with Alison May, she rewrites misunderstood classic fiction, with an emphasis on heroes who are not so heroic.

Her favourite food is tomato. She spends too much time playing silly computer games, and is an enthusiastic, if not always successful, cook.

Janet loves to hear from readers—so do drop her a line.

janetgover.com

facebook.com/janetgoverbooks

Twitter: @janet_gover

Also by Janet Gover

The Lawson Sisters
Close to Home
The Library at Wagtail Ridge

(Available in ebook)
Flight to Coorah Creek
Christmas at Coorah Creek
The Wild One
Little Girl Lost

The
LAWSON
LEGACY

JANET GOVER

First Published 2024
First Australian Paperback Edition 2024
ISBN 9781867230069

Published by
HQ Fiction
An imprint of Harlequin Enterprises (Australia) Pty Limited (ABN 47 001 180 918), a subsidiary of HarperCollins Publishers Australia Pty Limited (ABN 36 009 913 517)
Level 19, 201 Elizabeth St
SYDNEY NSW 2000
AUSTRALIA

® and TM (apart from those relating to FSC®) are trademarks of Harlequin Enterprises (Australia) Pty Limited or its corporate affiliates. Trademarks indicated with ® are registered in Australia, New Zealand and in other countries.

A catalogue record for this book is available from the National Library of Australia
www.librariesaustralia.nla.gov.au

Printed and bound in Australia by McPherson's Printing Group

MIX
Paper | Supporting
responsible forestry
FSC
www.fsc.org
FSC® C001695

I don't have a sister so this one is for
my brother, Ken. Just because.

PROLOGUE

18 years ago

Four figures slipped behind the shed next to the school sports oval. Kayla carefully peeped around the corner at the classrooms they had just left. If a teacher saw them, they'd get into so much trouble. Kayla shuddered at the thought of what her mum and dad would say. They'd expect this of her older sister Lizzie, but not her; she was the good one. She really didn't want to be here at all, but they were the four musketeers—all for one and one for all. She couldn't stay behind while the others had an adventure without her.

Her best friend Jen waved an urgent hand at her. 'Come on, before someone sees you.'

Further ahead, Lizzie and Jen's big brother Mitch were climbing through a hole in the cyclone wire fence that enclosed the school yard. Jen was next, but as Kayla followed, her skirt snagged on a bit of wire.

'Wait.' She tried to slip the fabric off, but it was too well caught.

'Hurry up, Kayla. You kids need to keep up.' Lizzie took hold of the skirt and pulled firmly. There was a ripping noise, but Kayla was free.

The sisters darted away to the shadows under a tree, where Mitch and Jen were waiting. Kayla examined the rip in her skirt. How would she explain that to her mother? This was the first time she'd worn the skirt. She'd seen the pretty fabric in a shop and her mother had bought it. They'd made the skirt together then her mother had drawn a lovely pattern of flowers around the hem. They had embroidered those flowers together too, and now they were ruined. Kayla could try to fix it, but even if she covered the tear, she would know it was there. The lovely skirt would never be the same again.

Somewhere not far away a dog barked and all four of them froze. Kayla's heart was pounding in her chest. When they'd discussed this, it had seemed such a great adventure; the four musketeers skipping school to sneak into the showgrounds for a preview of this weekend's annual show. But now they were actually doing it, she wasn't having fun at all.

'We should go back,' she whispered, but her companions weren't listening.

She followed as the older two darted between the trees towards the road at the end of the block. On the other side of that road, a high fence indicated the showgrounds. Sounds of voices and machinery came from inside.

Lizzie grinned. 'They're still setting up. We should be able to sneak in and no-one will see us.' As always, Kayla's big sister was the ringleader of their little gang. Mitch followed because he was her boyfriend. Jen followed because she desperately wanted to be like the teenagers, and because she adored her brother. Kayla followed for the very same reasons.

Lizzie led the way across the road and along the showground fence. She pulled on the wire mesh in a place hidden from the road by trees. 'The other kids said it was here.' She tugged again and two panels separated. It wasn't a big hole but it was enough for them to slip through one at a time. Kayla held her damaged skirt very close to her body, wishing that, for once, she'd worn jeans to school.

From there, they sprinted to the nearest building, a long set of wooden stables. Lizzie and Mitch would be back here in a couple of days, preparing their horses for competition. Kayla too, with her beloved pony Ginger. But for now, their focus was sideshow alley—or what would be sideshow alley when it was done.

Lizzie give the younger girls a stern look. 'You two be careful. We're just here for a bit of fun and to look around. Don't get lost and be careful … Don't get hurt fooling around with the half-built rides.'

Kayla never went on the rides at the show. She didn't see the point of scaring herself silly. They seemed even scarier today, the half-constructed Octopus and the Big Zipper looking like the skeletons of huge monsters. Even the giant Ferris wheel looked menacing as the bare iron frame towered above her, devoid of the lights and music that drew teenagers to it. The workers climbing over the rides with their tools looked like insects serving their queen. The amusement stalls, though, were a different matter. There was skill involved in them. You had to put the ball in the mouth of the clown at just the right moment. Or throw the balls at the skittles with just the right strength. If you were good enough, you could win a prize. A reward for your skill.

As they ducked between the marquees and stands, trying to avoid being spotted, Kayla stopped. One stall was already set up. Lying on the flat counter in front of her were some Kewpie dolls, their dresses sparkling in the sunlight.

'Look, Jen.' She grabbed her friend's hand to stop her walking past. 'Aren't they pretty?'

'They are. Are you going to try to win one on Saturday?'

'I never win.' Kayla wanted one of those dolls so much she could feel it like a pain inside her gut. Every year she tried to win one and every year she failed. Some of the stalls had them for sale, but the biggest and best dolls were the prize dolls. Kayla moved closer to the stall. A few dolls had already been removed from their packing. One in particular was lying a little apart from the rest. Kayla took one look at it and fell in love. The doll had blonde hair and a beautiful white dress covered with sequins. It could have been a wedding dress. Her pink plastic shoulders had been painted with glitter. She wasn't one of the sad dolls that had travelled too many miles from show to show, covered with dust and its beauty fading. This doll was new and clean and perfect.

'She looks like a beautiful bride.' Kayla's ten-year-old heart was pounding even more now than when they'd slipped away from school.

'Come on, Lizzie and Mitch are over by the stables. We need to find them.'

Kayla didn't want to find them. They'd be holding hands and staring at each other—or they'd be kissing, which was worse. A surge of jealousy was replaced by a sort of daring she had never felt before. She couldn't have Mitch, but she could have that doll.

Without giving herself time to think about what she was doing, Kayla darted to the stall and grabbed the doll. Then she ran. She heard Jen behind her but just kept running back towards that hole in the fence. They had almost reached it when she heard a shout. She looked over her shoulder to see a man running towards them. He looked angry. A final sprint took her and Jen to the fence. Jen was the first through and Kayla followed, taking care not to rip the doll's pretty dress. She and Jen were both panting now. Kayla was about to start running again when there was a loud cry of pain behind her. She spun around to see the man who had been chasing them sliding along the ground in a cloud of dust. She froze. The man stopped moving and just lay there. He didn't get up or move or even make a sound.

'Is he dead?' Jen sounded scared.

'No. He can't be.' Kayla wasn't at all sure. 'He tripped. Come on, now is our chance.'

The girls turned and ran. In a couple of minutes, they were back at the school gate, but they didn't return to class. They hid behind the sports shed, waiting for the final bell and the arrival of Kayla's mum to take them home.

As that time approached, Kayla realised that she couldn't take the doll with her. Her parents would see it and ask where she'd got it. Biting back the tears that were so very, very close, she pulled the doll off its long Bo Peep stick. Then she began folding the wide skirt. It didn't fold well. Some of the sparkle on the doll's shoulders rubbed off as she wrapped the stiff netting around them, but she had to get the doll into her school bag.

When the bell rang, the girls darted back to the veranda outside their classroom where their bags were stored. Kayla shoved the doll into the bag. Her mother's car was waiting by the gate and she and Jen climbed in.

Her friend was frowning at her and looking at the school bag, but Kayla just shook her head and avoided her eyes until her mother pulled up in front of the house where Jen and Mitch lived.

'Thanks, Mrs Lawson. See you, Kay.' Jen jumped out.

'You're quiet today,' Kath Lawson said as she drove her daughter away from town towards Willowbrook Stud. 'Is everything all right?'

'Yes. I'm fine.'

Kayla jumped out of the car as soon as it pulled up outside the two-storey stone homestead. She raced upstairs into her bedroom and shut the door behind her. Sitting on the bed, she pulled the doll out of her bag. The perfect dress was rumpled and a few of the sequins were hanging by a thread. She looked around the room wildly. Where could she hide it so her mother wouldn't find it?

She heard voices downstairs as her father came in from working the horses. She opened the door and listened. They were talking about the show, but only about the horses they'd be taking. Just when she was starting to relax, she heard a car pull up outside. That was Mitch and Lizzie. Now that Mitch had his licence, he and Lizzie drove back to Willowbrook after school each day.

Lizzie appeared on the stairs. She took Kayla by the shoulder and almost dragged her back into the privacy of her room.

'What happened to the two of you?' Lizzie whispered furiously.

'A man chased us, so we went back to school.'

'There was an ambulance called to the showgrounds. I panicked because I thought it was you.'

'An ambulance?'

'Yes. But we saw them load some bloke in blue overalls into it. He was hurt in a fall.'

'Was he … dead?'

'Dead? Of course he wasn't dead. Maybe a broken arm or something, that's all. Why?'

Kayla just shook her head. She couldn't speak.

'Anyway. Don't run off again if we let you follow us. All right?'

Kayla nodded.

'I'm going down to the stables. If I groom Apollo for Dad, he might let me ride him. Coming?'

Kayla shook her head. 'Homework,' she managed to whisper.

'All right. See you later.'

Her sister vanished in the whirl of energy that surrounded her wherever she went.

Kayla sat on the bed, mindlessly picking at a torn bit of lace on the doll's dress. She heard her father head back to the stables with Lizzie. When her mother went into the kitchen, Kayla picked up the doll and slipped quietly out of the house. She ran down to the creek, to the spot where a fallen tree formed a kind of bridge. She walked out onto the tree as she'd done a hundred times before and sat down. Heavy rain in the last couple of weeks meant the water in the creek was high and moving fast. Fast enough to wash a doll downstream so it would never be found. But what if it was found? She might go to prison.

Fear took Kayla and she leaped to her feet. It wasn't hard to find a rock. Without a moment's hesitation, she tore up the lace on the pretty dress, tied the doll firmly to the rock and dropped it into the water.

Kayla's last sight of the once-perfect doll she had loved was the ruined fabric sinking into the muddy water. She brushed tears from her eyes and turned back towards the homestead, vowing that she would never again do anything so stupid. She had learned a lesson today.

Nothing good could ever come from a bad act. How could something be beautiful and perfect when it began with a crime? Or with someone being hurt? From now on, she would always make sure everything in her life was right and perfect and beautiful—and stayed that way.

CHAPTER
1

18 years later

'It needs to be perfect,' Kayla told the hotel's events coordinator. 'Do you think it's perfect?'

The woman in the dark suit scanned the room. Kayla watched her assess the layout of the chairs and the flowers. Eyes almost as critical as Kayla's checked the shine and placement of the wine glasses on the tables along the wall and the crispness of the white tablecloths. The room was a symphony of silver and sparkle, the perfect tone for a winter wedding. Then the woman's head tilted slightly.

'One moment, please.' She walked quickly to the arch of white roses where the ceremony would take place. The lectern was polished mahogany, but its placement was not quite right. The events manager straightened it and returned to Kayla, nodding in approval. 'Now it's perfect.'

Kayla chuckled. 'I agree. You and your team have done a fabulous job.'

'Thank you. Coming from you, that means a lot.'

Kayla knew her high standards were hard to meet but this was one of Sydney's most prestigious hotels. It was accustomed to providing nothing but the very best, although it came at a high cost. Not that Kayla's clients cared. If you could afford the services of Elite Weddings, money was not a problem.

Kayla glanced at her watch and walked to the big double doors at the end of the ballroom. She nodded at the two uniformed staff standing by them. The men swung the doors open just as the first group of wedding guests appeared at the top of the escalators from the foyer. Kayla stood to one side as the stylishly dressed women and equally expensively outfitted men came through the door. There were a few 'oohs' as the guests took in the beautifully decorated ballroom, the subtly lit balcony and the big arc of the Sydney Harbour Bridge beyond. The wonder lasted only a few seconds, before the hum of voices and the clink of glasses told Kayla the important part of the evening was underway. The highest of the mostly very high-profile guests had taken their places and were beginning to hold court while lesser mortals gathered around.

What's wrong with me? Am I becoming this cynical?

She waved away a waiter offering Moët & Chandon in crystal glasses. The guests were in good hands. Her job now was to check on the bride and groom. Leaving the room, she took the reserved lift up one floor to the bride's room. Her knock was answered by a bridesmaid, who ushered her through the suite to a room full of mirrors, where the bride was having a last-minute touch-up done to her make-up. Kayla paused in the doorway. The girl was only nineteen and a vision in couture ivory silk covered with sequins and crystals. That gown cost more than many people paid for a car, but it was beautiful. The young woman was glowing with happiness. No second thoughts or uncertainties would mar this day that Kayla had made perfect for her.

Having assured herself that everything was as it should be in the bride's world, Kayla set out for the groom's domain. This time when she knocked on the door, the response was a long time coming. The loud music and rowdy voices inside the suite probably had something to do with that. At last, the door opened a few inches and one of the groomsmen looked out.

'It's the wedding planner.'

Kayla heard some scuffling inside and the door opened another few inches, just enough for her to see the stripper dash for the bathroom. The groom walked into view. His hair was ruffled and he was buttoning his shirt.

'Hi, Kayla. Everything all right?' He didn't even have the grace to look abashed.

'Are you ready? You need to be downstairs in five minutes.'

'I'll be there.'

Kayla bit her tongue and walked away. In her heart of hearts, she wanted to go back to the bride's room and tell the beautiful girl wearing the white dress that she should take it off now and find someone worthy of her. But she couldn't. She was being paid a lot of money to facilitate the perfect wedding. She fulfilled that role expertly, meeting even her own exacting standards. Sadly, no amount of money would change what was happening in the groom's rooms.

By late evening, the girl in the white dress was a wife, the groom and his friends were raucously drunk and the most important people had slipped away. Kayla was about to do the same, but as she turned to go, her stomach heaved, sending her rushing to the bathroom. She barely noticed the shiny marble counter, soft white hand towels and free Chanel hand cream. She dashed into a cubicle just before her stomach completely revolted and she lost what little food she had eaten today.

When she was convinced there was nothing more to throw up, she left the cubicle and used one of the fine towels to pat the sweat from her face. The door opened and a wedding guest tottered in on impossibly high heels.

'Are you all right?' she asked as she watched Kayla straighten her smart black dress.

Kayla looked at the woman and saw the unspoken words in her eyes—she assumed Kayla was drunk, or worse. The judgement and censure she saw in the woman's eyes broke through the barriers that had slammed down on Kayla in her bathroom that very morning. She was finally able to say to this stranger the words she had not yet been able to admit to herself.

'I'm pregnant.'

★★★

Another week passed and Kayla hadn't said those words again outside the walls of her flat with its tiny balcony that allowed her a glimpse of Sydney Harbour. She never worked Mondays during the wedding season, and this Monday morning found her emerging from the bathroom to pour the coffee she'd made down the sink. She opened the balcony doors to get rid of the coffee smell and poured herself a glass of apple juice, which seemed to be the only thing her stomach could handle first thing in the morning. She'd taken another two pregnancy tests, with the same result on each. She had also missed her second period and couldn't put it down to stress or overwork this time. She knew with absolute certainty exactly how far along she was. It was time she faced facts and made some decisions.

Of course, the job came first. Being a wedding planner required focus and long hours. She was very good at her job. At least, she always had been. Throwing up at the reception wasn't part of the job description. And that was just the start. She shuddered, thinking about the impact a pregnancy—or a child—would have on her work.

She should do this in person, but she wasn't up to it. She reached for the phone.

'Hi, Kayla. I didn't expect to hear from you today. I see the Crosby wedding was another triumph.' Her boss Pascale Bonnet was also her friend, but when she was in the office, Pascale was all business.

'It was fine. The hotel did a good job, although I'll put a note on their venue listing about staff phones. I caught one waitress trying to take a photo. Luckily, I got to her in time.'

Kayla could picture the frown on Pascale's perfectly made-up face. The money their celebrity clients paid for the services of Elite Weddings often came from an exclusive photo deal with some high-end glossy magazine. A guarantee of absolute privacy was important to Pascale's business.

'Point taken. I'm talking to the manager today about another booking. I'll mention that to her and see if I can get a discount.'

'I know it's short notice, but I've decided to head up to Willowbrook tomorrow.'

'But we don't have any more bookings there this season.'

'I know.' Kayla's family home at Scone had become a sought-after wedding venue in the twelve months since they had opened for business. The horse stud that had been in the family for generations was run by her big sister Lizzie and her husband Mitch, while the wedding business in the old homestead was Kayla's concern. During the spring and into summer, there was a Willowbrook wedding almost every weekend, but no-one was looking for outdoor venues in mid-winter. 'Pascale, I need to take some time off.'

In an instant the boss was gone, replaced by the friend. 'Are you all right?'

'Yes … no … I'm not sure. I need to take some time to think about things. I can't do that here in the city.'

'Can I help?'

'Thanks, but no.'

'Take all the time you need and call me if there is anything I can do.'

'I will.'

'Are you sure you'll be all right?'

'I have Lizzie. She's the sensible one in the family. I think I need a bit of her right now.'

'Is there anything—'

Kayla smiled. 'You already asked, Pascale. Thanks. Don't worry about me. I'll talk to you soon.'

'Take care.'

Kayla disconnected the call. Now that it was done, all she wanted was to be away from here as fast as she could. Sydney was suffocating her. If she didn't get away and clear her head, she had no idea what she would do next.

***

It was almost dark as Kayla approached Scone after a nightmare drive that involved traffic queues caused by an accident on the freeway, delays due to roadworks, and a scary few minutes dodging some roos. She was almost in tears and desperate to go to the toilet when she turned off the main road towards Willowbrook and the beautiful sandstone homestead her great-grandfather had built.

The house looked wonderful as the last glow of evening painted it gold. Where once it had shown signs of decay, it now looked as beautiful as it must have the day it was finished—maybe more. It was hard to believe that the homestead and horse stud had been on the brink of foreclosure just over a year ago. Lizzie had been trying to run it all on her own since their parents' deaths when the sisters were teenagers. Despite her best efforts, it had slowly slipped into decline. The project to turn it into a wedding venue had done more than save the homestead, it had also rebuilt Lizzie and Kayla's relationship, and brought Lizzie back to her first and only love, Mitch, with whom she had renewed her wedding vows. Now they lived across the creek from the homestead. With the two of them behind the stud and Kayla behind the wedding venue, Willowbrook was thriving. It would be ready to pass down to the next generation, as it had been passed down to the sisters by the generations before.

Next generation? Lizzie and Mitch didn't have any kids. Lizzie always avoided even talking about the topic. So what next generation was there going to be? The baby Kayla carried? A baby as unwelcome as it was unexpected.

She parked in front of the house. The veranda light was on. Another light shone through the windows from inside the house. That was a bit strange, but she was far too tired to think about it. She pulled her bag out of the boot and climbed the steps to the front door. It was unlocked, which it shouldn't have been. She walked into the foyer. The light was on, but one bulb had blown, leaving it dim, which perfectly suited Kayla's mood. In front of her, the curved staircase led upstairs to her room and the office from which she ran Willowbrook Weddings. That was her domain and a place where she always felt happy and content.

But first she had another urgent need. She dropped her bag on the carpet and dashed into the nearby bathroom.

Afterwards, she wandered into the big kitchen looking for some refreshment, but as she put the coffee on to brew, the smell sent her dashing back to the bathroom. Why was it called morning sickness when it seemed to strike her at any hour of the day?

Having once again lost the contents of her stomach, Kayla was washing her face with shaking hands when she heard what sounded like a car outside. Maybe Lizzie and Mitch had seen her arrive and decided to drop by. She usually told them when she was coming; this time she'd hoped to delay the meeting until tomorrow, but it didn't really matter. Lizzie and Mitch were her family, and the only people she wanted to be around right now.

Then she heard a child's voice in the hall outside the door.

'Is this our new home, Mummy?'

CHAPTER
2

Jen shifted the toddler on her hip and tried to sound happy. 'Yes, Dylan. This is going to be our home. Just for a while, sweetheart. Until Daddy is back with us.'

Beside Jen, her seven-year-old daughter's face fell. 'I miss Daddy.' There was a small sniffle.

'I do too. But it won't be long until he's back. Now, look after your little brother for me while I get some stuff out of the car. Then we can have something to eat. We'll all feel better then.'

Jen handed over her squirming son. He'd be safe with Suzi for a couple of minutes while she fetched what they needed for tonight. She had barely turned away when Suzi screamed. Jen spun back to see a figure emerging from the men's toilet in the dimly lit hallway.

'What's going on?' The voice was that of a woman, but in the dim light, Jen could hardly distinguish her features.

'Come here, kids.' Jen gathered her children to her.

'What are you doing here?' the figure asked.

'I live here. What are you doing here?' Jen tried to sound authoritative. She wasn't lying. As of about two minutes ago, she did live here.

'That's funny, because I live here too.'

'Mum, she came out of the boys' toilet.' As always, Suzi's curiosity overrode her fear. 'She shouldn't use the boys' toilet, should she?'

'Not now, honey.' Jen pushed the girl protectively behind her.

'Hi there—this is a surprise!'

Both women spun around as a man stomped up the steps.

'Uncle Mitch!' Suzi flung herself at him.

'Hey, kiddo. It's good to see you too.' He crouched down to hug her then stood up, holding her in his arms. Suzi was clinging to him in the bear hug she reserved for only two people—her Uncle Mitch and her father. 'Hi, sis. And Kayla too. We weren't expecting you.'

'Kayla?' Jen studied the person in front of her.

'Yes, Jen. It is.' The figure stepped forward into the brighter light.

For a second Jen didn't recognise the woman in front of her. Despite being best friends in primary school, they had drifted apart. When her parents had died in a horrible road accident, Kayla had been sent to boarding school and not long after, Jen and Mitch had relocated to Queensland with their parents. There had been letters and emails, but those had slowly stopped. Mitch and Lizzie's marriage had not included a traditional wedding and so no family get-together either. It had to be ten years, probably closer to fifteen, since Jen had laid eyes on Kayla.

Her friend was the same … but not.

Kayla had always been the pretty one. She'd been into clothes and make-up. She'd liked beautiful things and she'd always wanted everything to be perfect. By the time she was a teenager, any clothes that had a small tear or, even worse, a stain, had been consigned to the back of the cupboard. Kayla's things had to be the best and even the smallest flaw was not permitted. Jen could see something of that still. Kayla's jeans and jacket were obviously designer, as were her high-heeled boots. Only someone who knew her would know that her hair colour had been helped along. And she had obviously started this day beautifully made up. The problem was that nothing was perfect. The clothes were wrinkled, and one knee of her jeans was dark with … water? As if she had been kneeling on a wet floor. Water splashes darkened the lapels of the jacket too. Her face looked damp, with either water or sweat or perhaps a mixture of both, and her hair had obviously been pushed back from her face by rough fingers. As for her face … Kayla looked white where her make-up was smudged. She looked unwell.

'Mum?' Suzi had found her courage again and was staring at Kayla from her new perch on Mitch's shoulders. 'Who is this lady and why is she in our new house?'

'Suzi, this is your Aunt Kayla. She's Aunt Lizzie's sister.' As for the second part of the question, Jen didn't have an answer. Mitch and Lizzie had told her all about the wedding ceremonies and receptions held at Willowbrook by Kayla's bridal company, but they'd assured her there were no upcoming events and Jen and the kids would not be in the way. Nor would they be disturbed.

'Hello, Auntie Kayla,' Suzi said.

Jen could see by the look on Kayla's face that she wasn't coping with this unexpected gathering as well as her niece.

Mitch came to the rescue. 'I've got an idea. I guess everyone is tired after their journeys. Lizzie will be here in a bit. She's with a mare who's not doing too well. Why don't we go through to the kitchen and unwind a bit? We have tea and coffee or something stronger, if you feel like it. And for you, miss, cake.' He hitched Suzi higher onto his shoulders and she squealed in delight.

When Jen walked into the kitchen, she saw nothing left of the place where she'd spent so many hours as a child. The big glass-fronted coolers and professional ovens belonged in some fancy restaurant, not the family kitchen where she and her best friend had done their homework and talked about ponies and boys and clothes while Kayla's mother Kath prepared dinners for whatever collection of family and friends were at Willowbrook that day. A lot had certainly changed since then, and she guessed both she and Kayla had changed a lot too.

While Mitch kept his niece busy making tea and cutting a cake that had magically appeared from the fridge, Jen sat with her sleepy son on her lap. Kayla sat down next to her.

Jen broke the silence between them. 'You didn't know I was coming? Lizzie and Mitch didn't tell you?'

'No. But they didn't know I was coming up either. I haven't spoken to them for a couple of weeks.'

'Have you got a wedding scheduled? I'll make sure I'm not in the way. The kids too.'

'No. Nothing for a while.'

After all these years apart, there should have been something more than this. Excitement maybe. Or curiosity. But Kayla appeared pretty disconnected from what was going on around her.

'Kay? Are you sure it's all right that I'm here?'

Before Kayla could answer, Suzi said, 'We're going up to my room.'

'I need to rearrange a couple of things to fit everyone in,' Mitch said. 'Kayla, your room is fine as always. Sis, I'll put the kids and you all in one room, if that's okay, for tonight. We can sort out something more permanent tomorrow.' He didn't say it, but the meaning was obvious. They'd sort everything out when they'd had time to find out how long Kayla was staying and what Jen was planning to do in the longer term. Good questions, both of them.

Dylan was dozing in Jen's arms and she didn't want to disturb him. He'd had a long journey. They all had. And it had come at the end of a distressing time. She could still see her husband Brad's face as they led him through that courthouse door, taking him to a place where he might remain for years. Back in the day, when she and Kayla were as close as sisters, Jen would have told her everything by now, probably be crying on her shoulder. But they hadn't had that relationship for a long time. And as they sat there in silence, she began to suspect that Kayla had her own preoccupations.

They might have stayed like that for hours, not talking, each lost in their own thoughts, had Lizzie not come striding through the door.

'Sorry I wasn't here, Jen ...' Lizzie's voice trailed off. 'Kayla? We weren't expecting you, but it's good to see you. Where's Mitch?'

'Right behind you.' Mitch was alone as he re-entered the kitchen. 'Suzi fell asleep upstairs. I hope that's okay, Jen?'

'Of course. Poor thing. She's exhausted. We all are.'

'I'm not surprised.' Lizzie gave her a quick hug. 'These few weeks have been hard on all of you. Well, you can relax now and stay here as long as you need. Until the trial. Or longer, if you want.'

Until the trial. The words reverberated in Jen's head. She glanced quickly at Kayla. She was frowning slightly, but Jen had the feeling she hadn't really heard Lizzie's words. If she wasn't frowning at the mention of a trial, what was she frowning at? Jen would have to explain to her why she and the kids had invaded her space, but she'd find a better time and place to do it, when she'd had time to unwind after the long drive and, more importantly, when there was no chance the kids would overhear.

The boy in her arms was fast asleep and getting heavier by the second. Her own eyelids were drooping—she'd driven seven hundred kilometres in one day with two restless and upset kids in the car. Any minute now the room was going to start spinning.

'I have to get some sleep.' She stood up, doing her best to hide the wave of exhaustion that swept over her.

'Do you need a hand to get Dylan upstairs to bed?' Mitch was still looking out for her, as he always had.

'No thanks, big brother. We're fine.'

She could see from his face that he didn't believe that. Which was reasonable, because she didn't believe it either.

***

Jen woke next morning in a place that was both familiar and a distant memory. This wasn't the first time she'd woken up at Willowbrook. Or in this very room. This had once been Kayla's room and Jen had spent many sleepovers here as a kid. They had sat up late into the night, talking and planning for the future. They had laughed together and cried together and whatever problems they faced had seemed less because they were shared. But this time was different. She wasn't a kid any more. She was all grown up with no money, no home, no job and two kids to care for. All on her own because her husband was in trouble.

The kids!

Jen sat up and looked around the room. She was alone. Her heart skipped a beat and she struggled to her feet, reaching for her dressing gown to ward off the chilly morning. She'd told them not to leave the room without her.

Moments before she reached the door, it opened and her children walked in.

'I took him to the loo, Mum. We didn't want to wake you.'

Relief and love are a powerful combination. Jen crouched down to hug them both. She breathed in that special smell that children have for their mother and allowed herself a few seconds to think of their father, sitting in a cell more than seven hundred kilometres away. Then she tucked that thought into the furthest recesses of her mind.

'Thank you, sweetheart. Let's all get dressed and find some breakfast. What do you think?'

Squeals of delight were her answer.

This morning Jen was able to take a better look at the kitchen. It had clearly been designed for catering, but at the same time, it still worked as a family kitchen. One of the fridges had been stocked with butter and milk and juice, and in one of the cupboards she found cereal and bread and other basic necessities. It was the work of only a few moments to get the kids happily settled with juice and corn flakes, while Jen watched the coffee brew.

She was pouring a cup when Kayla appeared in the doorway.

'Great timing,' Jen said. 'Coffee?'

Kayla shook her head. She looked quite pale. 'I brought some juice with me last night.' She glanced at the kids' glasses. 'Is there any left?'

'Plenty.' Jen wasn't going to feel guilty. 'The fridge is well stocked. Mitch and Lizzie were expecting me and the kids so there's more than enough to go round. I was about to make some toast. Do you want some?'

'Please.'

'Honey or Vegemite?'

'Mum. Can we see the horses now?' The volume of Suzi's voice caused both adults to wince.

'Suzi. Remember, no shouting indoors.'

'Sorry, Mum.'

'That's better. You can't go and see the horses now. I told you that Uncle Mitch or Auntie Lizzie would take you. But you're not to go near the horses unless they're with you or I am. Understand?'

'Yes, Mum.'

'Horses!' Dylan screamed.

Jen could see Kayla glancing around as if looking for an escape.

'Why don't the two of you go upstairs for a bit now that you've had breakfast. Suzi, you know where Dylan's things are. Find him something to play with. You've got your books. I promise that if the two of you stay quiet for a little while so Auntie Kayla and I can talk, we can go and see the horses a bit later.'

Suzi nodded.

'Good. Now off you go, and remember, don't leave the house without me until you know your way around better.'

'Yes, Mummy.'

The tension in the air noticeably eased as the kids took their noise upstairs. Jen topped up her coffee and slipped more bread into the toaster. When she finally sat at the table, she slid a plate of toast towards Kayla. The butter and toppings were already out, but Kayla ate her toast dry.

'I'm sorry we surprised you,' Jen said as she slathered a healthy serving of butter and jam onto her own toast. 'I sort of assumed Mitch and Lizzie would have told you.'

'No. How long are you here for? And is …'

Jen could see Kayla was searching her memory for a name.

'Brad.'

'Sorry. Of course. Brad. Is he joining you and the kids?'

This was the question she'd been dreading. It was also the reason she'd taken her children away from their home and everyone they loved. Away from local media and town gossip. Mitch and Lizzie knew, but they wouldn't say anything to anyone. Not even to Kayla.

She could say nothing, pretend her life wasn't in a tailspin. Pretend her marriage was fine and her husband was simply tied up at work or that they had agreed on a trial separation. But both of those would be lies. Kayla had once been her best friend, as close as a sister, and right now Jen needed a friend more than anything else. If they were to renew their friendship, she wouldn't start with a lie.

'No. He … It's just me and the kids.' She took a steadying breath. 'We had to sell the house. That's why I'm here. I couldn't stay in Queensland. My parents' house is too small and besides, Brad didn't want us to stay there. He didn't want the kids to know what was going on.'

'But what is going on? Where is he?'

'In prison.'

CHAPTER
3

Kayla carefully took a sip of her juice and a bite of toast but suspected she hadn't managed to hide her surprise.

'Your husband is in prison?'

'Yes.' Jen kept her head high and looked Kayla squarely in the face. 'He's being held on remand awaiting trial.'

What should she say to that? 'I … I'm sorry.' It didn't seem the right thing to say but she couldn't think of anything else.

'That's why the kids and I are here. He didn't want the kids to visit him in prison. He didn't want them anywhere near that place. And we both wanted to protect them from the gossips. You know how people can be.'

She did.

'The house has been sold. He'll need the money for legal fees.'

'Are you going to divorce him?'

'No! Of course not. He's innocent. As soon as the trial is done, we'll be back together as a family.'

Everyone is always innocent until the jury found them guilty, and in many cases even then—at least in their own minds and those of their family. Even when small, Jen had been fiercely loyal; Kayla could hardly expect her to be different now. Although she did want to ask what his crime—alleged crime—was. But after all this time, she wasn't sure she had the right to ask Jen anything.

Besides, the smell of the coffee …

'Sorry.' She barely had time to gasp the word before she was on her feet and heading for the nearest toilet.

Once her stomach had emptied itself of her small breakfast, Kayla washed her face, wondering how it was the human race had ever survived. If this was what it was like being pregnant, it was a wonder anyone had babies, not when it was possible to avoid the whole thing. Or at least—

Her mind shied away from that thought, even though deep down she knew that was one of the reasons she had sought the comfort of Willowbrook, to consider whether or not she was going to have the baby.

'Anyone here?'

Thank God for Mitch. His arrival should save Kayla from difficult questions when she returned to the kitchen with a face as white as the one staring back at her from the mirror. From somewhere above, she heard the thumping of running feet, followed by a loud squeal descending the stairs.

'Uncle Mitch.'

Kayla winced at both the pitch and the volume. Another reason why human reproduction was something she did not understand. As the commotion moved on to the kitchen, Kayla washed her face one more time. She patted it dry and stared at the woman in the mirror. 'You can do this.'

She left the safety of the bathroom and returned to the kitchen. Mitch's arrival had obviously been the signal for chaos. The kids were leaping around the kitchen, yelling at the tops of their voices about horses and Aunt Lizzie. Oblivious to the noise, Mitch was helping himself to coffee, the smell of which almost had Kayla racing back to the bathroom. Jen seemed equally unconcerned by the chaos as she tidied away the kids' breakfast dishes.

'Auntie Kay, we're going to go and see the horses,' Suzi greeted her with enthusiasm.

'That's nice.' What else was she to say? She turned in the direction of the big fridges, but Jen caught her eye and nodded towards a bench where a glass of apple juice sat, apparently waiting for her.

'Thanks.' Kayla sipped the cold juice with appreciation.

Mitch was holding a cup of coffee, but for now, her stomach wasn't complaining. 'Hi, Kayla. Lizzie's with the horses. She'll be done soon.'

Of course she was. The horses had always come first. Although, to be fair, Lizzie had no idea that Kayla was here for anything other than a casual visit.

'Right,' Jen called and the kids immediately fell silent. 'Uncle Mitch is taking us to see the horses.'

This brought a rousing cheer.

'But you have to promise to be quiet so you don't frighten them. No opening any gates. No going near the horses unless one of us is with you. No climbing fences and do what you are told. All right?'

'Yes, Mummy,' the kids chorused.

'I can always take the kids and leave you and Kayla to catch up,' Mitch offered.

'No,' Kayla jumped in. 'I'd like a stroll around the place to see how it's looking.'

'Okay. Kids, let's go and clean your teeth. And get a jacket. It's cold out there.' Jen pushed back her chair.

A peaceful silence settled over the kitchen and as Mitch drank the last of his coffee and washed the cup, Kayla felt some of the tension leaving her body. She still had to explain why she had suddenly appeared and how long she was staying, but Mitch wouldn't ask. He'd wait for her to tell him and if she didn't, that was fine too. Mitch was a man of infinite patience. He'd waited for her sister for years; he wasn't about to hurry anything now.

They set off when Jen and the kids returned. Kayla walked slightly ahead of the others. It wasn't just that she needed some space, which she did, but since she'd been spending time at Willowbrook, she'd come to enjoy her first walk across the gardens, down the shaded path between the towering gums to the stables and the wooden-fenced paddocks where the brood mares grazed with their big bellies or, at the right time of the year, their foals stumbling and skipping around them.

She opened the last gate leading to the stables and saw a rider in the square exercise yard. Lizzie was riding Deimos, the stallion that was the heart of Willowbrook Stud. Kayla stopped walking for a few seconds to watch. The big chestnut horse was the spitting image of his sire, her father's famous horse Apollo. Watching Lizzie and Deimos together, Kayla was transported back to when she was Suzi's age, watching her father and Apollo working in this very exercise yard. Sam Lawson and that horse had been like one creature when they moved, embodying a beauty and grace that very few pairings ever reached. Now Apollo's son and Sam's daughter were the same. Where Deimos had inherited his sire's look and grace and power, so too had Lizzie inherited her father's affinity and skill and special talent for working with horses. That talent had given rise to the legend that was the Willowbrook horse, generally considered among the finest of the breed and eagerly sought after for work, competition and breeding. A Willowbrook horse could do it all.

But what did the future hold for Willowbrook and its horses? And for the Lawsons?

Lizzie and Mitch didn't have any kids, and Kayla had no idea if they wanted a family. Kayla might have come back to Willowbrook for a while, but her life was in the city. And despite the hours spent with ponies when she and Lizzie were young, Kayla wasn't a horsewoman. Her life was about beauty and design, about elegant gowns and gleaming crystal. She hadn't inherited her father's horse skills.

But there could be someone else. A grandchild for Sam Lawson. People often said some skills skipped a generation. For the first time since she'd seen that blue line on the test strip, Kayla placed her hand on her stomach. There was no bump there yet. No kick. But if she chose that route, there would be a baby. A grandson or grand-daughter who might inherit Sam's love of horses and his skill with them. There could be another generation of Lawsons for Willowbrook. Or … she could say no to that future. There were options. Tough options to be sure, but options all the same.

She dropped her hand quickly, but as she did she looked up and saw the others approaching from the direction of the stables. Kayla saw the question on Jen's face. Surely Jen hadn't guessed? Had she? She had two children of her own—she must have at least suspected what was behind Kayla's sickness this morning. What would Jen say if she knew the whole story about this pregnancy or knew the option Kayla was considering?

As she joined the group leaning on the wooden fence to watch Lizzie and Deimos, Kayla wondered if there was enough of her relationship with Jen left for them to talk.

For now, it was enough to stand quietly in the background and watch as Jen introduced her children to the delights of Willowbrook. This was their first visit. Lizzie and Mitch had seen the kids a few times at family gatherings in Queensland, but for the city-born children, Willowbrook was a wonderland of new sights and sounds and smells.

The morning passed quickly, until Jen called a halt.

'Okay, kids. We have to go to Scone soon. I need to go to the school and arrange for Suzi to start there next week.'

'Aw, Mum. Do I have to?'

'Yes, Suzi. You do. I've got an idea,' Lizzie chipped in as she walked out of the stall where the newly groomed Deimos was dozing. 'Why don't we all go into town together? Mitch and I have to collect some stuff that's coming on the train. We could have a nice lunch.'

'I don't—'

'That's a good idea, Lizzie.' Mitch cut Kayla off. 'This is the first time we've all been together as a family. We can celebrate.'

And so it was settled.

Kayla discovered that going out with two small children wasn't as simple as it might sound, but after several changes of dress (Suzi) and trips to the toilet (Dylan) and sorting out of school records (Jen), they were finally ready. Jen and the kids took their car, and Kayla slipped into the back of her sister's dual-cab ute.

While Lizzie and Mitch were at the rail station, Kayla strolled down the main street, looking in shop windows. At first she saw very little; her mind was far away. But eventually she began to take notice. Scone had changed in the last couple of years. It looked very prosperous. There were a couple of trendy-looking cafes, and hair and nail salons. There was even a flourishing florist. Kayla knew that she had played some part in all this. The high-end weddings she staged at Willowbrook brought money into the community. That knowledge gave her a sense of satisfaction, as did the occasional nod of greeting she got from the locals. It was almost like this was home again.

By the time they met up for lunch, Kayla was feeling more relaxed than she had in a while. It soon became clear that Suzi's view of the school had been favourable, with a potential best friend already met.

That reminded Kayla of herself and Jen. As kids, they'd met and become friends in a single day. And she realised she missed that now. Pascale was her best friend, but also her boss. She had friends in Sydney, but they were mostly people she worked with, or met through work. None of them knew much about her background. About who she had been and how she had become the person she was.

Perhaps it was time to rebuild what she had lost.

'The Stockman has been sold,' Mitch said to Lizzie, pointing at a two-storey brick building on the corner where the road turned to head out of town and back to the highway.

'I hope the new publican knows exactly what he's taken on,' Lizzie said.

'Why do you say that?' Kayla asked.

'It's a pretty rough pub. When they were building the bypass, some of the main roads crew stayed there. Even more of them drank there. There were a few fights. The police were called most Friday nights. None of the women would go there, certainly not alone. Most of the locals found better places to go. I guess that's why it sold. By the time the roadworks were over, it wouldn't have had many customers left. I guess it's just been hanging on since then.'

Kayla saw a man emerge from the front door of the pub. He was a big man, would be physically strong. If that was the new

publican, she didn't think the place was about to improve much. All
he needed was a leather jacket and he'd look like one of the bikies
behind many of the pub fights. He glanced up and down the street,
perhaps searching for customers, and his eyes came to rest on Kayla.
She couldn't see him clearly enough to be sure, but she felt as if he
was watching her.

She turned to follow her family in their quest for a more
suitable place for lunch, resisting the urge to turn and check if he
was watching her walk away.

★★★

Connor saw the little group turn away and head back into town, no
doubt looking for a better place for lunch. He didn't blame them.
He wouldn't bring kids into the Stockman either. He took a couple
of steps back to study the pub he now owned. Well, 'owned' was
possibly the wrong word. He had a hefty mortgage; one he'd been
lucky to get, given his history. And one he was not going to waste.

The pub must've been a showplace once, with those arched windows and that fancy wrought-iron railing on the upper storey. The
interior too must once have been a symphony of rich timber that
glowed in the lamp light. It must once have been the sort of place
Connor had dreamed of as a child, where people in smart clothes
went to be seen and have fun, while in the quiet corners, people
with power and money made important decisions. The sort of place
someone like him would never belong. But right now, it looked
like exactly what it was, a place that had fallen on hard times, faded
by the sun, battered by the years and stained with disappointment.
They kind of belonged together now, him and the pub.

The previous owner had sold the Stockman cheap, glad to see
the back of a business that was barely making a profit. Not only
that, but the pub probably saw almost as many on-duty police as

it had customers. That downhill slide and the fights and the police were a familiar story to Connor, one he had seen many times. One he had lived.

But he believed places like this could be brought back. People too.

He had to believe that.

A ute pulled into a parking space next to him and a man wearing blue overalls got out.

'Connor Knight?'

'That's me.'

'Pete Hearn.' They shook hands. 'So, you're the new owner of this place. Good luck with it. It needs a bit of work.'

'It does. That's why you're here. They tell me you're the best man for a job like this.'

'I'm good with my hands.'

'That's what the old place needs. There's a lot to do, but first thing, though, we need to put up the sign.' Connor stepped back through the front doors of the pub and emerged with a sheet of painted plywood. Between the two of them, it was soon screwed to the front wall beside the door.

CLOSED FOR RENOVATION.

JOIN US FOR OUR GRAND REOPENING ON FRIDAY 23RD.

'That's only four weeks. We'd best get to it.' Connor led Pete inside. They stood for a few minutes taking in the stained paint, the pitted lino on the floor and the cheap tables and chairs.

'Where do we start?' Pete asked as he dropped his toolbox on the floor.

'Got your ladders?'

'Yep. On the ute.'

'Then let's start outside.'

The sign above the door was old and the paint had faded, but the pub's name and the image of the man and his horse were still visible.

'You going to keep the name?' Pete asked as he unstrapped the ladders from his vehicle.

'No.'

'What are you going to call it?'

'I don't know yet. Something will come to me.'

It took them a while to get the sign unscrewed and down on the footpath. Connor was aware of the curious glances from people passing by on the other side of the road. Curiosity was good. It might bring them back in four weeks for the reopening.

The two of them carried the sign into the pub and stood it against one wall. There would be a new sign. Something freshly painted and welcoming. Something with a name that reflected what Connor wanted this pub to be. A place where people could feel safe and comfortable. A place families could come to for lunch. A place the police only visited when they were off duty and thirsty. To achieve that goal, the woodworking, metalwork and sign-writing workshops that had been part of Connor's rehabilitation would help his new home as well.

If he could find his way back, so too could the pub. And one of these days that nice-looking family and their kids would want to come inside his pub for their lunch.

He would make it so.

CHAPTER
4

'When's Daddy going to ring?' Suzi asked for the tenth time that afternoon.

'As soon as he can,' Jen replied.

'I miss him.'

'I do too, sweetie. Now, why don't you go and watch the TV?'

'Promise you'll call me when you hear from Daddy.'

'Of course I will. Off you go.'

Suzi slid off the bed and left the room. In the past couple of days, Jen and Kayla had sorted out the living arrangements at Willowbrook. The homestead had four upstairs bedrooms. Kayla had been using one as her office and the other as her bedroom. The remaining two now served as main living rooms for Jen and her kids. All three of them slept in the biggest and the last room had become a playroom for the kids. There were toys and games there, and a secondhand TV had been purchased and installed. It wasn't perfect, but it would do for now. How long 'now' was going to last was anyone's guess.

The phone lying on the bedside table remained stubbornly silent.

Jen leaned over and opened the drawer of the bedside table to remove the manila envelope she had hastily hidden there when Suzi knocked on the bedroom door. Now that the kids were occupied elsewhere, she could take another look at the documents that had arrived that morning. She steeled herself and read through the papers once more. There was a lot of legal jargon she struggled to understand, but she understood what was happening all too well. These documents were making her family homeless. That dreadful knowledge was hard to take, but it was, she knew, the only way. She might be losing her home, but in doing that, she was protecting her family. They could always buy another home, but she couldn't buy another family.

The phone rang and she grabbed it quickly, before a second ring could bring the kids charging into the room. 'Brad?'

'Hi, Jen.'

They didn't ask each other how they were. There was no point.

'The documents came this morning.'

'Honey, I am so, so sorry. I wish there was some other way. Maybe if we don't sell, we can find the money—'

'No.' They'd had this conversation many times and her decision was made. 'You need the money for your legal fees. When this is all over, we can start again. The house isn't the important thing.'

'I love you. You know that, don't you?'

She did. And she loved him too. 'This is what being a family is all about,' she said. 'What helps one helps us all.'

There was a long moment of silence. It wasn't that there was nothing to talk about; there was so much Jen wanted to ask about Brad's life in prison, days passing slowly as he waited for a trial date. She wanted to know how he spent that time. Was he eating? Was he sleeping well? Most of all, was he safe? She'd seen movies and read books that featured life in jail, and she didn't want to believe any of that. She longed to ask Brad for the truth, but she was afraid it would be too hard to hear. At the same time, she was sure he didn't want to hear about her life, living in limbo while she waited, trying to keep the kids from understanding what was really going on. They were smart kids. They knew something was wrong, but she'd shielded them from the worst as best she could. She'd tell them one day, but not now. They were too young. All they knew was that Daddy couldn't be with them right now. That he had things to sort out related to his work and would join them as soon as he could. Only Jen understood that could be months ... or even years. How would she and the kids live through that?

'I will make it up to you.'

'No. You did nothing wrong. There's nothing to make up for.'

'I was stupid. I didn't see what was going on. I should have known and done something about it.'

'We both made mistakes, Brad. If I'd stayed there you might have been given bail.' At the hearing, the judge had decided that putting his house up for sale and sending his family away made Brad a flight risk. Remanded in custody was the result they had not expected.

'We agreed to get the kids away from all this.'

They had been through this many times before. The media camped outside their gate had frightened Suzi. No doubt by now the gossips at school were in full flight, with the kids repeating things they'd heard their parents say, the same parents who had previously described Brad as a great teacher. Suzi didn't need to hear any of that. Dylan was too young to understand what was happening, but he was not too young to feel the change in the world around him. Better that change be one that was calm and fun and good. A change that involved living with relatives, meeting horses and being with a mother who could hide her tears when he was awake and cry into her pillow in the safety of midnight.

'Are the kids there? I haven't got much time on the phone.'

When Jen appeared with the phone in her hand, Suzi tried to snatch it away.

'Daddy? When are you coming to get us?'

'Not for a while, Suzi. I'm sorry, but it's very important that I stay in Queensland. Now, put the phone on speaker so I can talk to you and your brother. Tell me what you have been doing. Have you met Aunt Lizzie's horses yet?'

Jen sat quietly holding the phone while Brad and the kids talked. He was such a good father, and now it had come to this. Brad had always worked hard to give his family everything he could and more. Even though he wasn't perfect, he was a good man. But he was given to trusting people he shouldn't. That's how this whole thing had started.

'It's a good job, Jen,' he'd said. 'Sure, I'll be away a lot more, but it won't be forever. We need the money. If I do this for a while, it will make such a change in our lives.'

He'd been right, but not in the way they had anticipated. Now he was in jail, charged with—she could barely frame the words—drug trafficking. He was innocent, of course, but he was still fighting for his life. Criminal justice took so long, but in the end, he would be back with them. She was certain of it, because he had to be. She could not envisage life without him. Not for the kids nor for her. She could only hope he wasn't changed too much by whatever he was experiencing in that prison.

'Okay, I have to go now, so I'm going to talk to Mummy for a minute. All right?'

Jen waited until the kids had said their goodbyes, then took the phone off speaker and stepped back into the bedroom.

'Be strong,' Brad said.

'You too. I love you.'

The call ended.

Jen was fighting back the tears when her children came into the room. They jumped onto the bed and snuggled up close on either side.

'Daddy's gone,' said Dylan.

'He'll be back, my darling boy. Because he loves you. He loves all of us very much, and he'll be back.'

Suzi said nothing, but there were tears in her eyes.

The three of them lay like that as, outside, the sun sank behind the trees. The light dappled and faded. The children's eyes began to droop and they fell asleep.

Jen lay there holding them, wishing she could do the same.

★★★

After another morning that started on her knees in the toilet, Kayla wasn't in the mood to talk to anyone. The office next to her bedroom was the last place she wanted to be, and with winter settled in, there were no Willowbrook weddings to worry about. She slipped into the kitchen for a large glass of iced water, then found sanctuary in the groom's room. When the homestead had been converted into a wedding venue, the room became a relaxing space for grooms and groomsmen to prepare for the ceremony. It had the feel of a library, with bookshelves and comfortable armchairs, and suited Kayla's mood today far more than the bride's room across the hall, which was a symphony in cream and gold, and had far too many mirrors for her liking.

She put her laptop on the coffee table and sank into the soft leather of an armchair. She closed her eyes and tried to empty her mind. Relaxation didn't come easily and after a few minutes, she realised it wasn't going to come at all. Too many thoughts were racing through her mind. She had a decision to make. Well, many decisions to make, but the big one was hovering at the front of her brain in big lights, refusing to go away.

What was she going to do about this pregnancy?

The past few days had been something of an eye-opener. Watching Jen with her two children was the closest Kayla had ever been to parenting. Pascale was a career woman with no intention of having children. Kayla had always been similarly wrapped up in her work. She didn't have any real friends other than those she knew through work, and none of them had children. In the last two days, she hadn't seen Jen without at least one child at her side. There had been screaming at breakfast, arguments over lunch menus and noise. So much noise. Kayla had no idea how Jen coped with that, especially now she was on her own.

Kayla very much doubted she could do it. She knew she could count on support from Lizzie and Mitch. Pascale too. And her job made enough money to pay for childcare. At least, she thought it did. But could she continue that job if she had a small child, totally dependent on her?

Therein lay the crux of the problem. Could she be a single mother? Did she *want* to be a single mother? And if the answer to those questions was no, could she face either of the alternatives?

She didn't know.

When she heard a gentle knock at the door, she welcomed the distraction, her desire to be alone with her thoughts having evaporated. 'Come in.'

Jen appeared in the doorway. 'Are you sure you want to be disturbed?'

'Please.'

'Is it all right if I leave the door open, so I can keep an ear out for Dylan?'

'Where is he?'

'He's upstairs teaching a stuffed panda to drive a toy train. Suzi is with Lizzie, down at the stables. She's trying to convince Lizzie to give her riding lessons.'

Kayla chuckled. 'That's going to be a tough job.'

'No, it's not. Lizzie has already asked me if it's all right for her to do it. She's just got to find the right pony.'

Kayla was surprised. Lizzie had endless patience when it came to training horses, but she'd never really thought of her sister as being good with kids. 'Will you be here long enough for her to learn?'

Jen tilted her head on the side. 'Kayla, I know you didn't expect us to be here. But then, Lizzie and Mitch said your weddings were done for the season when they offered me this place while Brad ...' She hesitated and took a deep breath, obviously fighting for composure. 'While Brad faces his trial. But if it's a problem for you ...'

'No. No problem at all. It's a big house.'

'And it will give us a chance to catch up. It's been far too long.'

Kayla nodded.

'I suppose you're wondering about what happened with Brad. It's a long story. Perhaps one night soon, after the kids are asleep, we can have a glass of wine and talk.'

She wanted to be a good friend. She wanted to say *Hey, I'm here with a shoulder to cry on if you need me.* But she couldn't. She did not have the emotional strength for someone else's problems. She was barely coping with her own. The best she could manage was to stay silent.

A long minute passed before Jen spoke again. 'In the meantime, if you want us to leave ...'

Kayla wanted to say yes. Having Jen and her children sharing the house was only going to make her life harder. Make her secret harder to hide. And she did want to hide it as long as she could while she tried to decide. Did she want to be a single mother?

Could she give a baby up for adoption? Or should she end this now? She didn't want anyone to know she was pregnant until she had an answer to those questions.

'No. I don't want you to leave. It's good to see you again. You'll just have to give me a bit of time to get used to sharing the house. Especially with kids.'

'You are going to have to get used to that even if we aren't here.'

Kayla looked at her friend. 'You guessed?'

'I've had two kids, Kayla. It wasn't hard to figure out. And the morning sickness was a dead giveaway. Do Lizzie and Mitch know?'

'Not yet.'

'How far along are you?'

'Nine weeks.'

'You know exactly?'

She didn't want to think about that night, and she certainly wasn't ready to talk to anyone about it. 'Yes. Exactly.'

'Is the father …?'

'No. He doesn't know and he's not going to be any part of this.' Kayla steeled herself for the response.

'If that's how you want it. You have family who love you. We're all here to help.'

That was unexpected. No questions or recriminations or arguments about the father's rights or responsibilities. Or hers. Acceptance, Kayla realised, was what she needed right now. If someone else could accept her situation, maybe she would too.

'Thank you.'

'Have you found a doctor or midwife yet?'

'No. I've been fine, well, apart from the throwing up. I haven't even thought about it.'

'You should. For the baby's sake as much as yours. Once Suzi is back at school, I can come with you if it would help.'

'I'm not sure if ...' Kayla's voice tailed off.

The look in Jen's eyes told her she knew exactly what Kayla had been thinking. There was no judgement on her face or in her voice when she spoke. 'Whatever you decide, the first step is to see an obstetrician.'

She was right, of course. Kayla felt a wave of relief.

How different this was from when they'd been best friends as kids. Once Lizzie and Mitch had started dating and left the younger sisters to their own devices, Kayla had been the strong one. The one who had all the ideas and all the answers. It felt strangely good to let Jen take the lead.

'Okay. I have no idea about ...' Kayla waved her arms in the air.

'No-one does the first time. It helps a lot to have someone to count on. I had Brad.' Jen's voice broke a little but she hurried on. 'And Mum too, of course. I will be here for you, if you'll let me. If you want me.'

'Yes to both of those. Thank you, Jen. I'm glad you're here.'

A loud noise from upstairs called Jen away. She was smiling as she left, but Kayla wasn't at all sure she would have been. She didn't have Jen's calm strength. In the past couple of days, she'd quickly come to understand that Jen was a great mother. Kayla had doubts about her own ability, even with all the help in the world.

She glanced out the window at the crisp blue sky and the stables. Lizzie would be there. Maybe this would be a good time to talk to her.

Kayla found her sister in the tack room. Lizzie had the door shut against the cold as she cleaned a stock saddle, buffing the leather to a warm glow.

'Hi. Glad you came down. We haven't had a moment alone to really talk.'

'I know.' Kayla perched on an old feed tin. 'Is that Dad's saddle?'

'Yes. Mitch uses it sometimes when he's competing. It might have a few years on it, but it's a good saddle.'

'Dad would be pleased to know it was still being used.'

'I think he would too.'

The sisters sat in silence, both lost in memories.

'How is it living in the house with Jen and the kids?'

'It's not too bad. Jen tries to keep the kids quiet ... but it doesn't always work.'

Lizzie chuckled. 'And you were never exactly keen on babies.'

That took Kayla a bit by surprise. 'Wasn't I? I don't remember ever saying I didn't want kids.'

'It wasn't that you said it, it's just that all the time you spent playing with dolls, they were always brides with pretty gowns. You never had baby dolls.'

An image flashed in Kayla's mind: a Kewpie doll in a big white dress held tightly in the shaking hand of a frightened little girl.

'Well, you never had dolls at all,' Kayla countered. 'Seriously though, now you and Mitch are together again, have you thought about kids?'

Lizzie's hand stilled for a moment, then resumed its rhythmic polishing. 'Mitch would be a wonderful father. We would like kids, but it hasn't happened yet.'

Kayla was stunned. 'You've been trying?'

'Not exactly trying. But not *not* trying, if that makes sense.'

'How long for?'

'Not long. We're not worried. I'm sure it will happen for us.'

'Oh, Lizzie. I'm sorry. Have you talked to a doctor?'

'Don't be sorry. It's early days yet. It hasn't been long enough to talk to a doctor. Maybe we will eventually, but we're in no hurry. We've got plenty of time.'

Kayla studied her sister carefully. She couldn't detect any under-tones of sadness or worry, so maybe Lizzie really wasn't concerned. At least not yet. But this was hardly the time to confess to her own condition and ask for her help. After the accident that took their parents, Lizzie had been the strong one. She had supported Kayla, paid her way through school and university. That had taken its toll on their relationship. Rebuilding that relationship had taken time, but they were in a good place now. Kayla realised she didn't want to change that by once again asking her sister for help. Lizzie would give it in a heartbeat. Financial, emotional—whatever help Kayla needed. But she wasn't going to ask. It was her mistake that had brought her to this place. She had to fix it herself.

CHAPTER
5

'Are you expecting a delivery?' Pete asked as he prised open another can of paint.

'No. Why?'

'Because you keep looking through that window, leaving me to do all the work.'

'Well, there goes your free beer at the end of the day.' Connor chuckled to make sure Pete knew he was joking. 'Come on, I want to get these walls finished today.'

'Yes, boss.'

They settled down to the steady rhythm of work they had established. After ten days, the tired old pub was already showing the fruits of their labours. The tatty old lino had been removed and the bare floorboards were now waiting for the sander. When done, they would glow with a dark polish. The odd assortment of tables and chairs was gone and replacements were on their way. The biggest changes of all had been in the kitchen. On day one they had pulled out the filthy old grills, hot plate and oven. The new equipment was already in place and the stainless steel gleamed in an inviting fashion. The newly painted cabinets and cupboards held stacks of cheap, but good, plates and serving dishes—no mismatched or cracked dishes for Connor's customers. He tried not to think about the amount of money he'd spent; his bank loan was almost bottomed out. He'd have enough to get in stocks of food and drink, but after that he needed customers. And he needed them quickly. What was that line from the old Kevin Costner baseball movie? *Build it and they will come.* He could only hope that was true.

A few minutes later, the sound of a car outside caused him to lift his head from his work again. The person who got out of the driver's side was not the woman with the wavy dark hair he'd been hoping to see again. Nor was the passenger. The occupants of the car were not exactly unexpected, but he couldn't say he was pleased to see them. Although perhaps it was good to get this encounter over and done with before the pub opened.

He put his tools down and greeted the police as they came through the door. 'Morning.'

'Good morning.' The sergeant removed his hat. 'We're looking for the new owner. Would that be you?'

'Yes, it would.' Connor held out his hand. 'Connor Knight.'

The sergeant looked at Connor's hand for a second before he took it. Connor knew he was looking at the tattoos, dark stains that told the sergeant exactly what he needed to know, even if he hadn't already run the name of the town's new publican through the police system, which Connor assumed he had.

'Baker,' the sergeant said. 'And that's Constable Mills.'

'Pleased to meet you. How can I help you?'

On the other side of the room, Pete stopped painting and turned on his ladder to watch.

'Hey, Pete.' Baker nodded in his direction before turning back to Connor. 'Just thought I should drop by for introductions. In case, you know … in case you have need to call on us.'

'Thanks. Hopefully I won't.'

'We've been called here most weekends ever since I arrived in Scone four years ago,' Baker said. 'I imagine you've got an idea of the way it was then. Rough. Fights. Bikie gangs.'

So he had run Connor through the system. He knew about the gangs. Connor hoped the sergeant also knew about that last court case, when Connor gave evidence that put the gang leaders behind bars. If he'd talked to the parole officer, he'd know how hard Connor was trying to put that past behind him.

'When you shut the place to do it up, my Saturday night felt incomplete.'

Connor said nothing as the sergeant slowly walked around the room, inspecting the renovations.

'You're putting a lot of work in. That's good. It needed it. I'm told this used to be a nice pub. You know, the sort families would come to for lunch.'

'I was told the same thing.' Connor had been pushed around often in his life by tough men in uniforms. By even tougher men not wearing uniforms. He didn't scare easily, but he also knew when to stay silent.

Baker finished his round of the room and stopped in front of Connor. Their eyes locked for a very long minute.

Then the sergeant nodded. 'This is a nice town. Full of good people. I'd like to see this pub the way it used to be—safe and friendly on a Saturday night.'

'That's what I want too. I've had enough trouble in my life. Now I simply want to settle somewhere peaceful.'

'Fair enough. Let's hope that's how it goes.'

The police officers turned towards the door. Connor waited until both men were nearly there before he spoke again.

'Sergeant, maybe one day you'll drop in on a Saturday night—for a quiet beer, this time.'

The man didn't turn around, but Connor saw his shoulders move as he laughed. 'That sounds good to me.'

Connor knew he'd left the past behind, but some things had a habit of sneaking up on a man when he wasn't looking. The relief he felt as the officers left was real.

'He's a good bloke, really,' Pete said from his perch on the ladder. 'He comes across a bit … you know. But he's okay.'

'I'm sure he is.'

Connor bent back to his work. He'd seen good and bad cops in the past and he'd developed a bit of an instinct for telling them apart; a survival instinct of sorts. He suspected Pete was right and both Baker and his offsider were honest cops. More than honest—good cops. Maybe. But trusting anyone in a uniform was a skill he had yet to master.

He rubbed a bit of paint off his hands, thinking for the hundredth time that life would be a touch easier if he didn't have the tatts. But they were part of the experiences that had made him who he was. He'd removed some of the letters to make them less offensive, but the rest he'd left. He wasn't proud of his past, but to deny it would be to deny who he now was. And he wouldn't do that. And he hadn't been lying when he said he hoped the cops would drop by for an off-duty drink. A cop was as welcome as anyone else in his place.

By mid-afternoon, they'd repainted the whole bar and stopped for smoko. Breathing the fume-free air by the front door, Connor sipped a cup of coffee and watched the traffic go past. The town was quite busy. There would be mothers picking up kids from school, doing the shopping. Other people meeting friends at a coffee shop. Maybe one day soon, they'd be meeting their friends in his bar. He caught his breath as what looked like a beautifully restored red Datsun 260Z drove past. But not even that classic could hold his attention when he caught a glimpse of the woman behind the wheel. For a moment he thought she glanced in his direction as she drove past at a sedate speed that belied what ownership of such a car said about her. Most of what it said was that she was even further out of his league than he'd originally thought.

She hadn't looked his way, or if she had, it was the pub she was checking out, not him. She wouldn't even have seen him. Maybe one day, when the restoration was complete and his pub had found its place in the town, she would drop in for a beer. He would look forward to that much more than having the two policemen come back through his door.

Smoko done, he was ready to start sanding the counter when his phone rang.

'Hello.'

'It's Hayden. About the job.' Hayden was another ex-con. They'd met inside when Connor had taken the kid under his wing. While Connor had been doing wood and metal work in the shop, Hayden had learned how to cook. Connor had offered him the job cooking in the pub. He'd wanted to give the kid a break, but at the same time, Hayden was the only cook he could afford.

'G'day, Hayden. Have you talked to your parole officer?'

'Yeah, I have. He's willing to transfer me up there.'

'That's good. We'll be ready for you in a week. So I'll see you then.'

'Sure. Um … Connor?'

'What?'

'I heard on the grapevine that your old gang is looking for you.'

Connor's jaw clenched. His old gang was dangerous, and since he'd shopped them to the cops, he was top of their list for revenge. The last thing he wanted was them showing up here in Scone. His new start would be over before it had even got off the ground.

'What did you tell them?'

'Nothing, Connor. I wouldn't do that.'

'Okay. Thanks. Just try to avoid them. They're bad news and hanging out with them will do you out of a job and probably put you back inside.'

'I know. I'm not gonna blow it this time.'

'Good. Then I'll see you next week.'

'Okay, boss. See you then.' Hayden hung up.

Connor stared at his phone. The boy's words were disturbing, but there was nothing he could do about them. He put his phone away and picked up the sander.

By the time he and Pete finished work for the day, it was starting to get dark. Pete passed on their regular beer—he had a date. So Connor ripped the top off a can and stood alone at the window overlooking the street, watching as the lights blinked on in the surrounding buildings. The sarge was right. This was a nice town. One he hoped would accept him enough that he could feel at home.

CHAPTER
6

Jen put the phone down and thumped her forehead on the kitchen table. She glanced at her watch. Half an hour on the phone to the lawyer. At the rates he was charging, that was a pretty expensive way of finding out that they still didn't have a court date, something Brad could have told her for free when he called from prison tomorrow. She was really worried about money. The cash from selling the house had mostly gone to pay off the mortgage and the lawyers had already taken the rest. She wasn't sure how much more money she could raise. Brad's family weren't well off and had already given as much as they could. Her parents had offered to help, but they didn't have much spare cash either. Mitch and Lizzie had already given her and the kids a place to stay, and they'd make sure they never went hungry. But Jen knew there was nowhere else to go, except maybe a loan shark. And that was no option. Not really. Much as she hated the thought, it was high time she went to Centrelink and applied for benefits. And now Suzi was in school, maybe she could find a part-time job. But day care for Dylan would be expensive, and she couldn't ask Kayla or Lizzie to look after her kids.

She lifted her head off the table. Brad was her husband and the father of her children. She believed he was innocent and she still loved him. They would get through this somehow.

She put her phone on charge and went upstairs to find the kids. She'd left them playing in their makeshift family room. As she opened the door, she heard the TV. Dylan was humming along to the *Bluey* theme song but there was no sign of Suzi. Jen backed out of the room and looked in the bedroom, expecting to see her daughter with her nose in a book. No sign of her. That was strange. Jen went back downstairs and checked every room.

'Suzi?' She stood in the hallway and raised her voice, hopefully not enough to worry Dylan. There was no reply.

Where was she? Jen glanced upstairs to where the cartoon soundtrack could still be heard. Dylan would be all right for a second. She darted out to the front veranda and called again.

'Suzi!'

The name wafted through the trees on the breeze and down towards the stables. There was no answer.

Jen wasn't sure whether she was angry or scared. She'd told Suzi not to leave the house by herself. Her daughter knew better than that.

'Is everything all right?' Kayla appeared behind her. 'I heard you calling.'

'Suzi's gone.'

'Gone? What ... Where?'

'Probably down to the stables. I'll go and find her. Can you keep an eye on Dylan for me? He's upstairs watching cartoons.'

'Keep an eye on him? But I don't know how to look after a child. Why don't I go to the stables—'

'Really, Kayla? You're going to have one of your own in a few months; it's about time you learned. Go and sit with Dylan and make sure he doesn't do anything silly or hurt himself. Suzi can do it and she's only seven.'

Without giving Kayla time to answer, Jen set off for the stables, deeply disappointed and annoyed with her best friend—her former best friend.

The anger vanished as she approached the stable block, leaving only the fear.

'Suzi? Are you here?' She didn't call too loudly because a startled horse is a dangerous horse, especially around a little girl who did not know what she was doing. Jen went into the stables, checking each stall. The stallion's stall was at the far end. With her heart in her mouth, Jen looked over the stable door. Deimos was dozing quietly in the corner. Alone.

As she left the stables, Jen called for her daughter again, a little more loudly this time. There was still no answer. Where could Suzi be? She turned slowly in a circle and saw a flash of red in the yearling paddock on the other side of the training arena. Suzi was wearing a red top. Jen ran half the way, then dropped back to a walk. She could see her daughter now, surrounded by a group of yearlings. Even at that young age, the horses were already taller than Suzi. And those unshod hooves looked very sharp.

'Suzi, don't make any sudden noises or movements.'

'Mum?' When Suzi looked around, her face was shining with happiness. She showed no fear as she rubbed the nose of a colt.

'Suzi, walk over to the gate. Slowly, now. Don't frighten the horses.' Jen was already fiddling with the latch. Her hands were shaking and it took several goes for her to release it. The young horses were as interested in Jen as they were in her daughter, and Jen slipped carefully into the paddock, gently pushing her way through the group until she reached Suzi. Jen had been around horses when she and Kayla had been best friends, but that was a long time ago. She wasn't exactly scared—and certainly not for herself, but her daughter … that was a different matter. Even a yearling could hurt a small girl.

'Come on, we need to walk back to the gate.'

Keeping herself between Suzi and the yearlings, who were crowding close, Jen opened the gate and guided Suzi through. She followed and, with a sigh of relief, latched the gate behind her. The curious young horses stuck their heads over the fence. Suzi reached up to pat one just as another gave a sharp kick with a hind leg. A third horse squealed and half-reared and a moment later the group were galloping across the paddock, kicking and bucking as they went.

'Aren't they beautiful, Mummy?'

'Yes, honey, they are, but they're also a little bit wild and much bigger than you.'

Jen crouched and took her daughter by the shoulders. She looked intently at her face. Suzi was too brave for her own good. Jen didn't want to frighten her, but she had to make her understand.

'Did you see how they kicked and squealed? They don't hurt each other when they kick, but if they kicked you, they would hurt you. You need to promise me you will never come down here by yourself. You must always have me or Aunt Lizzie or Uncle Mitch with you.'

'What about Auntie Kayla?'

Jen didn't think there was much chance of that. 'Yes. Aunt Kayla too. One of us has to be with you. We don't want any accidents.'

'Auntie Lizzie said I could have a pony of my own. I thought maybe one of those, because they are the small ones.'

'They're small now, but they've got a lot of growing up to do. Like you. I'm sure when Aunt Lizzie has found the right pony for you, she'll tell you.'

'Sorry if I was bad, Mummy.'

Jen swept her daughter into her arms, trying not to cry. 'It's all right, honey. No harm done. Promise me you won't do it again. I was worried.'

The head tucked against her shoulder nodded.

'All right. Let's go back and find Dylan. There might be milk and cake in the kitchen if we look hard enough.'

'Yay, cake.' Suzi wriggled out of Jen's arms to jump up and down.

★★★

Kayla heard Suzi's footsteps and voice on the stairs. Then her niece bounded through the door.

'Dylan. Mum says come downstairs. There's cake.'

'Yay!'

'You can have cake too, Aunt Kayla.'

'Thank you. I'll be down in a couple of minutes.'

As the door slammed behind the kids, Kayla's shoulders sagged with relief. She was glad Suzi was all right, but it was more than that. She'd grown increasingly tense while sitting here with Dylan. Not that the boy had done anything to cause it. Quite the reverse, he'd been perfectly well behaved, watching the cartoon and occasionally singing along. The stress had all grown out of Kayla's mind. What if he wanted to go to the toilet and needed help. Did a two-year-old need help going to the toilet? And what if something had happened? If he'd fallen and hit his head or started to cry? Or maybe something worse. She would've had no idea how to deal with it.

She stood up, turned side on to the mirror over the dresser and put her hand on her stomach. The bump wasn't showing yet, but it would soon. And then, a few months later, she'd be responsible for a baby. If she was like this after babysitting Dylan for fifteen minutes, what was she going to be like with a fragile, terrifying newborn?

She couldn't do this. She really couldn't. She wasn't altogether sure she was cut out to be a mother at all—and certainly not a single mother. Wouldn't it be better just to end this now? She could return to the job she was good at, move back into the apartment she loved and go back to the lifestyle she had worked so hard to build. There would be plenty of time to have children later when she'd met the right man and was ready for a family. When she didn't have to do this on her own.

Yes. That was the sensible thing to do.

Behind her, the door opened. She turned quickly, not wanting to be seen checking her figure.

'Kayla?'

'Hi, Jen. Glad Suzi's all right. I guess she was down with the horses.'

'I've told her not to do that ever again. Are you coming downstairs? There's cake and milk ... although you'd probably prefer something else.'

'After the past few minutes, I need a stiff drink.' She wasn't entirely joking.

'Was Dylan a problem?'

'No. No. Not at all ... It's just that I know nothing about kids. Even less about babies. I can't be a mother.'

'I know it's daunting, but none of us know anything about having a baby the first time. I knew nothing either. There's all sorts of people out there to help. And you're one of the smartest women I know. You'll do fine.'

'But what if I don't? I'm all the baby would have. I'm not so sure I can go through with this. Not alone.' The words were out before she realised what she had said.

'You're not alone, Kay. You know that. Whatever you decide, your family is here for you.' Jen took a step closer and put her arm around Kayla's shoulders. 'You don't have to decide now. There's time for you to figure out the right thing to do. And you will. I'm here to talk to if I can help. In the meantime, why not join me and the kids for cake?'

'No G&T?' She tried to make it a joke.

'No. But I do have some nice chamomile tea. How does that sound?'

The tea sounded awful, but Kayla didn't have the heart to say so.

CHAPTER

7

Jen wasn't there to support Kayla on her first visit to the obstetrician two weeks later. She'd made a late-afternoon appointment at the private clinic, but that morning, Dylan had woken up grizzling and crying.

'He's running a temperature,' Jen said, her forehead creased with worry. 'I don't think it's too bad, but I think I should keep him in bed. And I don't want to take him to the clinic. He might pass something on to the other kids.'

'It's no problem,' Kayla assured her. 'I'm fine doing this alone. You stay here and look after him.'

'Why don't you ask Lizzie to go with you? I'm sure she'd be only too pleased to be there for you.'

'No. I think telling her I'm pregnant and then asking her to come to the appointment all in one day might be a bit too much.'

'You're kidding? Nothing is too much for your sister. She wouldn't bat an eyelid.'

Jen was right, of course, but Kayla just wasn't ready to tell Lizzie she was pregnant yet. She was still hoping that those little blue lines had been wrong.

'It's fine. Lizzie would fuss over me and I'd rather do this first one alone.'

'If you're sure.'

She was sure. She had dressed in a smart but simple linen outfit that always gave her confidence. She had this. She walked swiftly out to her little red sports car and slipped behind the wheel, getting the same lift from the act that she always did. The Datsun was a classic. It was fun and sleek and a little bit sexy. It always made her feel good to drive it and today was no exception, right up to the moment when she pulled into the clinic carpark. The little red sports car that she loved so much looked totally out of place among the sensible sedans and SUVs. There were cars with plenty of space for prams, and kids and kids' friends and sports equipment and dogs. Cars with baby seats in the back, shade devices stuck to the side windows and signs saying BABY ON BOARD. By comparison, her car shouted to the world that she was not ready—or fit—to be a mother.

'I'll need a new car. If I decide ...' She still struggled to say the words out loud. At that moment, she wished more than anything that Lizzie was with her. Kayla's whole world had lost its substance and purpose and direction, and she really wasn't fine doing this alone after all. Tears were not all that far away, but she took a deep breath and blamed them on hormones. Then, with determined movements, she pulled the keys from the ignition and got out of the car. If she couldn't even do this alone, what hope did she have of being a decent single mother?

Walking through the door into the waiting room was like stepping into an alien world. The walls were bright yellow and covered with artwork done by children. There were rainbows and stick figures of people and animals of indeterminate species. There were big yellow suns and even bigger red flowers in crayon and pencil and watercolour. Beneath this storm of colour, mothers sat on rows of plastic chairs. Some were trying to read magazines while their offspring climbed into their laps. Others were holding fast to the small hands of toddlers intent on running around. One kid had escaped and was standing in the far corner of the room stamping its feet. And the noise! Kayla wasn't sure which was louder, the children's voices or the sounds of the mothers telling them to hush and be quiet.

She stopped in her tracks, feeling a wave of something very like panic. Her first appointment would have ended before it began had not the receptionist behind the desk spotted her and waved her over.

'Good morning. You're new, so I guess you're Mrs Lawson.'

'Ms Lawson.'

'Of course. My apologies.'

Kayla could almost feel the eyes of the women in the room behind her. Some of them must know who she was. Or maybe they knew Lizzie. The small-town grapevine would be working overtime this afternoon.

'Could you take this form, please? It's for all your details and medical history and so forth. You can take a seat anywhere and fill it in.'

Kayla took the clipboard and pen and selected a seat in the corner as far away from the other patients as she could. She started filling out what seemed a pretty standard medical history form, but her hand stopped moving when she turned the page and saw the first line at the top of page two: Father's Name.

She'd known she was going to have to deal with that detail at some point, but she hadn't thought it would be quite this soon.

It wasn't just the name they wanted either. They wanted contact details. Then there were questions relating to the father's medical history. She certainly had no idea about that. She had a face and a name and a phone number. Well, email too. And she had a lot of feelings. Regret. Anger. Possibly something that was very close to shame. She willed the hand holding the pencil to stop shaking, left those fields blank and moved on. She had always considered herself a strong woman, but there was only so much she could deal with. One thing at a time.

When she was led through to the doctor's office, Kayla was proud that her hands were no longer shaking. Her armour was firmly in place as she sat down. A few moments later a woman in her mid-forties walked in.

'Ms Lawson, I'm Doctor Woods.'

'Pleased to meet you.' Kayla knew that if the woman congratulated her, she would scream.

'Welcome to our clinic. If you don't mind, I'd like to go through the form with you before we move on.'

'Of course.' The doctor's businesslike attitude steadied the nervous ache in her stomach.

It was the work of a few moments to check Kayla's details, then the doctor turned the page and saw the blank fields for the father's details.

'The biological father won't be involved at all moving forward?'

'No. He won't.'

The doctor made a small notation on the form and moved on to the next page. It was that easy. Of course it was. Kayla released the breath she'd been holding. Medical professionals were used to dealing with single mothers and didn't ask difficult questions. Her family might be a very different matter, but that could wait a little longer.

'Shouldn't we make sure I really am pregnant before we go any further with this?'

'You said here you took a home test.'

'Three of them.'

'And you have missed a period and have been vomiting.'

'It's two periods now.'

'Then we can be pretty sure you are pregnant. I will get my nurse to take a blood test before you leave today, so we will double check, but that blood test is mostly to monitor things like your sugar levels and general health.'

'Oh.' And that was that. Her last hope dashed.

Doctor Woods looked at Kayla. 'I'm sorry, but I have to ask this. You don't sound like you're certain you want to go ahead with the pregnancy?'

'To be honest, I'm really not sure.'

'I understand. I think the most important thing at this point is to make sure you're healthy. The receptionist can give you the information about all your options.'

'Thank you.'

'You don't have to make any decisions now, but remember, the longer you leave it, the more difficult it's going to be.'

The doctor went on, explaining about the care Kayla would need in the weeks and months ahead if she decided to have the baby.

'You might want to start thinking about a birth partner. It's never too early to have support during the pregnancy.'

'I'm sorry. A birth partner?'

'Someone to be with you for the actual birth. And they might also come to antenatal classes with you. Help you prepare.'

'I see.' Kayla understood that would normally be the father.

'And of course, they'd be around in the time immediately after the birth. Dealing with a new baby all on your own can be difficult.

The clinic is here to help you through those first few weeks as well. Do you have family for support?'

'Yes.' She knew Lizzie and Mitch would support her. But first she had to find the courage to tell them.

'As you're almost twelve weeks, I think we can do your first scan today. I have time to do it now.'

'What?'

'Your first scan. We do one at about twelve weeks to check for certain abnormalities and to confirm your due date. It won't take long.'

'Do you have to do it now?'

'No, but it would be best if we did. For both you and the baby. And you would get to see your baby.'

That was exactly what Kayla did not want, not while she was still struggling to make a difficult decision. She had always believed a woman had the right to make her own choices, but now that she was facing that choice …

'Ms Lawson?'

Kayla almost leaped from her seat. 'Sorry. Yes. Yes. Let's do the scan.'

The doctor pulled the ultrasound device to the side of the bed, turning it so Kayla had a clear view of the screen. But as the cold gel dribbled onto her stomach, Kayla turned her head and closed her eyes. If the doctor noticed, she said nothing until the scan was complete.

'That all looks fine, Ms Lawson,' the doctor reassured her. 'And I think we're right with the due date too. I'll give you a moment.'

Kayla opened her eyes cautiously as the doctor returned the ultrasound device to its corner. She wiped the gel from her stomach and straightened her clothes.

'Thank you.'

'If you don't have any more questions at this point, I'll send the nurse in to talk to you about diets and supplements and to get some blood, and as long as the results look good, I won't need to see you for a while. Unless you have any concerns, in which case, just give us a call and we can make an appointment for you.'

Kayla was still in something of a daze when she left the clinic, a million pamphlets in her tote bag and a small piece of cotton wool taped over the needle site on the inside of her right elbow. She hadn't been able to stop herself noticing the titles on those pamphlets. Everything from the stages of pregnancy through to the services offered by the clinic, to home births, the role of midwives, giving up a baby for adoption and, yes, termination.

That option had seemed totally reasonable until today. Until she'd peeped during the scan and glimpsed an image on the screen. An image that was already starting to look like a baby.

She was in no fit state to drive so she began to walk, not caring where, as she lost herself in her thoughts. It was all real now. No matter how many times she'd told herself she was pregnant, she *knew* it now. Really knew it. And was beginning to understand that her whole life was changing … irreversibly. It was almost beyond comprehension.

Kayla staggered sideways, putting out one hand to balance herself as the world started to spin. Someone had punched her hard in the heart—at least that's how it felt. Her knees shook and she struggled to draw breath. A pounding in her head overwhelmed her. She would have looked for somewhere to sit, but the world was lost in a haze. She opened her mouth to cry for help, but nothing came out.

Then a firm hand grasped her arm and another circled her shoulders.

'Here, this way. You need to sit down.'

Kayla let the unknown hands guide her a few steps. As the stranger gently turned her around, she felt something hard behind her knees and collapsed onto a bench.

'Drink this.'

Something cool and damp was pushed into her hand. A bottle of water. Kayla raised it to her lips and took two mouthfuls. Slowly, her head stopped spinning.

'Take it easy now,' the gentle voice continued. 'Do you need me to call an ambulance?'

She shook her head.

'You're shaking. You need to get inside out of the cold wind. Are you able to stand, do you think?'

Was she? She didn't know.

'Here, take my arm.'

The arm was strong but gentle. The person towered over her, but it didn't feel threatening, it felt safe. She allowed herself to be led to a small set of steps.

'There's just three steps. Be careful now. There you go.'

The stranger helped her through a door then a chair appeared from somewhere and Kayla gratefully sank into it. She took another mouthful of water and realised that her hands had stopped shaking. She shivered once more, aware for the first time that she had been cold. Or was it some sort of shock?

'Thank you.'

'Are you sure you don't need a doctor or an ambulance?'

'No.' The words came out as a whisper and she shook her head cautiously. 'I need a minute, that's all.'

'Take all the time you need. You're safe here. Let me get you a wet towel to wipe your face. That will help.' The figure vanished.

Kayla took another couple of deep breaths, feeling her control returning. She looked down at the water bottle between her hands. It was almost empty. She hadn't drunk that much, surely?

'Here. This might help.' The man—she had realised that much at least—was back and holding out a towel. As she took it, she realised it was a bar towel. She turned her head. She was in a pub?

'It's all right.' She could hear the humour in his voice. 'The towel is clean and the water bottle was unopened before I gave it to you.'

If she'd been feeling more herself, Kayla might have blushed that her thoughts—pretty unkind thoughts at that—had been so clear.

'Thank you.' She raised the towel to her face and patted away the sweat. Then she wiped the back of her neck. Those two small actions made her feel so much better.

She forced her eyes to focus on the person who was crouched in front of her. As the fog faded, she saw a man about her own age, concern and kindness written all over his handsome face.

★★★

'Welcome back. How do you feel?' Connor had been on the verge of calling the ambulance despite the woman's refusal, but now the colour was returning to her face and she was obviously far more aware of her surroundings than before.

'I'll be all right. I'm not quite sure what happened.' Her voice was stronger too.

'You were walking past and you looked like you were about to faint. I brought you in out of the wind. It's a bit cold not to be wearing a jacket. I saw that—' he nodded at the cotton wool on her arm, '—so I thought maybe you needed a doctor.'

'No. No. But thank you for your help.'

The woman looked around. Connor followed her gaze and realised how the place must look with the ladders and paint cans and the fridge sitting in the middle of the room waiting to be installed.

'I'm sorry for the mess.'

The woman waved his apology away.

'I'm Connor, by the way. Connor Knight.' He held out his hand, then noticed he was still wearing his work gloves and hastily pulled one off. The hand she placed in his had long red nails and a silver ring on the middle finger. The woman might still be shaky, but her grip suggested strength and competence. She was no wilting flower.

'Kayla Lawson.'

He could have stayed there all day holding that hand and looking into her eyes, but that would have been awkward. He let her hand go and got to his feet. She started to follow suit.

'Don't rush it. You're welcome to rest here for as long as you like.'

'I think I'm all right now.' She was on her feet again.

She was quite tall but, compared to his almost two metres, still quite short. And she was slender too. He shouldn't be thinking that she was very attractive, but he couldn't help it, because she was.

'I guess I should get on and let you get back to your work,' she said, turning towards the open door.

'If you're sure.'

'I am. Thank you again for your help. I appreciate it.'

'Don't mention it.'

They walked out of the pub and Kayla looked around. He saw the surprise on her face when she saw where she was and guessed that maybe she'd walked further than she realised while she was out of it.

'We'll be reopening in a couple of days,' Connor said. 'Drop by sometime.'

'You're the new owner?'

'Yes. Owner, barman and everything else.'

'I'll think about it. Goodbye, Connor.'

He liked the way she said his name and he liked the smile she flashed him.

'Goodbye, Kayla.'

As he watched her walk away, he told himself he was just making sure she was all right and not likely to faint.

'Oh, man, she's well out of your league,' he muttered to himself.

He went back to sanding the old, blistered paint around the pub door. He didn't think Kayla would be coming by the pub any time soon. Even with new paint and all the polish on the wooden bar, he didn't think his pub would be in her league either.

CHAPTER

8

Kayla was sleeping later each morning. Back in the city, she'd been awake every morning before seven and on her way to work by eight. After these few weeks back at Willowbrook, she rarely woke before eight, unless something disturbed her. Sometimes it was the kids yelling, but this morning it was a voicemail alert pinging into her phone at five past seven. She reached for the device, a bit bleary eyed. There could only be one person trying to contact her at this time of day; Pascale was always at her desk by eight, but she checked messages well before that. Sent them too.

Kayla put the phone back on her bedside table and pulled the doona over her head. She would call back later. Maybe. She didn't want to talk to Pascale. For a start, with winter in full swing, the spring wedding season wasn't far away and Pascale would want to know when Kayla was coming back to work. She had no answer for that. The next question would be why she'd needed time off—and she had no answer for that either. One more hour in bed, then she could face Pascale's questions. She'd been feeling tired, with good reason, and shouldn't feel guilty about resting a bit longer. It wasn't as if she had anything else she had to do.

She lay with her eyes shut, not sleeping, for a full ten minutes before reaching for the phone and calling her voicemail.

'Kayla, call me as soon as you get this. I have a rush wedding ... three weeks. Willowbrook would be perfect. It's small and profitable. Easy. Call me.'

Of course Pascale had a wedding. There was always one more wedding. Kayla heaved herself into a sitting position and dialled.

'Hi, Pascale.'

'How are you? I've missed you. Suddenly everyone is getting engaged. It's some sort of winter marriage madness. So many new bookings coming in for next year, even a couple of rush jobs for later this year. When are you coming back? I need you.'

Time to bite the bullet. 'I'm not sure. Not for a while though. You're going to have to manage without me.'

'Are you all right?' The change in Pascale's demeanour, from boss to friend, was palpable.

'Yes. Sort of. It's a long story and not one I want to get into now. I'll tell you when I've got everything sorted out myself.'

'Are you sure? I'm here if you need me.'

'I know.' She did too. Pascale was a friend, but Pascale's world was very different to Kayla's. Once Kayla had thought they were the same, but while Kayla had started to fall out of love with glamour weddings, Pascale never would. Or she'd never fall out of love with the very profitable business of organising other people's expensive weddings. Kayla couldn't fault her for that.

Kayla sighed. 'Tell me about this wedding. Three weeks, you said in your message?'

'Yes. It was a shock for me too. But you know this pair.' Pascale named a high-profile celebrity couple.

'But we've been planning their wedding for months. It's all set for January. Two hundred guests at the Intercontinental. What happened?'

'That one is still going ahead, but they've decided they want a small, private ceremony. Sort of like eloping. Just the two of them and a party of about a dozen. Fly in and fly out. Can you do it?'

Of course she could do it. That wasn't the point. Did she want to do it? She had more than enough on her plate right now. And there was Jen and the kids to consider. She was about to say no, but hesitated. She'd been spending her days sitting around, thinking. Way, way too much thinking. A distraction right now would be good for her.

'I'll do it.'

'Great. I'm emailing everything to you now.'

'Okay. I'll look at it today.' Kayla ended the call and dashed to the bathroom to appease the demands of her bladder, which seemed to be getting worse on an almost daily basis.

Great was not the response she got when she told Jen about the wedding. They were in the kitchen having lunch. The kids were eating spaghetti hoops on toast. Kayla was trying to eat the healthy food suggested by the clinic, but part of her really, really wanted canned spaghetti hoops on toast. Was that her first food craving?

'Doesn't it take a lot longer than three weeks to plan a wedding?' Jen asked.

'Normally it does. But this is going to be very small. And we have everything we need here. All I have to organise is flowers, catering and some serving staff. I can do it.'

'If you think so.' Jen did not sound convinced.

Kayla took a deep breath. 'Look, don't take this the wrong way, but usually Willowbrook is empty … I mean no-one lives here. I come here for the weddings and that's it. I'll need you to keep the kids out of sight on the day.'

For half a second Jen looked taken aback, then she nodded. 'Of course. Will it be outside? They could watch from an upstairs window?'

Kayla wanted to tell Jen to take them somewhere else for the day, but that wouldn't be fair. Jen lived here as much as Kayla did, and neither of them knew how long they'd both be here. 'It'll be too cold to be outside—we'll have the ceremony in the ballroom. The kids might get a quick peek if they sit very quietly at the top of the stairs as the bride walks through the hall. I'm sure that'll be fine.' She wasn't at all sure, but what else was she going to say?

It felt good getting back into the familiar routine. The pile of pamphlets from the clinic was sitting on her desk. Kayla gathered them up and dropped them in a drawer. They could wait. Then she started contacting her suppliers to organise catering and waiting staff. She needed a wedding celebrant too. On such short notice, a lot of them would already be booked, but her contacts list was long and she found someone with her fourth email. From storage cupboards in the homestead, Kayla brought out boxes filled with tablecloths and vases, candelabra and ribbon.

Normally she would have employed someone to help with preparing for the wedding. There were glasses and canape trays to be washed, wooden floors to be brought to a golden shine and every trace of dust to be removed from sight. But as this was the only wedding on her books, she decided to do it herself, taking a surprising degree of pleasure from some of the simple tasks. It might have been that planning a wedding was a welcome distraction, or perhaps it was because her morning sickness seemed to have stopped the moment she accepted the job.

Jen helped her, and Kayla made a mental note to make sure she was paid for her work. She deserved it and, given the circumstances, probably needed the money. After all these years, the two of them once more shared some things in common—not simply the wedding and the house, but also the uncertainty of their future. Maybe this was a chance for them to grow close again.

***

Two days later, the whole family gathered at the stables for Suzi's first riding lesson, following the arrival of Jango, a quiet old grey gelding who was to become her pony.

'Remember, Suzi, Aunt Lizzie has only borrowed the pony.' Jen wanted to make sure her daughter understood. 'We can only keep Jango for as long as we're here. When we go back home to Queensland, he has to go back to his real owners.'

'I know, Mummy.'

Jen suspected that when the time came, any parting of the ways would involve a lot of tears. But that was yet another thing she could put in the box labelled 'one day I'll have to deal with this'. Compared to some of the other things in that box, her daughter's attachment to an old grey pony was going to be relatively easy to manage.

'All right. Now, you listen to your Aunt Lizzie and make sure you do everything she says, all right?'

'Yes, Mummy.'

'She'll be fine,' Kayla assured her as Lizzie led the pony into the railed exercise arena and waved at Suzi to join her. 'Lizzie's good at this. And Suzi is a smart kid. She'll learn.'

'I know.' Jen's heart was in her mouth as her daughter approached the pony and, under Lizzie's guidance, stroked first its nose then its neck. The pony didn't move a muscle.

'You were never frightened of ponies when we were kids. I used to ride more than you did and while neither of us was as horse mad as Lizzie and Mitch, you weren't afraid.'

'I wasn't a mother then. I worry far more about the kids than I ever did about myself. But I guess you'll find that out.' There was no chance Lizzie or Mitch would hear—Lizzie was too busy with the riding lesson and Mitch had taken Dylan into the stables to help him mix the evening feeds.

'I never saw it that way. I guess I've got a lot to learn about being a parent.'

Silence settled for a few minutes as they watched Lizzie lead the pony slowly around the yard, Suzi sitting in the child's saddle that had once been Kayla's. The little girl's back was ramrod straight and her hands steady and gentle on the reins. She had her head tilted to one side, listening to every word her instructor said.

'She has her Uncle Mitch's love of horses,' Jen said. 'I wish I was able to give her a pony of her own. And lessons and a life like this. But ...' Her voice trailed off as the weight of her circumstances came crashing down on her. The woman standing beside her had once been her best friend and now, at this almost impossible time, she didn't feel she could turn to her because this Kayla was not the one she had known. This Kayla was wrapped up in her own problems, which was totally understandable. But right at this moment, Jen wished for her old friend back, because she needed all the help she could get.

A lump formed in her throat as she forced herself to smile and nod at Suzi as she rode past, grinning wildly. This was not the time for tears, but they came none the less.

Almost the same moment that Suzi dismounted and hugged the pony, Mitch and Dylan appeared from the direction of the feed room. Her son was sitting on his uncle's shoulders and carrying a couple of carrots that were no doubt destined for Jango. Mitch leaned on the railing next to her, keeping a firm grip on his nephew.

He frowned as he looked at Jen and she blinked away the last couple of tears.

'Jen, is everything—'

Mitch's question was cut off by the arrival of Lizzie, Suzi and Jango.

'Mummy, did you see me? I was trotting. Jango is the best pony ever.'

'I know, I saw how well you did. I think your brother has some carrots. Why don't you both give Jango one?'

Under cover of the fuss involved in feeding the carrots to the eager pony, Jen caught Mitch's eye and smiled. It wasn't much of a smile, but she hoped it would tell him that she was all right, considering the circumstances, and that the tears were only a momentary weakness.

'I've got an idea,' Mitch said as they walked to the stables. 'Once Suzi has got Jango happily settled back in his stall, why don't we go into town? I have some things to pick up, and we could all have lunch to celebrate the newest member of the family.'

He meant Jango of course, but Jen cast a quick glance at Kayla, who seemed not to interpret it any other way.

'That's a good idea,' Lizzie said. 'What does everyone think?'

'Why don't we try the Stockman? It should have reopened by now,' Kayla suggested.

The kids cheered and Jen nodded, happy for the distraction.

CHAPTER
9

'They'll come, boss. Give them time.' Connor's new—and only barmaid—Laura, was a local single mum in her early forties with a round face and a robust sense of humour. She'd been recommended for the job by Pete, who'd described her as honest and a hard worker, and that's all Connor could ask for. He was happy to arrange her shifts around her family needs. If every day was as quiet as this one, it wouldn't be hard.

'I know. And we'll be ready when they do.'

Maybe he should have had balloons. Or a band. Or something more impressive than a sign saying GRAND REOPENING. His posts in the community Facebook groups had attracted a few thumbs up. A couple of the local shops had let him put announcements in their windows and Pete had been spreading the word. But that wasn't enough. An ad in the local media would have been good, but Connor couldn't afford that. After the repairs and restocking, he only had enough cash left to pay a month's salary for his new cook and barmaid. What he needed now was a few customers to give them something to do.

He took a few steps away from the door to look up at the new sign: THE GATEWAY HOTEL.

He had painted that sign himself, with the image of an open gate. He had hoped his customers would see that open gate as a welcome. He saw it as a gate leading to something in the future. Something new and better. Something he could be proud of.

Connor walked back into the bar. Standing out there was not helping attract customers. He decided to put some music on the jukebox. It would at least make the place seem—not alive so much as less dead. The pub looked pretty good now the refurb was finished. There was still a hint of a smell of fresh paint, but that would vanish as soon as the kitchen and bar were working. There was still more to do. He'd like to redo the bathrooms, but at least they were clean now. The counter was newly polished and behind it, Laura was making sure the glasses gleamed too.

He pushed open the door leading to the kitchen, where the radio was playing country music to an empty room. The back door was open and Connor smelled smoke. Cigarettes. Ordinary cigarettes and totally legal when smoked outdoors.

'Hayden?'

'Hey, Connor.' A head appeared in the open doorway. 'We got customers?'

'Not yet.'

Hayden took another drag on the cigarette and stubbed it out before coming back inside. 'It was an ordinary fag. Honestly.'

'I know.' Connor was willing to give a young ex-con the sort of break he'd needed himself a few years ago, but he'd made it clear that the first time anything illegal was found anywhere near his pub, Hayden would vacate his small room above the bar and hit the road.

'I won't let you down, Connor. I won't.'

'We'll be fine, as long as you really can cook.'

'Just hit me with that first order.'

If only, Connor thought.

And yet seconds later, the door to the bar swung open and Laura's head appeared. 'We got customers, boss.'

'On the way.' The relief that Connor felt was almost matched by the smile on the barmaid's face.

Connor recognised her the moment he walked back into the bar. She looked so much better now than that day he'd helped her through his door and made her sit down. And by 'better', he wasn't referring to her health. She was smiling and laughing with the people around her. He recognised the rest of the group as the one that had turned away from the pub not long after he'd first arrived; one of many families who'd avoided his establishment was now the first to give it a try. Was she the one who'd brought them back? His heart gave a little skip at the thought. Of course, it might just be her way of saying thank you … or maybe something else. Something else would be nice.

'G'day. Welcome to our Grand Opening. I'm Connor Knight, the new owner.' He greeted the group as a whole then turned to the one face he had been longing to see again. 'Hi, Kayla.'

'Hello, Connor.'

'I hope you're feel—' He didn't finish the sentence. The surprised looks on the faces of Kayla's companions told him she hadn't mentioned their previous encounter.

'I didn't know you two had met?' The man standing next to Kayla sounded surprised rather than annoyed, which was good.

'I bumped into Connor one day in town, that's all.' Her beautiful eyes held his, asking for his discretion.

'I'm glad you've all decided to drop in. Now, who do we have here?' Connor crouched in front of the kids.

'Look, Mummy—he has letters on his hand. Like in my book.'

That was something Connor was used to. People saw his hands and most of them judged him by what they saw. But this small boy had not yet learned about judging people.

'That's right. Can you tell me what the letters are?'

Connor loved the straightforward way in which the boy took hold of the fingers of his right hand.

'That's L. And that one is O. That's an E.' The boy pointed to Connor's middle finger. 'What's that one?'

'That's a V. Do you know what word those letters spell?'

'No.' The boy's blue eyes were wide with interest.

'That spells love. That's a good word.' Connor glanced at the woman standing next to the boy. He guessed she was the mother. He was pleased to see she was nodding slightly. The boy grabbed his left hand and pointed at the letters tattooed there.

'What word is that?'

'It's not a word. It's only two letters. C and K.' Connor had never been more thankful he'd had the first two letters of that word removed for times just like this. 'These letters are my initials. C for Connor and K for Knight.'

The boy screwed up his face. 'But night starts with n.'

'Not all the time.' Connor laughed. 'When you're a little bit older, you'll understand.'

'That's what Mummy says all the time.'

'Mummy is right.'

Out of the corner of his eye, Connor saw a pair of stylish ankle boots take a half-step backwards. He didn't look up at her face because he didn't want to see the look in the eyes of the beautiful woman who had suddenly realised what the tattoos represented.

He'd seen that look too often. Nor did he want her to see the disappointment that her reaction must have put on his face. He wasn't proud of his past. Well, not of some parts of it, the parts that had eventually led him to the place where those tattoos had been done. But he was proud of what he'd achieved since then, and he wasn't about to let anyone, not even a woman as attractive as this one, force that shame upon him.

He avoided looking at Kayla when he stood up and turned to the only man in the group. 'You looking for lunch? I've got a big family table in the lounge if you want it.'

'Sounds good. Come on, kids.' The man led the children away, but their mother hung back.

'That was kind of you. Thank you.'

'No problem. He seems a nice kid.'

'He is.'

She followed the rest of the group through to the lounge.

Connor flexed his inked fingers, pushed the past back where it belonged and went to collect menus from the bar.

***

Kayla watched the publican from the corner of her eye, her mind for once not focussed on the problem that had brought her back to Willowbrook.

'Those tattoos … they looked like …' She kept her voice low so the kids wouldn't hear.

'Prison tattoos? They did.' Mitch seemed unconcerned.

'But that means he's been … you know.' She cautiously nodded in the direction of Suzi and Dylan, who had left the table seconds after arriving to check out the bright old-fashioned jukebox that stood against the nearby wall. 'Jen, are you sure you want the kids to be around someone who's been in jail?'

'He was good with them. Dylan liked him.'

'But doesn't it worry you? You don't know what he did. He could be violent—or worse. I thought you were protecting the kids. You shouldn't let the kids near someone like that.'

'By "someone like that" you mean?' Jen's voice was soft.

'A criminal.'

'Just because he's been to jail, that doesn't mean he's dangerous. Or could harm the kids.'

Mitch frowned. 'Kayla, what happened when you bumped into him the other day? Was he a problem?'

'No,' she said quickly. 'But I didn't see the tattoos. I didn't know he'd been in jail. If I had, I never would have suggested we come here.'

'And when Brad gets out of jail?' Jen's voice cut like a knife. 'Are you going to avoid him then? Are you saying the kids can't be with him any more?'

Kayla winced. 'No. Of course not. That's different.'

'Is it?'

'Of course it is. We know he's innocent of …' Her voice trailed off.

'You don't even know why he's in jail. You've never even bothered to ask.' Jen paused for a deep breath. 'You don't know anything about why that man was in jail either. Don't be so judgemental, Kayla. Not everyone is as perfect as you want people to think you are. And while we're being honest with each other, don't you dare tell me how to raise my kids.'

Kayla blinked in shock. The Jen she'd grown up with had never fought back like that.

'Fine. If you're happy for them to be around some criminal you don't know, that's your business. I only hope nothing happens to make you regret it.' As Kayla spoke, she saw the others freeze. She knew why without turning around.

'Here are the menus,' a controlled and quiet voice said. 'When you're ready, come up to the bar and order. You can order drinks then too.'

Lizzie was the first to speak after Connor walked away. 'Kay? What's going on with you? That was so rude. That's not like you.'

Her sister was right. It wasn't like her at all. She couldn't explain why she had reacted so strongly to Connor. Maybe it had something to do with being pregnant? According to those pamphlets she'd collected from the clinic, pregnancy could change behaviour. That must be it. There was no other reason why he would provoke such strong emotions in her.

'The two of you are acting like you're eleven again. Come on, this is supposed to be a happy family gathering.' As always, Mitch was the voice of calm and reason. 'Kids, come back to the table and tell us what you want for lunch.'

Kayla stood. 'Sorry. I'll be right back.' She dashed to the bathroom, at once cursing her pregnancy bladder and thanking it for giving her a chance to escape the awkwardness at the table. She took her time washing her hands and splashed some water over her face, but she was still feeling chastened as she made her way back to the others. She didn't talk much during the riotous procedure of getting the kids to agree on something for lunch. She was thinking about Jen's words. Her friend was probably right. She could be judgemental, but there was nothing wrong with being a bit protective of the kids. Wasn't that just what she and Jen had talked about earlier, down at the stables? Being more afraid for them than for herself?

She watched surreptitiously as Mitch went to the bar to place their order. He exchanged a few words as the publican was making their drinks. Was he apologising for Kayla's behaviour? Connor probably deserved one. He seemed to bear no ill will towards

Mitch, serving the drinks with a friendly air. It was the same when he brought their meals. Jen had opted for a sandwich, while big juicy burgers were placed in front of Mitch and Lizzie.

'Here's your salad,' the publican said as he placed a plate in front of Kayla. 'With grilled chicken, no cheese and no dressing. I hope it's to your liking.'

She didn't dare look at him. 'Thank you.'

The salad did look good, but she didn't each much of it. Her stomach wasn't feeling very strong—nor were her emotions. There were a couple of moments when she thought she might have to make a dash for the bathroom, but in the end, she was fine. Lunch, it seemed, did not upset her stomach as much as breakfast or dinner.

While they were eating, a few more people came into the pub and the place seemed friendly, bordering on festive. Although there was a waitress looking after other customers, the publican himself came to clear their plates.

'You didn't like the salad?' He seemed determined to force her to acknowledge him.

'It was fine. I wasn't really very hungry.'

'Do you want me to put it into a takeaway for you?'

'No. No. Thank you.'

'Okay. Any more drinks? Coffee? Dessert?'

Kayla was pleased to hear everyone else decline when she did, and soon Mitch was at the bar taking care of the bill and they were hustling the kids out the door.

As Mitch joined them outside, Kayla suddenly said, 'Wait for me. I'll only be a minute.'

She darted back inside the hotel. Connor was alone behind the bar, stacking glasses from the dishwasher. He looked surprised to see her, but not displeased.

'I just wanted … wanted to apologise.' She was stammering like a guilty schoolgirl. 'I was rude and I am sorry. Especially after you were so kind to me the other day.'

His face relaxed into a smile. 'Thank you. You're not the first to think that, but not many people have the courage to say sorry.'

'There were two other letters on your first two fingers once, weren't there?'

'Yes. And you can probably guess what they were. You were right, it was a prison tattoo, but I had those first letters removed when I got out. It's hard enough to make new friends when you've done time. I didn't want to be flashing that at everyone who came near me. Especially kids.'

Always-in-control Kayla had no answer to that. 'Well … I'd better catch up with the others. Thanks, Connor.'

'I hope you'll be back soon, Kayla.'

***

He watched her go.

'She is way, way too good for you,' he told himself again as he reached for his polishing cloth and another glass. And that was a shame. Not only because she was beautiful, which she was, but even during the family lunch he'd sensed a sadness and vulnerability underneath the controlled exterior. He understood that. He'd been there too. He thought he had the dynamics of that group figured out. A mother and two children. A couple. And Kayla. She was part of the group but slightly on the outside. Slightly removed; whether by her own design or not, he wasn't sure.

He was drawn to her, but that was the end of it. Despite the apology, she was clearly disturbed by his having done time. Connor had met a lot of people like that and he knew from experience it was not an easy thing to get past.

CHAPTER
10

In the safety of the wood-railed exercise yard, Lizzie unclipped the leading rein from Jango's bridle and signalled Suzi to ride on. From her spot on the fence, Jen smiled. Suzi was a natural, taking after her Uncle Mitch and the grandfather who was still training racehorses in Queensland. These moments seeing her daughter smiling and laughing were a lifeline for Jen. Every morning she woke afraid of what the next few hours would bring. And every night she went to bed glad to have made it through another day. She missed her husband. She missed her home. And she missed the security and happiness that had once been the hallmark of her family. She missed the life that she and Brad had built and loved. And hanging over her head was the threat that Brad might go to jail. Not for a few weeks, but for years.

Her eyes were misting over when she heard footsteps approaching. She knew at once who it was. The footsteps were too light to be Mitch and anyway, he was with Dylan, cleaning tack in the stables.

'Jen, I need to apologise to you,' Kayla said.

Jen kept her eyes on her daughter. She wasn't worried about her safety—at least not more than a mother's everyday background worry—but she didn't want to face Kayla right now. And she wasn't in the mood to be forgiving.

'I shouldn't have said what I said in the pub.'

'No. You shouldn't have. When did you get to be so judgemental?'

'I'm not …'

'Yes, you are. You're judging the publican. And Brad too. You know, you're lucky you've never found yourself in that sort of trouble.'

She felt Kayla bristle beside her. 'I've never committed a crime.'

'Yes, you have.'

'What?' Kayla's voice quivered with outrage.

Jen shook her head. 'Don't you remember? When we were kids. We followed Lizzie and Mitch and broke into the showgrounds. We went for a look, but you … you had to steal one of the Kewpie dolls.'

'It was only worth a few dollars …' Kayla's voice was soft. She sounded uncertain.

'It was still stealing. And that guy got hurt chasing us. Remember?'

From the corner of her eye, Jen saw Kayla slowly nod, her face frozen.

'But I was just a kid.'

'Yeah. And if you'd been caught? Kids not much older than we were go to juvenile detention centres. And once you're in the system … well, some people come out worse than they went in. Even if they go in innocent, they can come out—' Jen's voice broke.

'No. Don't think that.' Kayla's voice was low enough to shield Suzi from the words, but Jen heard the vehemence in them and recognised the voice of the friend she thought she had lost. 'You can't think that, Jen. Look, I know I've never met Brad. And I'm sorry

I didn't come to the wedding. But you said you believe him. You can't give up. You never did when we were kids, no matter what the problem. You can't start now.'

Jen sniffed. She wasn't going to let the tears come.

Kayla put her hand on Jen's arm. 'It was all my fault we lost touch. I was hurt and angry after Mum and Dad died in that crash. I was only eleven. You'd moved to Queensland. I was stuck at boarding school and hated it. Lizzie and I barely spoke. I withdrew from everyone. That's no excuse, though, and I am sorry I let us drift apart.' Kayla sounded honestly contrite. 'I am still your friend even though I haven't acted like one. I'm sorry for that too. These past few weeks I've been too caught up in my own troubles to think about yours.'

That was understandable, but Jen was not going to make it easy for her. She remained silent.

'It's no excuse for what I said yesterday though,' Kayla continued. 'I don't know what's happening with you and the kids and their father. I don't want to pry. But I am here to help if I can. A sympathetic shoulder to cry on, if nothing else.'

Jen swallowed the lump that suddenly appeared in her throat. 'Thank you.' She paused but Kayla said nothing more. She was obviously leaving it up to Jen to decide what, if anything, to tell her and when. That was more like the Kayla she remembered, considerate and kind. And now Jen did want to tell her.

'When you meet Brad, you'll understand. He is a good man. He's kind and loving. Determined to do the right thing by his family. It was a bit of a rushed wedding, but I was pregnant with Suzi.'

Jen looked at Kayla and this time their eyes did meet. She saw something that might have been sympathy there before turning back to watch Suzi, who was now riding circles around Lizzie without a leading rein.

'Do Lizzie and Mitch know that?'

'We've never talked about it, but they can count.' Jen chose her words deliberately. When Kayla shuffled her feet, kicking the dirt under the railings, Jen knew her message had hit home. Kayla was running out of time to talk to her sister. 'It was a small wedding. We would have married even if I hadn't been pregnant. That just hurried things along a bit. I was—we were very happy.' *Still are*, she wanted to say. But that wasn't true any more. Not for the reasons some people might expect. She and Brad were still very much in love. That, at least, hadn't changed.

'He is … was … a teacher, but teachers don't get paid that well. We had a small house with a big mortgage, but that wasn't what he wanted. He wanted to give us everything. And that's where it all went wrong.'

Suddenly she wanted Kayla to believe in Brad's innocence too. If Kayla believed, then it wasn't only his wife who was on his side. So, while her daughter finished her riding lesson and her son played with his uncle in the stables, Jen told Kayla everything. About the money problems brought on by Brad's desire to give his family everything. Too much of everything. There were some schemes he tried, but they never seemed to work out so he took a second job, driving cars for a firm that traded used vehicles. He was away from home a lot, delivering cars, sometimes interstate. But the money was good and it looked like they would be able to clear their debts. Her voice trembled a little as she explained how, unknown to Brad, not only had the cars been stolen, but some had also contained secret stashes of drugs. At least the one he was driving when he was arrested had.

'He didn't know. As soon as he understood what was going on, he told the police everything. He volunteered to be a witness against the others.'

'What does that mean for him?'

'The lawyer hopes that he'll get a light sentence because he helped. He may even be let off with the time he's already spent in jail. He might get to come home to us.' How she clung to those words. She needed to believe them so much. 'He's on remand until the trial. It's partly for his own protection, they said. Apparently there are people involved with this who still haven't been arrested. The police think they might …' She couldn't say the words that had been haunting her.

'Oh, Jen.' Kayla's voice was soft. 'I am sorry. It'll be all right. You have to believe that.'

Jen gathered her wits about her and resumed her place at the fence. She waved and smiled at Suzi. Her daughter was smart—too smart for her own good sometimes. It wouldn't take her long to figure out something was wrong if she saw her mother crying.

Jen kept fighting the tears, as she did virtually every day when she thought of Brad sitting in a prison cell. All she could see was the images from the TV shows and movies she used to watch; desperate men sitting in small, uncomfortable beds in small, open rooms with no privacy and no hope. She couldn't bear it.

An arm went around her shoulders and Kayla gave her a gentle hug.

'I'm so sorry, Jen. I'm here if you need me. Anything I can do to help.'

That was the old Kayla speaking. Her best friend. How Jen had missed her.

'Thank you.' Jen turned and hugged the friend she had rediscovered. The tears flowed.

In the centre of the yard, Suzi pushed the pony into a trot and it obliged. Jen dashed the tears from her eyes and gave an encouraging nod to her daughter. Her job right now was to hold it together for the kids, and she would do that, whatever it took. But at least she didn't feel as alone as she had.

CHAPTER
11

Her office was a mess. Well, perhaps not by most people's standards, but since the arrival of Jen and the two kids, it had become something of a depository for anything that didn't already have a proper place. Empty suitcases, hers and Jen's, were stacked in a corner. There was a pile of wedding magazines on her desk she hadn't yet read. A dressmaker's dummy she had inherited from her mother had been put here to make way for the kids' beds in the other room. And for some reason, there was a box of old VHS video tapes on the floor. What had happened to her tidy, well-organised office? For that matter, what had happened to her tidy, well-organised life? It was time she got things a bit sorted out.

She spied a small block of red-painted wood in the middle of the floor. She wasn't sure what it was or how it had come to be there, but she swept it up and dropped it in the bin. There! That was a start. Then she paused and rescued the block. It probably belonged to Jen's kids. She suspected there was going to be a lot more child-related untidiness in her future. She was pretty sure she wouldn't like that either.

She slowly turned in a circle, looking for the next offending item, and spotted a large cardboard box that she had wedged between a bookshelf and a filing cabinet in the corner of her office after one of the first weddings at Willowbrook. She picked up the catalogues that had been stacked on top of it and looked around for somewhere to put them. There was room on one of the bookshelves, so she picked up the dusting cloth and gave it a good wipe. Not that there was any visible dust on it, but Kayla was tidying her office, and that meant dusting everything. She frowned at the dust on top of the box as, with a little bit of effort, she pulled it out of its hiding place. It was light enough for her to easily lift it onto the desk. She opened the box to reveal a layer of tissue paper, then buried her hands in the soft white fabric that lay beneath the tissue. She lifted it out of the box.

The light streaming through the window caught the fabric, giving it a slightly silver sheen as Kayla let the folds fall. She draped the fabric carefully over her chair and reached back into the box. This fabric was firmer, but layer upon layer of gathering made it spring from its resting place like a waterfall or fluffy white clouds rolling across a clear blue sky. The ruffles filled her arms, spilling over onto the desktop as she leaned forward to peer into the box to discover what else might be hidden there.

'It's a bit early for you to start nesting.' Jen's voice held a hint of laughter.

'Nesting?'

'It's something pregnant women do—preparing for the baby's arrival. But not usually until the third trimester. And it does tend to involve baby clothes and cribs not— What is that? A wedding dress?' Jen crossed the room and reached for the fabric.

'Just odd bits of material. I was working on designs for the decorations in the ballroom. Draperies for the cake table, that sort of thing. It was ages ago. I ran out of time, or ideas or something, and stored everything up here.'

'This looks more like a dress.'

'Yeah … I got a little bit carried away.'

Jen dug deeper into the box and pulled out a sketchpad. She leafed through the pages. 'These are good.'

Kayla tried to pile the vast amount of tulle onto the chair, then shrugged as it slowly cascaded to the floor. She took the book from Jen. It was filled with sketches of brides in wedding dresses. Each was different. Each was beautiful. And every one of them was hers. She could remember the joy she'd felt doing these sketches. The gowns she had drawn were gentle and romantic and beautiful. They were the wedding dresses she had dreamed of when she was a little girl, tempered by what she'd learned in her years as a wedding planner. Gowns that embodied everything she had always thought a wedding should be, but no longer believed in.

'I was a terrible romantic back then. Too many soppy movies.' Kayla slammed the notebook shut. 'I know better now.'

'Really?'

'Jen, if you'd seen as many weddings as I have, with grooms making out with bridesmaids or brides eyeing off the best man, you'd lose some of the stars in your eyes too.'

'Not all of them are like that. I want to believe most aren't.'

'Maybe I've been to the wrong weddings.'

'Maybe. Or maybe you started feeling like that when you turned weddings into a job. When we were kids, we both used to dream about our weddings. The things we wanted: horse-drawn carriages, huge meringue dresses. I seem to remember I wanted a blue gown at one point.'

Kayla laughed. 'I remember you had a photo cut from some magazine. It was hideous.'

Jen was laughing too. 'It was, wasn't it.'

'We were such kids. And look where we are now …' The words were out before Kayla could stop them.

Laughter gave way to silence.

'I'm sorry, Jen. I didn't mean that the way it sounded.'

'Don't be. We all grow up. We have to be happy with the decisions we make. I have no regrets. I have two wonderful kids and a husband I love. He'll be back with me soon and we will go on building our life.'

'I hope so.'

'I know so. What about you, Kay? You haven't made your decision yet, have you?'

She shook her head. 'I'm afraid of making a choice—the wrong choice—and regretting it later.'

'Have faith in yourself. You'll know the right thing to do.'

Kayla wasn't so sure.

Before she could reply, an ear-splitting scream caused them both to rush to the doorway. Dylan was lying face down on the hall carpet, bits of broken toy all around him. He was screaming as if he was in terrible pain. In a flash, Jen was at his side, her arms around him. She held him gently as she searched for the cause of his anguish. She found a tiny scratch on his hand.

'There, there. Look, it's just a scratch. Mummy will make it all better.' Jen kissed the child's palm and the screaming subsided. 'We'll go into the bathroom and wash that, then you can have a plaster on it. That'll make it feel better.'

'I want an elefont plaster.'

'Well, I'm not sure we have one with an elephant on it. Shall we go and look?'

The prospect seemed enough to stop the tears streaming down Dylan's face. 'I broke my Bluey car.'

'That's all right. We'll ask Uncle Mitch if he can fix it. Okay?'

Dylan nodded.

With a rueful glance at Kayla, Jen picked up her son and turned down the hallway towards the bathroom.

Back in her office, Kayla searched for something to keep her mind busy. As she folded the white fabric to put it back, she caught a glimpse of the rest of the box's contents, sparkly, shiny things to warm a bride's heart, but not hers. She flicked through the pages of the sketchbook one more time, then put it on a shelf next to a cheap china figurine of a horse with a white blaze on its face. The figurine had taken pride of place on her father's desk for years after Kayla had presented it to him on his birthday. It had also been broken and glued back together, just like her relationship with her sister. Her fingers rested on the figurine for a moment. The window of her office faced the wrong way, but she didn't need a window to picture the hill that rose above Willowbrook, looking down on the homestead and the horses grazing the paddocks. She didn't need to see the place to remember the single tree that grew on that hill nor the tiny graveyard with its simple stone markers.

'Mum. Dad,' she whispered. 'I don't know what to do.'

When no answer came, she turned back to her desk.

With her laptop powered on, Kayla settled herself to working on the upcoming wedding. More than two of the three weeks had now passed and she had everything under control. Cars were booked to pick up the wedding party at the airport. With such a small party, she'd arranged local catering, and Scone's famous Cupcake and Cake Lady was preparing a small but elegant cake with white textured icing and trimmed with the palest of pink roses. The last thing on Kayla's checklist was the drinks. The supplier had promised to email her today, but her inbox was worryingly empty. She reached for her phone.

The call was short and when she put the phone down, Kayla was tapping her desk impatiently. Her supplier had let her down—she was facing the prospect of a dry wedding. That would never do. Famous as the Hunter Valley was for wine, the producers were mostly well south of Scone. She didn't know the local wineries well enough, and besides, she was hardly able to go sample their wines. With only a couple of days to go, her options were limited. Maybe there was someone local she could use. She turned back to her computer for a few minutes, then turned it off and reached for her car keys.

Kayla gave one of the town's two bottle shops a miss. Her online search had shown it stocked mostly beer and the wines weren't of the standard she required. Clutching a faint hope, she was on her way to the second bottle shop when she caught a glimpse of the Gateway pub. The doors were open and it looked quite busy for a weekday. An image of the publican flashed through her memory, while the embarrassment she'd felt on her last visit made her face flush. She had apologised, but somehow now that didn't seem enough. Without thinking too carefully about it, she did a U-turn at the next intersection and headed back towards the pub. There was no way she'd get what she needed for the wedding at a simple country pub, but asking was also another way of apologising to Connor for her rudeness. Then she could drive on to the bigger bottle shop and check it out.

She parked in front of the pub and glanced at herself in the mirror, tidying her hair before she got out.

★★★

'Boss, she's back.'

Connor carefully finished rolling the keg into its position in the cold room. 'Who's back?'

Laura was standing in the open doorway, wiping her hands on a bar towel. 'The one who was so rude the other day.'

Kayla. 'She wasn't rude, she just expressed an opinion. She didn't know …' Connor's voice trailed off as the barmaid grinned widely.

'Aha. I knew you had a thing for her.'

'I do not have a thing for her. I've only met her twice.'

'Twice is enough. Are you coming out to serve her or shall I?'

The keg could wait. 'I'm coming.'

'I knew it … you've got the hots for her.' Laura chuckled as she moved away.

As he walked into the bar, Connor had a sudden suspicion that Laura was right. Kayla had paused to speak to someone sitting at a table. The light streaming through the open door made it seem as if she was actually glowing. She was wearing a pair of jeans and a red silk shirt cut low enough to set any man's pulse racing. He liked the curves of her body and the way she held her head slightly to one side as she listened to the people talking to her. He liked the way her mouth lifted into a smile and the sound of her light laugh. And he knew that when she looked at him, he would like those brown eyes.

He took up his position behind the bar, reaching for a cleaning cloth to give himself somewhere to look other than at her. As a distraction technique, wiping an already spotless counter didn't work very well.

At last she finished her conversation and he could watch her approach without feeling like he was out of line.

'Hi, Connor.'

'Kayla. What can I get you?'

'I didn't come here to drink. I wanted to see you.'

Their eyes met and something deep inside Connor did a cart-wheel. 'Well, that's—'

'I have a proposition for you … a business proposition.' The faint blush that spread across her cheeks only made her more attractive.

'I'm always ready to listen to one of those. Do you want to come into the office?'

'It won't take long. It's more a question than a proposition.'

'Ask away.'

'I've got two days until the wedding and my wine supplier has let me down. I was wondering if you can help me?'

Connor didn't hear the last half of her statement. At the word 'wedding', his brain seemed to seize. Damn! That was unexpected and … disappointing wasn't the half of it. Then he realised she seemed to be expecting an answer to a question he hadn't even heard. 'Ah … well … congratulations.'

'What? No. You misunderstand. When I said "the wedding", I meant a wedding I'm organising, not a wedding with me in it.'

The big block of concrete that had dropped onto his shoulders vanished again and he smiled. 'Sorry. And you need my help to …?'

'Wine? I need supplies for the wedding.'

'Right. Of course. Sorry.' He must look like an idiot.

'I know I'm right in the middle of the wine country, but I've only got two days. I was kind of hoping you would have some on hand. Something better than the local bottle shop can offer. I have picky clients.'

Connor's mind was racing. There were other places to buy wine in and around Scone and most could reasonably be expected to have a better range and better quality than his pub. So why on earth had she come here to ask? Whatever the rea-son, he had to be the one to supply the wine because that would bring her back. He didn't have much wine in his storeroom. He was trying to slowly build up a stock and that took money he didn't have.

'How much wine do you need? And what sort of wine?'

She told him. It was all top-end stuff, far better than anything he had in his stock room. He didn't have much time, but he had to find a solution, because he was determined to do this. And not just for business reasons.

'It's just a small event. About two dozen people. Can you do it?'

'Let me make a quick phone call and see what I can do. In the meantime, would you like a drink … on the house?'

'A lemonade, lime and bitters would be nice. Thanks.'

He mixed the drink then excused himself. In his office, he rang his supplier in Sydney, who happened to be a friend of sorts.

'Sure, I can do that,' the supplier said after listening to the list of wines. 'I can have it on the truck on Monday for you.'

'Monday's too late.'

'Sorry. I really can't do it any earlier.'

'What if I was to drive down this afternoon? I could be there by six.'

'All right. I'll wait for you.'

'Thanks. I owe you.'

'For this lot, you will. Those aren't cheap wines.'

'I'm good for it.' He wasn't actually sure that he was, but he trusted Kayla would pay him before his bill came due at the end of the month.

'See you later.' The supplier rang off.

Yes! Where was his shining armour and his white horse?

Connor was smiling as he returned to the bar. 'It'll all be here sometime this evening. When and where is the wedding? I can bring it out for you tomorrow.'

He watched Kayla blink in disbelief, then her smile lit the whole place. 'Connor. You are a star. Thank you.'

'My pleasure.'

'Let me give you my phone number in case you need it. What's your email? I'll send you directions to Willowbrook.'

Details exchanged, Kayla held out her hand. 'Thank you.'

Connor took her hand in his, but it really didn't feel like shaking hands over a business deal. Her hand looked tiny and delicate wrapped inside his large fingers with the letters L-O-V-E roughly inked into the flesh. Her grip was firm and her skin soft. Connor wanted to caress the back of her hand with his thumb. He wanted to hold her hand forever. As he looked into her eyes, he would have sworn he saw a reflection of the same longing.

The shaking of hands was such an ordinary gesture, so why had he stopped breathing? Why had the world stopped turning on its axis?

After an eternity, Kayla gently removed her hand from his. 'I'll see you at Willowbrook tomorrow.'

Connor watched her walk out the door, then turned to find Laura at his elbow.

'I'm going to be out for a few hours. I have to go to Sydney and pick up some wine.'

'You know, boss, there are easier ways to get her phone number.'

He didn't answer.

'Why don't you just ask her out?'

'Why don't you go serve some drinks or something?'

The barmaid laughed as she turned away.

She was right about one thing. He did want to ask Kayla out, but he wouldn't. Starting a new life after prison had been tough. There was a lot of prejudice to fight. And mistrust. No-one would ever know how hard it had been for him or how many times he'd faltered. He was still trying to earn that better life. He didn't have time to think about a relationship, even if he could find a woman who might be willing to get involved with someone like him. Kayla certainly wasn't that woman. This was a woman who wanted perfect. Who would expect nothing less. And he was far from perfect.

CHAPTER
12

It was so good to wake up without feeling sick that Kayla almost bounced out of bed. She flung open the curtains. Outside, a light mist gave the garden of Willowbrook a magical aura. Spring was still a month away, but Kayla had always loved this time of year. If she were ever to marry, it would be in a misty garden like that, cold or not. And speaking of weddings, she had a lot to do today to make sure tomorrow's event would be perfect. But she had it all under control … except for the wine.

She picked her phone up from the bedside table and checked for calls or messages. There weren't any. No email from Connor either. Her spirits sagged. She told herself it was because she was worried about the wine. She didn't want to believe Connor would let her down, but she wasn't entirely sure she could trust him. He was an ex-con. Though to be fair, he'd done good things with that old pub, but good wasn't enough for Kayla. She wanted perfect and there was no way Connor was that.

No way he was a perfect businessman, she corrected. This was all about business.

An image of his tattooed hand holding hers leaped unbidden into her mind. That hand had been warm and felt so strong. Capable. But she'd seen how gentle those hands could be. And when he'd looked at her yesterday ... She felt the heat rising to her face. Her thoughts then had been far from perfect. And that was wrong. This was not the right time for her to think those thoughts. And he was the wrong person to think them about. She didn't know what crime had sent him to prison, and while part of her longed to know more, another part of her was afraid to find out he had done something she couldn't ignore. Enough to stop them working together or maybe even being friends. More than friends? No.

The good feeling was seeping away, so she pushed those thoughts to the back of her mind and headed for the shower.

As she dried herself, she turned sideways to the mirror and ran her hand over her stomach. Was there a bulge? She was fourteen weeks pregnant. Should she have a bump by now? She straightened her back and tightened her muscles. No. Nothing yet. Maybe a slight suggestion of thickening. Not a real bump. But there would be soon and she was still no closer to knowing what she wanted to do about the ... the pregnancy. Yes, that was the best word to use. She needed to keep emotion out of her thoughts when she made her decision and that would have to wait another couple of days. She didn't have time for that today.

Her phone beeped at her as she re-entered her bedroom.

When would you like me to deliver the wine?

Any time. I'm here all day. Did you get the directions?

Yep. See you about 10.30.

Kayla sent a thumbs-up emoji. Some of the stress had drained away.

As she tucked her shirt into her jeans, she ran her hand over her stomach again. Nothing there that anyone would notice. Her secret was safe for a while longer. She grabbed her laptop from her office and set off downstairs for breakfast followed by wedding prep. She might even attempt a cup of coffee now the morning sickness seemed to be fading.

By ten thirty the venue was taking shape. The dining room had been laid out with tables set for the celebratory feast that would follow the wedding. The bride's chosen candles were waiting to be lit and the crystal chandeliers sparkled. The kitchen was spotless, the food warmers and serving trays ready for the arrival of the caterers. The wine cooler was empty, but that would be rectified shortly.

Her kitchen list nicely ticked off, Kayla headed outside to check that arriving guests would be suitably welcomed. With no likelihood of rain overnight, the bows and draperies around the front door were being installed today. The florist would be here first thing tomorrow with buckets of blooms and ribbons to complete the setting here and inside the ballroom, where the actual ceremony would take place.

A battered single-cab ute appeared in the driveway. Kayla checked her watch. Connor was right on time. She waved to attract his attention and indicated where he should park to give easiest access to the kitchen door.

Connor whistled under his breath as he got out of the car, turning slowly to take in the homestead and grounds. 'This is quite a place.'

Kayla allowed herself a twinge of pride. She and Lizzie had worked hard to rescue Willowbrook Stud from bankruptcy and then to restore their old family home. The wedding venue had been all Kayla's work. And although weddings didn't make her cry any more, she was still proud of that work.

Connor shook his head a little. 'I bet whoever owns this never had to evict drunken road workers on a Friday night. You're lucky to work in a place like this. And now, with luck, I guess I might be. If you need someone to serve the wine tomorrow, or any time, I'm available. I scrub up all right when I have to.'

Kayla froze as her brain struggled to find the right thing to say. Everyone knew that she and Lizzie had grown up at Willowbrook and now owned it. Everyone except Connor, it seemed. She could tell him. It would be so easy to say, 'This is my family home and I'm glad you like it.' But if she did that, he would look at her differently. He'd obviously had a tougher upbringing than hers, an upbringing that had led him to prison.

'Anyway, enough of admiring the scenery. Where do you want the wine?'

'Yes. Of course. Through here.' Kayla led the way to the door.

Connor seemed equally impressed when he saw the interior of the homestead. He deposited the first box of wine by the cooler at Kayla's direction, then took a moment to peer through the door into the house.

'Wow. Nice. Some people have it easy.'

We didn't, she wanted to say. Surely, of all people, he would understand that things were not always what they seemed. She mustered her courage to speak, but before she could, Connor set off for the next load of wine.

★★★

When Connor returned with the second box, Kayla was nowhere to be seen. She'd never answered his question about acting as a waiter. She was probably busy, so he'd find her again when he'd finished bringing in the wine. That took a few trips. Kayla had said a small wedding, but who knew how small was small when it came to fancy weddings? And what did he know about how rich people drank?

The sound of running feet distracted him and he turned to see a small boy heading in his general direction.

'Whoa, there.' He swept the boy up in his arms. 'Hello, Dylan.'

Dylan smiled and reached for his tattooed hand. 'Connor Knight,' the boy said, touching the letters.

A moment later his mother appeared. 'Thank you,' she said as she took the boy from Connor. 'Dylan. Remember you promised to stay close to me. Aunt Kayla has lots of people here and things to do and you promised not to get in the way.'

The boy nodded.

'All right then. Now, here's your sister. Go with her upstairs and you can watch cartoons.' She put the boy down. 'Can you keep an eye on him please, Suzi? Take him upstairs and I'll be up in a few minutes. I need to talk to Mr Knight.'

Connor watched the kids walk back into the house.

Jen sighed. 'I'm going to have my hands full tomorrow keeping them out of the way.'

'This is your place?' Connor couldn't mask his surprise.

'Well, I live here. I don't own it.'

'Lucky you.'

'It's just temporary. I needed …' Jen hesitated. 'Mr Knight—'

'Connor.'

'Connor. I was wondering. Would you mind— I mean. Could I come and talk to you some time?'

'Sure. Any time. What about?'

'Well, my husband, Brad,' she said softly, not meeting his eyes. 'He's in Queensland. In jail, awaiting trial. He didn't do what they say he did. And his lawyers say they're hopeful he'll come home to us.'

'I hope they're right.' Connor managed to hide his surprise at her admission.

'Anyway, he won't let me or the kids visit him.'

'I can understand that. A prison is no place for kids.'

'I know. But he won't even talk to me about … about what it's like. I want to— No, I need to know what his life is like, so that when he comes home I can help him.' She looked at him then. 'Will you tell me? I don't want to pry into your life, but I need to know what he's been through.'

Connor closed his eyes and let the memories wash over him. They weren't good. He didn't want to talk about them, but when he opened his eyes and saw Jen's face, he knew he would.

'He's a lucky man.'

'Not all the time.' Her lips curled in the faint echo of a smile.

'Any time you want to talk, I'm here. Don't hesitate. If I can help with that, or with anything else, I will. Glad to.'

'Thank you.'

The sound of another vehicle on the driveway caused them to turn their heads.

'I'd better get my old ute out of here and make way for whoever that is,' Connor said. 'But first I need to find Kayla and check if she wants me here tomorrow as a waiter.'

'Good luck pinning her down for more than thirty seconds. She's been so busy the last couple of days, even I've barely spoken to her. It's probably easier if you simply show up ready to do it. And if she doesn't need a waiter, I could use someone to give me a hand keeping the kids out of the way. Although that job doesn't pay.'

'Deal.'

He watched Jen set off in the same direction as her kids. He admired her courage and strength. When—if—her husband got out of the joint, he'd better treat her right.

As he opened the door of his ute, he saw Kayla on the veranda of the homestead. He shut the door and turned in her direction, but she raised a hand in a casual wave and went back inside. She didn't want to speak to him. He had a feeling he'd said something wrong but wasn't sure what. Maybe it was that crack about the owner of this place. Or it might be that she was tense when she was working.

He shrugged and walked back to his ute. He would take Jen's suggestion and turn up tomorrow morning, nice and early. He'd be there to serve the wine or babysit the kids or Kayla could send him home. It would be her choice, but he hoped she'd make the right one—at least, the right one for him.

CHAPTER

13

How early was too early for a wedding? Connor had no idea. It was only eight thirty. That was probably too early for a barman to arrive at a wedding venue. But maybe the wedding was early. He began fiddling with his tie. He could never get it straight, but at least he looked the part. One of his first jobs on parole had been as a waiter in a restaurant. His parole office had helped with that. Then he'd moved to a slightly better restaurant. The smart black trousers and spotless white shirt from those days still fit properly. His only tie was black and his shoes, while showing a bit of wear and tear, had come up all right with some polish and elbow grease. He would grab a white apron from behind the bar on his way out. It might not be good enough for Kayla and her posh wedding, but it was the best he could do. And if she told him to clear off ... well, he'd clear off.

As he walked through the bar, his ears were assaulted by a wolf whistle louder than any indoor whistle should ever be.

'You scrub up all right, boss.' Laura was behind the bar, slicing lemons.

'And you're early. Don't think you'll get overtime just because you whistled at me.'

'Wouldn't dream of it.'

'The new barmaid is starting today,' Connor said. The need for a new part-time barmaid was a sign that the pub was heading in the right direction. He wouldn't be here for her first day, but Laura would. 'Are you sure you'll be all right—'

Laura gave him a look that would have shattered stone.

'Okay. Okay.' Connor held his hands up in defeat. 'I know when I'm not wanted. Call me if by some chance I'm needed.'

'You won't be. You've got better things to think about today. Good luck.'

He wanted to say that all he'd be doing was pouring wine and he didn't need luck for that, but he had a sneaking suspicion that wasn't what she was referring to, and that was a conversation he didn't want to start. He got into his freshly washed ute and headed towards Willowbrook.

As soon as he pulled off the road at the Willowbrook gate, two uniformed men stepped into the driveway. One held up a hand to stop the car and Connor tensed. His hands tightened around the wheel and he glanced from side to side, looking for more uniforms— or perhaps a way out. He lifted his foot from the accelerator, and forced his face to relax. These men were neither police nor prison guards, and he had no reason to fear either any more. But the instincts of half a lifetime are hard to put away.

He opened his window as the first guard approached.

'Good morning, sir. I need to check you're on the list.'

He hadn't expected this, although if this wedding was as posh as it seemed, he should have. 'I'm not a guest. My name is Connor Knight. I'm here to work as a waiter.'

The man ran his eyes over his tablet. 'I'm sorry, sir. I don't have your name on my list.'

'I was a late addition. Can you call—' Connor stopped. Kayla hadn't invited him. She didn't even know he was coming, so it would be pointless calling her. And he doubted Jen had the authority to authorise his entry.

'One moment please.' The security guard was already pulling his phone from his jacket. He stepped away from the car, turning his back so Connor couldn't hear the conversation. His partner, however, did not turn away. He stood about a metre from the car and although he looked relaxed, Connor knew his every muscle was tensed. Connor knew because his own body was equally ready to act.

Old habits and fears are hard to shake, but Connor did not lower his gaze to avoid eye contact with the guard as he once had. He didn't paint pictures in his head of what could happen next. He waited, and was proud of the calmness he exuded, even if deep inside him, in places he tried never to visit, traces of the frightened teenager in the detention centre were pleading with him to turn around and leave.

The first guard returned. 'Thanks for waiting, sir. Your name is on the vendors list up at the house. You can go ahead.'

'Thank you.' Connor pulled away, telling that frightened teenager he had once been that something important had occurred. A man in a uniform had called him 'sir'. That had never happened before. He'd been called many things by men in uniforms, but never that. He would tell Hayden about that later. The kid would understand, as no-one else did, how important that moment was.

When he reached the homestead, it was as busy as it had seemed the day before. Possibly even busier. An attendant in a crisp white shirt directed him away from the main driveway into a gravel area that he assumed was staff parking. There were a couple of vans and people movers there, with logos that identified them as belonging to caterers and florists. As he walked towards the house, he could see people around the front door placing flowers in an arch that was already half-covered with blooms and white ribbon. It was, he had to admit, quite pretty, if not exactly his cup of tea. There was no sign of Kayla, so he headed around the side of the house to the kitchen door and stepped into a tornado.

'Not like that. How dare you treat my souffle in such a manner!' a man in white was berating a girl as he stared at the plates in front of her. 'My souffle is a work of art and you toss it on the plate like a burger.'

'Duck,' another woman whispered at Connor as they walked past. 'Chef's in a mood today.'

Connor swept a rapid glance around the room, looking for either Kayla or some place to hide.

'You.' The man fixed his angry glare on Connor. 'What are you doing in my kitchen?'

As Connor looked for the right words, the man turned to another of the white-clad staff.

'You, why are the canapes not yet complete? The salmon ... get the salmon.'

'Yes, Chef.'

'Well? I asked you a question?' The man turned back to Connor.

'I brought the wine.'

'Then get on with it. The silver coolers are over there some-where. I hope they're clean. If not ...' He didn't finish the threat as another imperfection caught his eye, pulling him to the other side of the room.

Connor went looking for the silver wine coolers.

'Hi. I'm Ali.' The girl cast a quick look around, but the chef was nowhere to be seen. 'You're new.'

'Connor.'

'Hi. Sorry about Chef.'

'He must be hard to work for if he's always like that.'

'He's not easy, but he's always a bit hyper whenever it's a Willowbrook wedding. Man, can you imagine him and Kayla Lawson together? That must—'

Whatever she was about to say was forgotten as the chef stormed back into the room and the girl vanished.

This man and Kayla? Connor cast a discreet sideways glance at the chef, who had paused in his shouting long enough to carefully sample some delicate bit of his food. It made sense. They worked in the same industry, caught up in making perfect fantasy weddings. Perhaps they made a perfect relationship as well? Not that it mattered one bit, he told himself. It wasn't as if he had any chance with Kayla, so what business of his was it who she got involved with? Although, as he listened to the man yelling at another kitchen hand, he found himself hoping the chef was nicer to his girlfriend than he was to his staff.

Kayla walked through the door, looking cool and totally professional in a smart black dress and jacket. She didn't look in Connor's direction, her attention immediately grabbed by the chef.

'Lachie?'

'Kayla. My love. My angel. My rock in this storm-tossed ocean,' the chef said. 'Let's leave all this behind. My boat is waiting, we can cast off and sail away into the sunset.'

'Not until after the wedding, Lachie. And besides, that would leave your souffle without anyone to watch over it.'

'Pah. The souffle is a masterpiece. I am no longer needed here. Come, show me the ballroom. Let me see your genius.' The man linked his arm through hers and they made a dramatic exit.

Connor stood blinking as the door shut. The man was a drama queen and about as sincere as a three-dollar note. Couldn't Kayla see that? Why would she link up with someone like that when there were men around her who were— Were what? Better for her?

How could he think that? He didn't know what Kayla needed or wanted. And surely he wasn't thinking of himself, because an ex-con wasn't good enough for someone like her.

'Pay no attention.' Ali was back and smiling at him again. 'It's all bluff. And he is a brilliant chef.'

'Why do you put up with him?'

'Because he's the best in the business and I'm learning all his secrets. Maybe one day, I'll be the one giving the orders. In the meantime—' she looked up at him through long dark lashes, '—he'll calm down once the food is served and leave early. Then the rest of us can relax. Maybe even share a glass of this expensive wine.'

The offer was right there for him to accept. Ali was pretty, with a cute smile. Spending some time with her might be fun. It had been a long time …

Connor wished her luck with her dreams and turned back to his work, not meaning to be rude, but the last thing he wanted was a flirting kitchen hand to turn the chef's attention to him. And nice as she seemed, Ali wasn't the reason he'd come here today.

★★★

'I've missed you, Kayla.' As soon as they were out of the kitchen, Lachie dropped all his acting and was once more the man she had known for years. 'Willowbrook looks lovely as always, but why on earth have you decided to bury yourself up here?'

'I have not buried myself.'

'You weren't at the Intercontinental last week. Or at the Ivy two weeks before that. They were your weddings, Kayla, and you weren't there.'

'They were fine without me.'

'Fine, yes. You planned them, so of course they were fine. But they both lacked that final edge you always bring on the day.'

'I needed a break from work, Lachie.' She patted his arm. 'You of all people should understand that.'

'I do. There are times I even think about taking time off.'

That made Kayla smile. In the years she'd known him, Lachie had never taken a break of more than a few days.

'I mean it, Kayla.' He pulled her gently into a quiet corner of the hallway. 'I miss you. We were good together. Why don't we take a few days off, hop in the boat and sail off into that sunset together like we used to? You look wonderful. Maybe if I took some time off, I could look wonderful too.'

'At some point, the sunset will turn into a sunrise and you'll want to get back to the kitchen.' She smiled at him fondly. 'It's a nice idea, but let's hold onto the good memories we have. Besides, you always look wonderful and we don't want to disappoint all the many women who, according to social media, you seem to be dating. We'll still be working together. Here and in Sydney if I come back. So—'

'*If* you come back?' He sounded shocked. 'Surely you're not going to stay here forever?' The look on his face was as serious as she had ever seen him.

'Maybe. I don't know. Things are changing for me, Lachie. I'm not sure what direction they are going to lead.'

'Are you okay? Really?'

She was touched by his concern. 'Maybe not right now. But I will be. You are a good friend. Thank you.' She kissed him quickly on the cheek.

As they pulled apart, there was a scream from the direction of the bride's room.

'That does not sound good,' Kayla said.

'No. You'd better go work your magic.' Lachie turned back to the kitchen. 'While I work mine.'

CHAPTER
14

By the time Kayla reached the door of the bride's room, the scream had morphed into sobbing and a hubbub of loud voices. Before she could investigate, the door to the groom's room flew open and an anxious face appeared.

'Is everything all right?'

'Of course,' Kayla replied automatically. 'Don't worry. And you keep yourselves inside there. You don't want to see the dress before the wedding. It's bad luck, you know.'

He didn't seem convinced, but slowly withdrew and closed the door, giving Kayla the chance to enter the bride's room. It was chaos.

The bride was standing in the centre of the room, her face twisted with horror as she stared down at the red stain on her gown. A bridesmaid was on her knees, reaching for a wine glass that was spreading a similar red stain on the room's cream carpet. The mother of the bride was wailing loudly and wringing her hands.

'Oh my gosh! How could you do that?' Another bridesmaid had turned on the kneeling girl, bringing a fresh cry of despair from the distraught bride.

'It's ruined. My wedding dress is ruined!'

It was time Kayla stepped in.

'Please, everyone. Calm down. It's going to be all right.'

'No! It's not … look at her dress.' The mother of the bride collapsed onto a chair and reached for a box of tissues.

The offending bridesmaid got to her feet and carefully placed the empty wine glass back on a tray. The rest of the glasses were champagne, but Kayla didn't think this was the time to point out that white wine seldom caused this much trauma when spilled. Not to mention the damage to her lovely carpet. She quickly picked up a bottle of white wine and poured some over the stain. It might not work, but she had to try. It was an expensive carpet. She ducked into the bathroom for a damp towel to cover the patch. At least that might stop the wine from staining the hem or train of the wedding dress. Not that it mattered. It was clear the dress was ruined.

'What am I going to do?' The tearful bride grabbed her hand. 'We'll have to call it off. I can't go out there looking like this.'

Kayla almost smiled. The bride was a well-regarded actress and stunningly beautiful as well. No spilled glass of wine could detract from that. But a wedding dress was special. Especially your own wedding dress. Kayla crouched in front of the bride and smoothed the fabric of the gown. The wine stain covered a large section of the lower half of the skirt, beginning just below knee height, with the final dribbles on the hem. It was ruined. Nothing was going to get that stain out and certainly not before the ceremony, which was due to start in about twenty minutes.

She stood up and looked the bride squarely in the face. 'I think I can fix this.'

'What? How? That stain—'

'Won't come out. But I can alter the dress. Redesign it and give you something lovely to wear.'

'It's too late for that.'

'No. It's not. Not if you trust me. You hired Elite Weddings, and me, to make your wedding perfect. I can make this dress perfect again if you'll let me.'

The bride looked deflated. 'What have I got to lose now?'

'Let me try. If you don't like what I do, then you're really no worse off than you are now.'

'All right. What are you going to do?'

'Wait here. I'll be right back.'

She darted out of the room and almost collided with a waiter who was clutching a tray of drinks. He skilfully balanced the tray as she stepped back.

'That was close.'

'Connor? What are you— Never mind. I'm glad to see you.'

'Thanks.'

'Don't thank me yet. I need you to tell the groom and the celebrant and everyone that there is going to be a delay. Thirty minutes or more. Probably more but let's not say that yet. Serve drinks and keep them away from the bride. Got it?'

'Yes.'

How she appreciated his swift acceptance. She had no time to explain.

'Great. Do it.'

She ducked past him and headed for the grand staircase that led upstairs to the residence and, more importantly, her office. It took only a few moments to gather up what she needed then she slipped back into the bride's room, glad that no prying eyes had seen her.

'What's this?' The mother of the bride had recovered from her shock and was now in full mumzilla mode.

'It could be a solution.' Kayla dropped the armload of white fabric and opened her sketchbook. She put it on a table and waved the bride over.

'We can cut the ruined skirt here ...' Kayla waved her pencil in the direction of the stain. 'It gives a sort of a slit. Then I can do this.' She started sketching, her hand moving with confidence across the page. 'The tulle I have is the right colour. And some of it has sequins to give it shine. I could make an underskirt that gathers here, where the cut is. The tulle will fluff out through the gap, a bit like a kick pleat. And then I'll make a multilayered tulle overskirt. From here, on the hips, around the back. The same tulle. Some embellishments around the top will highlight your waist. I'd have to look, but I might have a belt or something that I can turn into a belt. The underskirt and overskirt go on for the ceremony. After, if you want, you can take one or both of them off and you have a second look for the meal.'

The whole bridal party had gathered around to look.

'That's a great idea.'

'The tulle would look lovely. See how it sparkles?'

Even the mumzilla seemed impressed. But it all came down to the bride.

Kayla gathered up a section of the tulle. It was already sewn into gathers, part of the design she had been playing with for a table decoration. But no-one had to know that.

She turned the bride to face a mirror and draped the tulle as best she could. 'What do you think?'

The bride fiddled with the fabric and for a minute Kayla thought she was going to say no and cancel the whole thing. Then she smiled. It was faint but it was what Kayla had been hoping for.

'It might work. And I do like the idea of looking different for the after bit. But can we get it done in time?'

'There's only one way to find out. I have a sewing machine upstairs. It's ready to go.' Kayla brandished the scissors she had brought with her.

The bride nodded, the look of despair on her face starting to fade. 'Let's do it.'

★★★

It took a lot longer than the thirty minutes Kayla had suggested, but eventually the ceremony was underway. From an inconspicuous corner near the bar, Connor watched the bride walk into the flower-studded ballroom. The scene was like something out of a glossy magazine, especially when he took a closer look at the happy couple. He blinked with surprise as Kayla appeared next to him.

'Thanks for looking after things while I was sorting out the dress disaster,' Kayla said, casting a critical eye over the scene in front of her.

'Dress disaster?'

'Red wine and white gowns are a bad mix.'

'Ah.' He chuckled. 'The dress looks fine now. You must tell me your secret for getting wine stains out—it's something every pub owner needs to know.'

'It involved scissors.'

'Wow.' Connor took a long look at the dress. 'It looks all right from here. Not that I'm any expert on wedding dresses.'

'It does look good, doesn't it? But it doesn't look much like the dress she brought with her. I did some running repairs.'

'Pretty impressive repairs. And ...' Connor hesitated, not sure of the protocol. 'I don't want to pry, but is the woman wearing that dress who I think it is?'

'If you are thinking of an award-winning actress, yes, it is.'

'And him too?'

'Yep. But please don't say anything. It's one of the things this place is known for: privacy for celebrity weddings.'

'I won't say a word.' And he wouldn't, but he cast a sideways glance at Kayla. When he'd thought she was out of his league, he hadn't known how far. If this was the crowd she ran with …

'I didn't expect you to be here today. I have plenty of wine waiters.'

'Jen suggested it. I hope it's not a problem. I can sneak out if it is … given, well, you know.' He nodded in the direction of the bride and groom.

'No. It's fine. I'll make sure you get paid.'

He wasn't doing it for the money, but in his current financial state, he wasn't going to say no. Every bit helped.

Under the flower-draped arch on the other side of the ballroom, the bride and groom kissed. What began as a gentle kiss quickly deepened, to the cheers of the crowd. Connor looked away but doing that only brought his gaze to rest on Kayla with her very kissable red lips.

'I guess I'd better get ready to pour wine,' he said hurriedly.

'Oh … yes. Of course.' Kayla avoided looking at him, sounding a little flustered herself.

Weddings, Connor thought. *They do strange things to people.* Kayla must be thinking of her boyfriend, so close in the kitchen. Maybe she was thinking about marrying him. That idea didn't appeal to Connor at all.

The rest of the event seemed to pass smoothly. Connor served wine, taking extra care with the red. When the bride and groom took to the dance floor, he tried to see signs of Kayla's running repairs, but to him the dress looked like a wedding dress should.

Once the food was on the table, the tension in the kitchen calmed down a lot and Lachie stopped shouting. Connor appeared to be the only person he hadn't shouted at, and a small part of him, the part that had gotten him into so much trouble in his teens, almost wished he had. Then Connor could have taught him some manners. But that would only create a fuss and he didn't want to let Kayla down. If only she'd chosen someone who was better for her ... someone like Connor.

What was he doing, thinking he was better for someone like Kayla? Who right now was talking to another face that Connor recognised from her nightly appearances on his TV. He was fooling himself. As soon as the guests had left, he'd be out of here so he didn't have to watch Kayla and the idiot chef together.

He was walking to the ballroom carrying yet more wine when he heard a giggle from the direction of the grand staircase. He laid his tray on a sideboard and went to investigate. One of the bridesmaids was seated on the stairs and next to her were two kids Connor recognised.

'Connor!' Dylan jumped up and darted over to take his hand and point at the letters on his fingers. 'L–O–V–E. See, I can read that now.'

'Yes, you can.' Connor lifted the boy and swung him onto his shoulders, while at the same time moving him out of eyeline and earshot of the ballroom.

'They're cute kids. Are they yours?' the bridesmaid asked.

'No. They live here with their mum ... and ...' Connor looked at Suzi, who was still sitting next to the bridesmaid. 'I thought you were told to stay out of the way today.'

'Mum's on the phone to Dad,' Suzi said. 'She shooed us out so we didn't hear what she was saying. And I just wanted to see the bride's dress.'

'I'm sorry, you can't go in there.'

'Of course she can.' The bridesmaid leaped to her feet. 'Well, maybe a glimpse through the doorway. What do you say?'

'Oh, yes, please!' Suzi's eyes were shining.

The bridesmaid led her to the double doors that opened into the ballroom. Suzi peeked carefully around the corner. From his perch on Connor's shoulder, Dylan did the same.

'Oh. She's beautiful. And the dress is too.'

'Did you know your Aunt Kayla helped make that dress so beautiful?' Connor couldn't resist.

'Did she?' The little girl's face lit up.

'She did, and I'm sure she'll tell you all about it, but only if you and Dylan are both good and go back upstairs with your mum.'

Suzi nodded. 'All right.'

Connor swung Dylan down from his shoulders and gently pushed the kids in the direction of the stairs.

Before they had taken more than three steps, their mother appeared.

'Kids, I told you to stay away from the wedding. I hope you haven't—'

'It's fine,' Connor said. 'They were just sitting on the stairs. One of the bridesmaids let them peep quietly through the door. No-one was disturbed.'

Jen's relief was visible. 'Right, you two, back upstairs. Now.'

'Yes, Mum,' came the answering chorus.

'Thanks, Connor,' Jen said. 'How's it all been going down here?'

'Fine. Interesting.' He hesitated. It was none of his business but he had to ask. 'The chef—Kayla's boyfriend—is a bit over the top. Not her sort at all, I would have thought.'

Jen raised both eyebrows. 'Boyfriend? I don't think so. Lizzie told me she was dating a chef last year when they first opened Willowbrook for weddings. But I think that's long over.'

Connor wasn't sure he hid his relief very well.

Jen gave him a questioning look. 'Why? You're not—'

'No. No. Nothing like that. Not at all. No. Look, thanks for suggesting I work here today. I guess I'd better get back to it. Can't let the guests get thirsty.'

He turned away, knowing he wasn't fooling anyone, least of all himself. But he was no longer in such a rush to leave as soon as the wedding was done.

CHAPTER
15

The wedding was over and the clearing up had taken a surprisingly short time. Lachie had vanished as soon as the guests were gone and in little more than an hour, his crew had also packed all their belongings back into their vans and left. Connor nibbled some of the leftover canapes that had been laid on for the staff as he sorted out the wine bottles. He thought the chef was a bit of a wanker, but credit where it was due, his food was very good. Following the catering team's example, Connor left the open bottles of wine in the kitchen for anyone who felt like a glass, then went in search of Kayla.

He found her in the bride's room. She had changed into faded blue jeans and a T-shirt and was on her hands and knees, a bucket of soapy water nearby, scrubbing at a red wine stain in the carpet.

'Can I give you a hand with that? After all, it was partially my fault.'

She looked up at him and brushed a stray piece of hair from her face. 'Why was it your fault?'

'I was the one who gave them red wine. I know you said champagne, but one of them wanted red. I'm sorry.'

'Don't be.' Kayla waved his apology away. 'You had to give her what she wanted.'

'But still ...' He dropped to his knees and wrung out another cloth that was in the bucket. 'I have some skill at this.' As he began to scrub the stain, Kayla sat back on her heels to rinse her cloth before continuing her attack.

They worked in silence for several minutes. 'It's starting to shift,' Connor said at last. 'You might get away with this.'

Kayla shrugged. 'I don't know. Even if it's only a faint mark, it'll still show.' She dipped her cloth back into the bucket and started rubbing again even more vigorously.

Whoever owned this place, they must be tough, Connor thought as he bent once more to help her. He wouldn't want to work for someone who would find even the faintest blemish unacceptable. Not that he was ever likely to. People like that didn't hire ex-cons.

As he and Kayla worked, their hands brushed together a couple of times by accident. Connor found himself thinking more about her hands than the job. They were small, shapely and quite perfect next to his own scarred and tattooed hands. Hers looked like they should be playing a violin. His showed signs of hard manual labour. Her hands would drive a man to madness if they were on his skin. The image in his mind was so strong, his hand stilled on the carpet. He turned his head to find Kayla looking at him.

His breath caught in his throat and the cleaning cloth fell from his fingers. The woman kneeling there in the stained carpet with him was no longer the impeccably dressed, incredibly efficient wedding planner. Her face was free of make-up and her working clothes flattered every curve of her body in a way that the severe suit had not. Her hair was clipped back, stray wisps falling over her face and clinging to the sweat on her neck. She was the most beautiful and alluring thing he had ever seen. He wanted to touch her to make sure she was real.

Then she leaned forward and kissed him, a short, gentle kiss that ended far too soon. As they parted, he could feel her breath on his skin and in his mouth and he reached for her, pulling her body against his as he sought her lips in a kiss that was no longer gentle. She raised her hands to his neck to hold him closer, their bodies coming together as his hands slid under her T-shirt to caress the silkiness there. She pushed him away and for one moment he thought ... but no. Her hands came between them to tug at the buttons of his shirt. When it fell open and her fingers touched his chest, he stopped breathing.

'Kayla ...' Her name was a whisper. He wanted to hear her say his name. To know she wanted this as much as he did. Instead, she held him even tighter, the demands of her lips giving him her answer. She moved away from him for an instant and he felt bereft. Then she pulled her T-shirt over her head. He experienced such joyful agony as he saw the soft firm flesh of her stomach and a white lace bra. As he reached for her again, she tossed the T-shirt to one side.

They gently fell sideways onto the wet carpet, their breath coming in gasps as he rolled Kayla on top of him, looking up into her face, her eyes dark with a passion that reflected his. Kayla moved her legs to bring their bodies closer together, then suddenly cried out—in surprise, not passion. They had bumped the bucket and knocked it over, sending a wave of soapy water along both their bodies. Ignoring the water, Kayla reached for his belt buckle but Connor gently took Kayla's hands in his.

Carefully, he rolled his body away from hers and sat up. He was breathing heavily, fighting to control his body's desperate need, and it was a few moments before he could speak.

'Kayla ... I can't. I want to, but I don't have anything ... protection.
I can't ...'

★★★

The spilled water had been warm, but his words were a cold wave.
Kayla froze, her face turned to stone. What was she doing? She
rolled away from him and reached for her T-shirt. It was wet, so
she wrung it out, not caring where the water went. She pulled it
over her head. A wet T-shirt was better than no T-shirt, but only
just. She got to her feet, backing away as Connor did the same.
She forced herself to take longer, slower breaths. She had never felt
desire like this before, an aching need that even now was telling her
to reach out, to touch that firm, muscular body and continue what
they had started.

She took another step back, tugging her wet top down. 'I, I
don't—'

'Kayla, I'm—'

They stopped. She couldn't meet his eyes.

After an uncomfortable minute of silence, he spoke again. 'I
guess I should go?'

She nodded, still far too embarrassed to speak.

'Okay.'

As the door closed behind him, she released the pent-up breath
she hadn't even been aware of holding. She listened to his retreating
footsteps, her anger at herself fighting down the urge to call him
back. Had she been afraid that he wouldn't go or that he would?
She lowered herself into a nearby chair, then leaped out of it—her
wet T-shirt might stain the gold and white brocade covering and
that would be one more problem in an already disastrous day. She
collapsed onto the floor instead, reaching for the cleaning cloths
lying nearby. She barely managed to drop both into the empty

bucket before tears started to course down her face. She brushed them away but they didn't stop. Before she had time to wonder why she was still sitting in the middle of a wet and ruined carpet, she was sobbing as if her heart was broken.

That's where Jen found her.

'Kayla?' Jen shut the door behind her, sank to the carpet and put her arms around Kayla's shoulders.

Kayla buried her face in Jen's shoulder and sobbed until she had no more tears. Then she straightened her back and pushed her hair out of her face.

'I don't know what's wrong with me. I never cry.'

'What's "wrong" is that you are pregnant. Your hormones are having a field day. It would be amazing if you didn't spend half your time crying. I'm pretty sure I did when I was pregnant with Suzi.'

Kayla sniffed and grasped the excuse with both hands. 'That must be it. I didn't think of that. Did you cry with Dylan as well?'

Jen laughed. 'No. With Dylan it was … well, let's just say I became very … affectionate towards Brad.'

Kayla frowned as she watched the half-smile of a memory creep across Jen's face. 'You mean you …?'

'Yep. Not everything associated with being hormonal is bad, you know.'

Kayla's hand flew to her mouth as realisation struck home. 'Oh my God! That's why—'

'That's why what?'

When Kayla didn't answer immediately, Jen raised a questioning eyebrow. Sometimes, her friend was too smart for anyone's good.

'All right.' Kayla raised her hands in capitulation. 'I had a moment with Connor.'

'Oh, did you?'

'Stop it.' If Kayla hadn't been so upset she might have laughed at the look on Jen's face. 'It was nothing. Not really.'

'And this nothing involved spilling a whole bucket of dirty water all over the perfect carpet that you love so much.'

'No! Yes, but it wasn't. You said it yourself. Hormones. It looks like I can't be trusted anywhere near a man at the moment.'

'Any man? Or this particular one?'

'Jen, I hardly know him.'

'But he is very hot. And nice as well.'

'And an ex-convict who owns a pub. Not my type at all.'

'And the father of your baby? The man you seem to want nothing to do with? Was he your type?'

Kayla didn't answer. She started to get to her feet.

'I'm sorry, Kayla. That was out of line.'

'No, you're right.' Kayla collected the bucket. 'I still don't know what to do.'

'I get that,' Jen said. 'But you're running out of time. You need to figure it out.'

'I know, but every time I think I've made a decision, I realise I haven't. Not really. I've only got a few weeks before the decision is made for me. Maybe that's what I'm doing. Procrastinating until I don't have a choice any more.'

'You haven't told anyone else, have you? Except the clinic.'

Kayla shook her head.

'And how many times have you been to the clinic?'

'Only once. They have texted a couple of times about another appointment. Some tests.'

'And?'

'I've been busy. There was a wedding to organise.'

'That's not an excuse. You're what—nearly fifteen weeks? Those are important tests.'

'But ...'

'No buts. For your own sake, if not for the child, you have to start dealing properly with this. It won't magically go away. Why don't you start by telling Lizzie? She'll understand. Mitch will too. They'll support you whatever you decide is the right thing to do.'

'Thanks. You're right. I have to stop running away.' The girl Kayla had known had grown into a sensible woman—perhaps even a wise one.

'You do. Promise me you'll tell Lizzie soon.'

'I will.'

'Good. Now, do you want me to help clean this up before I go to bed?'

'No, Jen. It's fine. Thank you.' She didn't mean just for the offer. She stepped closer to her friend and hugged her hard.

'Whatever you need. Now, I'm exhausted. Keeping the kids occupied inside for most of the day was hard work. Goodnight.'

''Night.'

Kayla stayed where she was as Jen left the room. She considered getting clean water to try to repair the damage to the carpet, then stopped. The stains on that carpet would never come out.

Perfection didn't exist, at least not for long. It was time she came to terms with that. She left the bucket where it was and walked out of the room.

CHAPTER
16

Kayla woke up feeling the best she had felt since seeing that blue line on the test strip. Her body felt alive, glowing even. She winced at the term, but today she understood what it meant. After prevaricating for so long, she was ready to take one very important step. She considered postponing it for a few hours, and instead hold on to this feeling a little longer, although she suspected that what she was about to do would actually add to today's joy.

There was a second task ahead of her—talk to Connor. But that could wait. She had no idea how to explain to him what had happened and why. He might think she was looking for a relationship and she wasn't. Not at all. Or perhaps he felt as used as she had on that night nearly four months ago. She couldn't escape the thought that she had treated Connor the same way she had been treated. That she had done to him what had been done to her. She had to apologise, but not today.

After breakfast, she made herself some of the herbal tea that had become her favourite to begin the day with. She didn't miss coffee one bit. Even if it no longer triggered her morning sickness, she felt no desire to go back to it. She poured the tea into a travel mug and pushed the lid firmly into place before setting off in the direction of the stables.

She heard Lizzie before she saw her; she was in the round yard lunging one of the horses. Her voice, as she called instructions to Deimos, was clear and firm but never harsh. Kayla leaned on the wall of the round yard to watch her sister. Mitch joined her, but didn't speak. Lizzie finished the horse's workout, then called the animal into the centre and rubbed his nose. He bent his head and gently nudged her.

Kayla cast a surreptitious sideways glance at her brother-in-law. His eyes were on his wife, and the look on his face was part love, part admiration, with a goodly hint of awe. His love for Lizzie showed in the light in his eyes and every line of his face. In that moment, Kayla understood why Mitch had waited all those years for Lizzie. No man had ever looked at her like that. Not the boys she had dated in uni. Not Lachie. And certainly not her baby's father. She wondered how it would feel to be looked at like that. It must be magical.

'Hi, Kayla,' Lizzie said as she approached, leading the stallion. 'We don't usually see you down here this early.'

'I'm heading into Sydney soon. But before I go, I need to talk to you.'.She had hoped to find Lizzie alone, because that might have been easier. But perhaps it was better this way. 'Both of you. Have you got time?'

Kayla and Mitch exchanged a glance.

'Sure,' Mitch said.

'Just let me put Deimos away.'

When the horse was happily dozing in his stall, the three of them settled on hay bales in the feed room.

'So?' Lizzie was as straightforward as always.

Kayla took a deep breath and tried to calm the nervous rioting in her stomach. She braced herself. 'I've got something to tell you and I guess the only way is to come straight out and say it. I'm pregnant.'

Lizzie almost knocked her over as she swept her into a hug. Kayla tensed for the shortest moment, before giving herself up to her sister's love and support. Over Lizzie's shoulder, Kayla saw a smile spread across Mitch's face. He nodded.

About the time that Kayla began struggling to breathe, Lizzie let her go and sat back to look intently into her face. 'When you came home so unexpectedly, I wondered why. I wanted to ask, but figured you'd tell us when you were ready. But this ...' Lizzie stopped speaking then nodded. 'So this is why you asked about Mitch and I starting a family?'

'It is. And after that, I didn't want to bring it up.'

Lizzie dismissed that with a wave of her hand. 'More importantly, how are you?'

'Fine. Healthy as a horse.' No-one seemed to notice the poor joke.

'I don't mean physically. You look great. But ... you know. About the baby?'

That was the important question, wasn't it? 'I honestly don't know.'

'The father?'

'He's not in the picture. And before you ask, no, I haven't told him.'

On the other hay bale, Mitch's face stiffened. 'Kayla, did he ...? I mean, were you forced in any way? Because if you were, I'll deal with him.'

'Mitch, you are the best man I know. It's fine. It was a stupid mistake, but it was my mistake and I'll manage the consequences.'

Lizzie's smile faded a little. 'What are you going to do?'

Kayla shrugged. 'I've gone back and forth with this a thousand times a day. I didn't plan to have a child. I'm not sure that this is the right time in my life to have a child—especially on my own.'

'But you're not on your own. We're with you,' Mitch said quickly.

'I know, and I'm so glad you are.'

'I was thinking.' Lizzie had turned to look through the open door to the graveyard on the big hill that rose above the stables. 'They would be so pleased to have another Lawson generation for Willowbrook.' Her voice was little more than a whisper.

Kayla's heart clenched. 'Lizzie. I'm not even sure I will have this baby.'

Lizzie turned to smile at her. 'You are my little sister. *Our* little sister. I have always looked after you as best I could. I'm not going to stop now. Whatever you decide.'

This time, Kayla reached for Lizzie. 'I know. Thank you.'

'So, what next?' Lizzie asked, gently pulling back from Kayla's embrace.

'I'm going back to Sydney for a day or two. I need to tell Pascale and sort out the work situation. I'll come back after that.'

'All right. Whatever you need. Willowbrook will be here for you.'

'Thanks.'

Kayla got to her feet. 'Oh, yes, one more thing. Jen knows.'

'You told her before you told me?' Lizzie did actually look annoyed.

'No. She told me one morning after I finished throwing up. She's got two of her own. She knows a pregnancy when she sees one.'

★★★

The drive to Sydney seemed to take forever. In the past, Kayla had enjoyed the run; driving her little red sports car had always been a pleasure and she'd liked the feeling as the open paddocks began to give way to homes and towns. The river views and scenery of the Hawkesbury had always been such a welcome green after the dryness west of the ranges. And then dropping down into Sydney itself, she'd felt a rising excitement for the city and the lifestyle she loved.

But this time was different, because, as a single mother, that lifestyle would change dramatically. She wasn't ready for that. She had to fight down an urge to turn around and drive back to Willowbrook, where everything was easier. Working there and organising a few weddings would be so simple. As she drove the last few blocks and pulled into the carpark of Elite Weddings, she was rehearsing in her mind the things she had to say to Pascale.

'I wasn't expecting you,' Pascale said as Kayla entered her office. 'Good to have you back. You look great. Have you put on some weight? Country living may suit you, but I need you here in Sydney for client meetings and venue inspections. Our list for the upcoming season is almost full. I've got at least three major events that need your special touch.'

'Hello to you too,' Kayla quipped as she sat in the armchair opposite Pascale's desk.

Pascale chuckled. 'It's been almost two months, you know.'

Kayla knew exactly how long it had been. 'I know it's hard, but can you forget work for a few minutes? We need to talk.'

Pascale frowned and closed her laptop. 'Sure. Is something wrong?'

'The reason I took a break … well. I'm pregnant.' It did not get any easier to say.

Pascale hesitated. 'Before I say anything else, tell me—is this good news or not? For you, I mean.'

'I'm not sure.'

'The father?'

'I'm not going to tell you. I haven't even told him. But it's really nothing to do with him … at least, not any more.'

'How far along are you?'

'Nearly sixteen weeks.'

'You sound very sure.'

'I am.'

Pascale frowned again, which Kayla found quite disconcerting. Pascale never frowned. She didn't want lines in the perfect skin of her forehead.

'Sixteen weeks ago, you were at the Forbes wedding.' Pascale raised an eyebrow.

'Pascale—please stop being my boss. I need a friend right now.'

'I am not your boss. I might be your business partner, but first and foremost I am your friend. So, tell me—are you happy about this? I assume you're planning to have the baby?'

She still didn't have an answer for that one.

'You know I'll support you whatever you decide, don't you? But you're leaving it very late to make that decision.'

'I know.' There were those damn tears again. She sniffed. 'Pregnancy hormones are the worst thing ever.'

Pascale's smile was back. Before she could say anything else, Kayla switched the topic to work and the rush wedding at Willowbrook.

'They were thrilled,' Pascale said. 'You did a brilliant job as always. But according to the bride, you also modified her dress?'

Kayla explained.

'She was really pleased with what you did. She kept going on about it. I know you used to sketch dress designs. Have you thought about maybe doing a bit of that while you're up there?'

'No. That was just coping with an emergency. I fixed the dress while Connor helped cover the delay with extra wine and canapes.'

'And tell me, who is Connor?'

His name had slipped out. 'No-one. He owns a pub. He managed to get me some wine when my usual supplier let me down.'

'Forget the wine—you probably need to explain why you just blushed like a schoolgirl with a crush on the captain of the cricket team.'

'What? No, I didn't. It's those hormones again. That's all.'

'Are you sure?'

'Of course I'm sure. Look, I'm pregnant. The last thing I need is to get involved with some barman. No matter how hot he is.'

Pascale grinned and waggled her carefully sculpted eyebrows. 'How hot is he?'

'Stop it!'

Pascale held up her hand in capitulation. 'But there is one thing I have to ask. Are you going to tell the father?'

'I don't know.'

'He does have a right to know. It's his child too.'

Those were the words that kept spinning through Kayla's head after she left the office with Pascale's blessings for an extended stay at Willowbrook, working from there. Her cleaner had kept her apartment in good shape during her absence, but it did feel cold and lifeless to her. When she opened the doors to the balcony, the city noises seemed harsh to ears that had become accustomed to the gentler sounds of the bush. She ordered takeaway food, which she didn't eat, and after a regretful glance at the bottles on her bar, made herself some herbal tea.

Kayla and Pascale had been business partners for several years and friends long before that. And one thing Kayla had come to accept was that, more often than not, her friend was right about the important things.

She picked up her phone and scrolled through the contacts.

CHAPTER
17

'Mum. Come on. I'll be late for school.'

That was a change. Most of the time, it was Jen hurrying Suzi along. 'I'll be right there.' She looked at herself in the mirror again.

Instead of her normal jeans, she was wearing her third best outfit: a smart skirt with a pretty top and a jacket that had seen much service at parent meetings, birthday dinners and the occasional work do with Brad. It wasn't anywhere as smart as the sort of clothes Kayla owned, but it was the most appropriate thing she had. Her hair badly needed trimming, but it was freshly washed and she'd pinned it back into some semblance of order. She'd even applied a touch of make-up. Not too much, just enough to make her feel confident.

Today was important.

'Muuuum!'

'I'm coming.' Jen took a deep breath, picked up her bag and left the bedroom.

Lizzie was in the kitchen with the kids. 'You look really smart.'

'Thanks. And thanks for looking after Dylan.'

'It's my pleasure.' Lizzie ruffled the boy's hair. 'There's lots of really hard work to do down the stables this morning. I could use the help.'

'You behave yourself, darling boy.' Jen bent down to kiss him. 'And you do whatever Auntie Lizzie says you have to do.'

'Okay, Mummy.'

'Come on.' Suzi was practically jumping out of her skin. 'I'll be late.'

'My daughter loves school. Who would have thought it?'

Lizzie walked out to the car with them. 'You know, I understand why you are doing this, but you know you'll be fine even if—'

'I know.' Jen watched Suzi run ahead and buckle herself in. 'The problem is that I really don't know how long it's going to be. The lawyers said a few weeks and it's been a few months now, with no sign of it ending. You know I appreciate everything you and Mitch are doing for us. At some point I do have to face reality. I need a job.'

'Well, good luck.'

'Keep your fingers crossed for me.'

Jen started the engine before Suzi could complain again. After dropping her daughter off, Jen drove into the centre of town. She parked next to the supermarket. She didn't check her appearance in the rear-view mirror; she knew if she didn't get out of the car now, she would just drive back to Willowbrook and put this off to another day.

How many 'other' days would there be? She didn't want to face the thought that Brad might spend years in jail. Her stomach clenched with fear. He might miss the kids growing up. As for herself, she still missed him every single morning when she woke up and he wasn't beside her. If he spent too long in jail, would they grow apart? She couldn't imagine not loving Brad, but if he spent too long in that dreadful place he might come back a different person.

No. She pushed that thought aside. Brad would always be Brad. Her Brad. And she would make him proud of her.

She marched out of the carpark and into the main street. A week of looking at online job sites had not offered a single job in Scone that she could do. She had no qualifications and very little previous work experience. She'd worked in various coffee shops and in a department store after leaving school. Then, since marrying Brad and having kids, she'd been a happy stay-at-home mum. Still, she could wait tables or deal with shoppers. She would even stack shelves at that supermarket if that's all there was. She had to make some money.

She reached the main street and looked up and down the long lines of shops. Time to put her plan into action. Coffee shops, restaurants and cafes always needed waiting staff. She could do that.

The first place she tried was new and looked quite trendy. It had big windows, closed now because of the cold, yet it still maintained a light, airy atmosphere. Coffee here wouldn't be cheap, but there'd be a better chance of tips. She took a deep breath and opened the door.

'Hi.' A head popped up from behind the counter. 'I'm sorry, I've only just opened. Please take a seat anywhere. I'll be over to take your order in a minute.'

'Oh, I'm not here for coffee,' Jen said. 'I'm hoping you might need some extra staff. Another waitress perhaps?'

'Oh.' The man wiped his hands on a cloth. 'I'm the manager here. I'm sorry. We don't have any positions open at the moment.'

'Could I leave you this?' Jen pulled an envelope out of her bag. 'My details are in there. If you have something come up …'

'Yes. Of course.'

'Thank you for your time.'

Jen left the coffee shop. She wasn't disappointed; that was only the first stop. There were many more places to try. She walked a little further down the street to the next coffee shop.

By the time Jen ran out of coffee shops, her feet were starting to hurt but she was still determined. The restaurants were opening. She'd have a better chance there. She didn't like the idea of working nights, but with family to help babysit the kids, she could make it work. She bought a bottle of water and continued.

After the restaurants, she approached some of the general shops. She could serve behind a counter. She was good with people. Then it was time to start with offices. She began with the Stock Horse Association. She knew the name Lawson carried weight there.

'What experience do you have?'

She heard the question again and again as determination was replaced with exhaustion and disillusionment. At last, she dropped onto a bench in the park at the far end of the main street. All her envelopes had been handed out and she imagined by now most of them were in the rubbish. No-one needed a willing but untrained assistant, no matter how much she tried to impress upon them that she was smart and organised and could do the jobs. Without experience, no potential employer was prepared to take a risk.

Except perhaps one.

The Gateway Hotel was just across the road from the park. The doors were open and she knew Connor would be inside. If anyone was going to take a chance on her, it would be Connor. Even though he didn't know her well, it was probably well enough to want to help. And after all today's setbacks, she wasn't too proud to ask.

She stretched her aching feet inside her shoes and stood up. Instead of crossing the road, she turned back to her car in the parking area of a supermarket that had her details but didn't need any new staff at this moment.

It appeared she did have a little pride left.

The house was empty when she arrived. She changed into jeans and went looking for her son.

Dylan and Lizzie were in the stables. Lizzie had a mare tied up and was holding Dylan as he ran a grooming brush over the horse's gleaming coat. His face glowed with excitement.

Jen leaned against the stable wall just out of their view as a sense of failure washed over her. Her children depended on her and she couldn't even get a minimum wage job stacking shelves in a supermarket or clearing tables in a coffee shop. She tried to ignore the nagging voice at the back of her mind that said she wouldn't have to get a job if Brad was with them. If he'd stayed clear of those dodgy associates. If he wasn't in jail. The more the voice spoke, the more her emotions slid from shame to anger. Anger at Brad for doing this to his family. To her.

She took a deep breath and pushed those feelings aside. She wouldn't go down that path. She didn't have the emotional energy for that. Her kids needed everything she could give them right now. And she would give them everything she had.

CHAPTER
18

Kayla looked at her phone for the fifth time in as many minutes. He wasn't late yet, but in another minute he would be. She wasn't sure that he was coming. She'd left a message last night asking for this meeting, but he hadn't replied. Not even a text. How long past ten o'clock did she have to wait? Would five minutes allow her to say he wasn't coming and leave? Maybe, if this was going to be her only attempt to contact him, should she at least wait ten minutes? How much time for her to be able to say she'd done her best? Or, more to the point, to feel honestly as if she had done her best? Perhaps she should get some juice if she was going to be here a little longer.

Before she could move, he walked in the door.

He saw her and smiled. Quite a few heads turned in his direction as he made his way across the room. As well they might. His face was easily recognised and he was considered one of the most handsome and eligible bachelors in the country. Was he handsome? Obviously she had thought so once or she wouldn't be here. But his looks did not set her pulse racing. Two days ago, her hormones had sent her crawling all over a man she barely knew. A man who was so wrong for her in every way, he should not even have caused a flutter. But today those same hormones were rejecting the very man who was responsible for ... everything. Stupid pregnancy hormones!

'I was so pleased to get your call. Sorry I missed it. I was on air.'

She had been very aware that he was working. In fact, she'd turned on her television to make certain he was in the studio for a live show before she called his mobile number. This was a conversation that could only be had in person.

'Hello, Dean. I'm glad you could make it.'

'I wasn't busy this morning and it's good to see you.' The smile he gave her said everything she needed to know about why he'd come. 'Now, let me get us some coffee. Where's that waitress?' He raised one hand and snapped his fingers to attract attention. He was a man who liked attention.

Kayla found herself studying his hands. They were well manicured, the skin obviously benefiting from hand cream and a job that required no manual labour. His long fingers were elegant, but the memory of those hands on her body almost made her shudder. Uninvited, an image came into her head of a pair of work-roughened hands, fingers carrying the marks of a tough life. Yet those hands had ruffled a young boy's hair. Had gently touched Kayla's face, had made her feel—

'Coffee?' Dean's voice dragged her back.

'No. Water please.'

'So, how are you? Busy planning more dream weddings?'

'It's our quiet time now. How have you been?'

'Excellent. I don't know if you saw my special on the election. They're talking about awards.' He droned on about a new show and the famous guests he was expecting to interview.

Had she not noticed on that night how very full of himself he was? Probably not. She'd only spent a couple of hours with him.

'I've been thinking about you. That night. It was great. We were very good together. I'd like to do it again.'

He smiled and reached for her hand. She pulled it away quickly. She didn't ever want to feel his flesh touch hers again. This was excruciating. She wanted it over.

'Dean, I needed to see you to tell you that … well. I'm pregnant.'

She'd kept her voice low, but the first thing he did was check over both shoulders, in case anyone was listening. 'Pregnant?' His voice was a harsh whisper. 'And you are telling me this now because?'

'It's yours.'

He shook his head. 'Don't try to pin this on me. We were only together once three months ago …. more. It could easily be some-one else's.'

'No. It couldn't.' The words came out louder than Kayla had intended.

'For God's sake, keep your voice down.' Dean was looking over his shoulder again. He smiled at a couple of women who had glanced their way, supremely confident that would be enough to put them on his side in case of an argument.

'It is your child.'

'Well, even if it is, we are both responsible. I seem to remember you were a very willing participant.'

He was right, of course. How could she have been so stupid? She'd had a bad day and she was tired and disillusioned. She'd had to break up a clinch between the bride and the best man in order to get the woman away on time with her new husband and had had an unaccustomed drink at the bar. That was where Dean had found her. He'd been handsome and charming and she'd accepted another drink. Then another and after that, an invitation to his room. She had been a willing participant and had regretted it the moment she woke next morning.

'I was. Neither of us took precautions.'

'I assumed you had that under control. The pill—ever heard of it?'

Kayla was struggling to contain a mix of anger and contempt. 'And have you heard of condoms?' She took a deep breath. Getting angry wasn't going to help.

'All right. I'm sure we are both eager to avoid any unpleasantness.'

She heard the unspoken word—*publicity*. Of course social media would go wild if the pregnancy became known. She didn't want that, but he didn't want it more.

'So I'm prepared to pay for half the abortion.' Dean waited for her reaction—or maybe her thanks.

Spoken out loud like that, the word hit her like the kick from an angry horse. *Abortion*. It was a horrible word. So hard and clinical and final. It no longer mattered that she had been thinking in terms of whether or not she wanted to have the baby—said like that, by this man, the idea was horrible.

'Who said I was going to terminate this pregnancy?' She spat the words, trying to hide the emotional impact of his callousness.

'Well, of course you're going to. Something like this could wreck my career—and yours, for that matter. Don't forget who I am and what I do for a living. I can ruin you. And your business.'

'I know exactly who and what you are. I could just as easily ruin you.' Kayla gathered her things. 'I also know that you are not nor ever will be this baby's father. You needn't be so scared for your precious reputation. I don't want you anywhere near my child. Or me.'

Kayla stood, holding her head high as she walked out of the coffee shop. A couple of those women who had noticed Dean arrive now cast interested looks her way. She wanted to scream at them to stay well away from him, not to let themselves be fooled by a handsome face and a smooth voice.

Clutching her dignity around her like a cloak, she stepped into the street. She felt like she needed a shower. She needed to get home. It was only a short walk back to the flat.

But as she approached her building, she realised something important. The flat was not her home.

This certainly appeared to be a day of revelations. She had to clear her head and think. The nearby park had always been a favourite spot of hers, and without thinking too much about where she was going, she wandered into its comforting embrace. The trees rustling above her and the glint of sunlight on the harbour water in the distance had a calming effect as she settled onto a bench.

She put her hand on her stomach and tried to examine her emotions. In the coffee shop, she had used the words 'my baby' for the first time. Her protective instincts had leaped to the fore. Was that because of Dean and his arrogance and assumptions? Or had she suddenly decided to keep the baby? If she was to become a mother, it had to be because she wanted to, not because of her anger at that man's words.

Until now, all she'd been thinking about was whether or not she wanted to have this child. It was time she started thinking about being a single mother. Could she make that work?

First of all, her flat was no place to raise a child. Maybe when they were small, but she would want any child of hers to have open space to run and play. Somewhere safe too. And she'd want the child to be part of a family, as she had been. If she was to be a single mother, the only family the child would have was hers, and they were at Willowbrook. So, she could sell her flat. There wouldn't be a lot of money left after she paid off the mortgage, but probably enough to keep her going until after the baby was born. So that was a box ticked.

Next—work. If she had a child, she had to be the best mother. She couldn't do that with her current work arrangements: the long hours and the weekends. She wouldn't leave her child with a nanny or carer, so she had to cut back on work. Maybe just do the Willowbrook weddings. Tick.

Which of course led back to money. Cutting back her work would mean a smaller income at a time when she needed to start thinking about schools and universities and God only knew what other costs a child meant. Lizzie and Mitch ran the Willowbrook Stud and all that income was theirs. The Willowbrook Weddings business was a partnership with Pascale and half the proceeds went to her. So how else was Kayla going to have the income and the time she needed to be a good parent? There was always Pascale's suggestion of designing wedding dresses. She wouldn't have to leave the child to do that. It was something Kayla had often thought about, so she'd be giving herself a chance to realise that ambition. That could tick another box. Two boxes really.

How many boxes did she need to tick to make this work? Money, time, place. Surely that was all of them?

Logically, she could have this baby. She fought down the insistent voice in the back of her mind that was saying this was not just about having a baby. It was about being a mother, and that was a very different story.

She got to her feet and strode out of the park. Her first stop at the real estate agent's office didn't take long. The market, she was told, was a ravening beast and her flat would sell quickly for a good price. And yes, the agent could organise everything, including hiring removalists to take Kayla's belongings to her new home.

She didn't tell him that her new home was in fact her old one. Instead, she thanked him for his advice and said she would be in touch. She collected a few things from the flat that she wanted and loaded them into her car. She did not look back as she headed for the Northern Suburbs and the highway home.

She made it as far as Singleton.

As she slowed down to pass through the town, her hands started to shake. Her legs felt too weak to properly operate the pedals and she could feel a lump growing in her throat. She pulled off the highway and into a side street, finding herself in the main shopping area. She quickly found a park and turned off the engine. Her head dropped onto her hands where they still clutched the steering wheel. She stayed like that until she felt strong enough to get out of the car. What she really needed was a cold drink, then she'd finish the drive back to Willowbrook.

She locked the car door to go in search of a bottle of water. But when she turned around, she found she was looking into a shop window filled with clothes. Not the sort of clothes she would want for herself, but tiny pastel clothes. Soft pink jackets and blue beanies. There was some sort of one-piece outfit in pale green, a cartoon lion appliqued on the front. One outfit looked like a tiny bear suit. Another had butterflies embroidered all over it.

Kayla approached the door of the shop like a sleepwalker.

Once inside, she moved between the displays, touching the soft fabric, marvelling at the colours. Not only pink and blue, but every colour of the rainbow. There were blankets so soft they felt like clouds and plastic plates and cups festooned with cartoon figures. She found herself in front of a display of stuffed animals.

The horse was made of brown fur, with a fluffy mane and a tail that had a greater resemblance to a possum's than anything she'd ever seen on a horse. It was the animal's face that drew her. A piece of white fur had been incorporated to show a blaze on the horse's forehead. Just like that cracked china horse, held together by glue and love, on the bookshelf in her office. The cheap figurine that meant so much to her because it was all about family. Her father. Her sister. And now here was this horse. A horse for a baby that Kayla had neither planned nor wanted. She picked the toy up and, as her fingers closed around the soft fabric, everything changed.

She placed her hand gently on her stomach and the bulge that was only beginning to form.

'Well, little one,' she whispered, 'we Lawsons have a legacy, you know. You may as well start early.'

She carried the horse to the counter.

CHAPTER
19

'Jen, I won't talk about it. I just won't.'

She heard the beginnings of anger in his voice and she didn't like it. 'Brad, I'm only trying to understand. I want to know what you are going through so I can help you.'

'You can help me by keeping our kids safe and well away from this.'

'I'm doing that. But I am your wife. I don't want to be kept away from it. I want to help you—'

'No, Jen.'

His voice was so harsh Jen had to bite back a tiny sob. This wasn't her husband. This wasn't the gentle and considerate Brad she knew and still loved. A heavy silence fell.

Brad was the first to speak. 'This is wasting money and phone time. I should go.'

'No. Don't you want to speak to the kids?'

'Just tell them I love them, okay? I'll call again next week.'

'I love—' He was gone before she could finish the sentence.

She sat on the side of the bed staring at the phone as the screen went dark. She should never have left Queensland. She should have stayed there so she could go to Brad. Help him. Give him moments of something good in a life that must be all sorts of hell. It had been his suggestion she come to Willowbrook when they sold the house. But now …

Her thoughts were interrupted as Suzi opened the door and looked inside.

'Has Dad called yet?'

'He has, honey, but he couldn't stay. He had to go.'

Her face fell and Jen's heart contracted.

'He said to tell you he loves you very much and he'll call again next week.'

'I miss him, Mum.'

'I know. I miss him too. And he misses all of us.'

'Mum?'

'What is it?'

'Why isn't Dad here with us?' It wasn't the first time Suzi had asked.

'I told you, honey, Dad had some things he had to do up in Queensland. He'll come and join us as soon as he can.'

Suzi was shaking her head before Jen finished speaking. 'Mum. Please tell me what's going on. Some of the kids at school, before we came here, they said Dad was a criminal. And in jail. They said he was a bad man.' Her daughter's eyes shone with tears.

'No, no, honey. No. Your father is a good man.' Jen had known this moment would come, though she'd hidden the truth from Suzi as long as she could. Suzi was going to grow up a lot faster than she should and it broke Jen's heart. 'Your dad had some friends. They were criminals, but your father didn't know. He got caught up with them. As soon as he knew what was happening, he went to the police and tried to make things right. That's what he's doing now up in Queensland. He's helping the police to stop the criminals from hurting any more people.'

Suzi's eyes were wide. 'Is it dangerous? He won't get hurt, will he?'

'No, honey. He'll be fine. And he'll be back with us as soon as he can.' Jen held her arms out and Suzi moved into them, wrapping her arms around her mother in a tight hug. Jen allowed herself this moment to lean on her daughter for comfort, while at the same time fighting down anger at her absent husband. All this was so unfair. Suzi should never have had to deal with it. She was a child who shouldn't ever have to talk about her father being in jail.

Jen fixed a smile on her face and moved away. Being angry wouldn't help anyone. 'Right. It's a lovely day. Let's collect Dylan and get some fresh air.'

'Can we go see Jango?'

'Maybe. We might also walk down to the creek. We can look for kingfishers and kookaburras in the trees. Come on.'

The three of them were making their way down the stairs when Mitch came through the front door.

'Hi, sis,' he said. 'I was wondering if the kids wanted to come down to the stables with me.'

Jen realised that Mitch had provided her with an opportunity too important to miss. 'Sure. In fact, I have to go into town for a bit. It would help if I can leave them with you.'

'Sure. Is Kayla back yet?'

'Not yet. I'm expecting her in the next couple of hours.' It would be helpful to do this before Kayla was there to look at her with those piercing eyes, asking questions she did not want to answer.

Mitch nodded and raised his voice slightly. 'Kids, who wants to come down the stables?'

He was answered by enthusiastic cheers.

'I've got it under control, sis. You go and do what you need to do.'

In town, Jen parked her car in the street outside the Gateway and glanced at her watch. It was well after lunch and too early for the evening crowd; she hoped the pub would be quiet and Connor would have time for her. There was one couple drinking at a table in the corner and one man at the bar, but otherwise the pub was empty. A barmaid was doing something with the bottles on the shelf behind the bar, but of Connor there was no sign.

'What can I get for you?' the barmaid asked as Jen approached.

'Um. A lemonade, lime and bitters please.'

'Sure.'

As the barmaid poured the drink, Jen mustered her courage. 'Is Connor here?'

'Yeah. Hang on a second.'

The woman placed Jen's drink in front of her and then disappeared through a door at the side of the bar. She returned only a few moments later, Connor close behind her.

'Jen, it's nice to see you. How's everything?'

'Fine, thanks.' Jen's reply was automatic. 'Connor, have you got a few minutes to talk?'

'Sure.' He started to sit on a bar stool but changed his mind. Perhaps it was the look on her face. 'Why don't you come through to my office?'

Connor's office was clean but cluttered. The desk was the clearest part, and even that was covered by papers and a laptop. Connor waved Jen into what was obviously his chair at the desk, while he lifted a folding metal chair from the top of a pile of boxes and sat on that. He didn't say anything, just waited for her to be ready.

'You said I could come and talk to you … about prison.'

'I did. What do you want to know?'

'I had the most awful phone call with Brad. My husband. Being in that place … it's changing him. And I don't know what to do or say any more.'

'Prison does change a person. There's no denying that. But mostly what it changes is the outside. It's like self-preservation. You shut everybody out so you don't get hurt. But what's inside, the heart of the person—it's still there. It'll come back when he's home with his family again.'

'I'm so scared it won't.'

'It will. Trust me. It might not happen for someone who's been there a long time and who doesn't have anything to come back to. But he has you. He has two great kids. He will find his way back.'

Jen clutched those words to her like a life vest. She had to believe Connor was right. Had to. 'He doesn't talk about being there. The sort of things that happen. Can you tell me what it's like?'

'Are you sure you want to know?'

'Yes. I want to be able to help him when he gets out.'

Connor nodded. 'All right. I think it's important to understand that the hardest thing to bear, at least for me, was that prison takes away your ability to choose. You can't choose when to eat or sleep. What to do or where to be. It's not just that you are locked up, it's that your life is no longer under your control.'

★★★

Connor had talked about his prison life before. He'd volunteered to talk to youth groups and the occasional troubled teen who was a lot like he'd been. Those talks had been aimed at convincing the kids to change the sort of behaviour that was leading them to the same place he'd ended up. 'Scared straight' was the term he'd heard used. He didn't like it. He would never deliberately scare someone, but if he'd known at fifteen what he knew now, his life would have been very different. He wanted to give other kids the chance he'd never had.

But this—this was very different.

The last thing he wanted to do was scare Jen. But at the same time, she deserved his honesty. She too had come looking for help. He would do what he could. But there was nothing to be gained from scaring her. He didn't tell her about the violence from both prison officers and inmates. He didn't talk about the fights or the near riots. Instead, he talked about loneliness. About being unable to trust anyone. He talked about the boredom that was almost enough to drive a man mad. He told her that, upon release from prison, the one thing he had needed more than anything else was privacy, something totally denied to him while he was inside.

'I drank a lot when I got out,' he said slowly. 'I guess it was because that's something else denied to you inside. I drank to forget what my life had been like, but I also drank to numb myself and drive away the anger and disappointment and regrets. Luckily, I came to my senses before it was too late. I enjoy a few social drinks now, but I drink because I want to, not because I have to.'

'What about your family?' Jen asked quietly. 'How did you feel going home to them?'

'I didn't have a family to go home to. I was an only child. My father had run off years ago. My mother was an addict. She died of an overdose while I was inside.'

'Oh, Connor. I am so, so sorry.'

'The only people waiting for me on the outside were the gang members I had always thought were my friends—family, even. I was wrong. It was because of them that I was inside in the first place. They were the ones who had led me to where I was. I'm not trying to avoid the blame. Maybe I grew a brain in jail, but I was determined not to go back. When I got out, I stayed well away from them.'

'That must have been so hard for you. How old were you?'

'I was fifteen when I first went inside. I got out for the last time at twenty-three. And let me say this, if I had been lucky enough to have someone like you and the kids to come home to, everything would have been better. Not easy … It's not going to be easy for your husband either. And there are no guarantees. But he has you. Be patient and most of all, love him. There will be times it might seem too hard, but you more than anyone else can help him come back.'

'Suzi was asking about him today. Some of the kids at her old school … well, I guess they were repeating what their parents had said.'

'What did you tell her?'

'I told her that her father was a good man who had some bad friends. And that he was trying to make everything right again.'

Connor nodded. 'I don't know much about kids, but the charities I work with say it's best not to lie. They always say tell them a truth they are able to understand. Those kids are a lot older, but I think the same principle probably applies. Your kids will be fine as long as they have you.'

Jen nodded, obviously fighting to control her emotions. 'Thank you, Connor.'

'And if there's anything I can do to help you or them, you know where to find me.'

Jen sniffed and ran a hand across her eyes. 'One of these days, you're going to make a great dad. You know that, don't you?'

'I hope so. One day. In the meantime, when your husband comes home, I'm here if he needs to talk to someone who has been through the same thing.'

Jen got to her feet and as he did too, she hugged him. 'You are a special person, Connor Knight. Whatever happened in your past.'

'Thank you.'

He walked back to her car with her.

As she was about to get in, he took his courage in both hands. 'How's Kayla? I haven't seen her since the wedding.'

She paused, one hand on the car door. 'She's fine. She went to Sydney today to talk to her boss.'

'Oh.' A spike of guilt made his voice rough. 'Is she moving back there for good?' He couldn't blame Kayla after what had happened the night of the wedding, but he had hoped for a different reaction.

'I don't think so.'

He began to smile at the thought of seeing her again. And maybe soon.

'I see.' Jen's voice brought him back down to earth.

'No. No.' Was he blushing? 'Nothing like that.'

'Of course not.' She was laughing at him, but he didn't really mind because her assumptions were right.

By the time Jen got into the car and drove away, Connor was laughing gently too.

CHAPTER
20

Do you want music playing in the delivery room?
  Do you want to give birth standing, squatting or lying down?

How was she supposed to know? Kayla dropped her pen back onto the birth plan templates strewn across her desk. She'd been back to the clinic that morning to discover that she and her baby were fine and it was time she started defining how she wanted to give birth. The clinic had given her another load of pamphlets and offered her a session with a midwife when she was ready to make some decisions. The internet had offered her so much information, she was now thoroughly confused. The templates she had in front of her were all different. How could one ask about bean bags while another seemed concerned mostly with what drugs she might want? Then there was the birthing pool option. She was intellectually aware of what that entailed and guessed there were plenty of videos online that she definitely did not want to watch. How was she expected to make decisions she knew nothing about?

So far, the only part of any of these plans that made any sense was the first question at the top of every form. Maybe it would be easier if she simply picked a form and started answering the questions she knew the answers to.

She grabbed a form at random and slid the rest to one side. Then she picked up a pen and without hesitation answered the first question, writing 'Kayla Lawson' on the top line. She read question two.

Your birth partner's name:

She put the pen down. Birth partner. Someone to be with her as she gave birth. Someone to share the experience with. Did she even want to share that moment? There was no man in her life or the baby's, apart from Mitch and, good man that he was, there was no way her brother-in-law was going to be that much a part of her or her baby's life.

What about Lizzie? Her sister might be the perfect choice. There was that nagging concern over Lizzie's own attempts to fall pregnant. Would it be fair to ask this of her? Besides, Lizzie was busy enough with the stud and show season, and foaling would be starting soon. Foaling? Images flashed into Kayla's mind of her sister kneeling in deep straw in the stables, assisting a mare with foaling in ways that made Kayla's eyes water. Maybe Lizzie wasn't the best choice.

If asked, Kayla would probably say Pascale was her closest friend. She snorted at the thought. Pascale—perfectly groomed, designer labelled, beautiful Pascale—in a delivery room listening to Kayla scream. Holding her hand and bathing her sweaty brow. She was sure that Pascale would do it if she asked, but she was equally sure she'd be pretty bad at it. She probably wouldn't pass out, but Kayla wouldn't have put money on it.

From down the hallway, she heard a faint thump followed by a yell. Dylan was the clumsiest kid she'd ever seen. Not that she'd seen many. The yelling subsided in seconds. Jen would have sorted him out. She was such a good mother. Far better than Kayla imagined she would be.

And there it was—the answer. If only Jen would say yes.

When she entered Jen's family room, Dylan was playing with some toy cars, obviously none the worse for whatever disaster had occurred seconds ago.

Jen put down the book she was reading. 'Hi. Sorry about the noise.'

Kayla waved that away. 'Have you got a few minutes? I need to ask you something.'

'Sure. What is it?'

Kayla nodded towards the door.

'Dylan, I'm just down in Aunt Kayla's office if you need me.'

With her office door left open in case Dylan yelled again, Kayla got right to the point.

'While I was in Sydney, I saw the father.'

Jen sat in Kayla's spare chair. 'How did it go?'

'I have no idea what I saw in him that night. He is …' Kayla took a deep breath. 'But that's beside the point. He says he will pay and he expects me to …' Kayla found she couldn't actually say the words out loud now.

'And?'

'I've decided to have the baby.'

Jen smiled broadly, then hesitated. 'Please say you decided that because you want the baby, not because he made you angry.'

'He did make me angry, but that's not it. That may have been the first time I really faced the decision—and I can't do it. This baby is part of me and I want to have her.'

'Or him.'

'Or him,' Kayla agreed, although deep down she was hoping it was a girl.

'I'm so glad.' Jen's smile was back. 'You won't regret it. Being a mother is the best thing in the world.'

'I've been back to the clinic, and now I have to prepare something called a birth plan.'

'I can help you with that. It's an easy way to make you think about what is going to happen. And to prepare.'

'I do need your help, but with more than the plan.' Kayla saw the small frown form on Jen's forehead. 'It's not a big deal, at least, I don't think it is. Will you be my birth partner?'

To Kayla's shock, Jen burst into tears.

'Oh, Jen, I'm sorry. I— You don't have to, I just thought …'

Jen started shaking her head wildly. 'No. I'd love to. It's an honour. It really is.'

'Oh.' Kayla was confused. 'But why …'

Jen took a moment to compose herself. She rubbed her eyes with her hands. 'I had a sudden memory of Brad when our two were born. He was …' She sniffed loudly. 'But this is about you. I am so glad you asked and I would love to. Are you sure you don't want it to be Lizzie?'

Kayla shook her head quickly. 'No. I love my sister, but she spends her life helping brood mares drop foals. I'm not letting her anywhere near me when I'm in labour.'

'I can see that. Well, then, a resounding yes. This is such good news, Kay. I needed something to cheer me up. Have you told Lizzie and Mitch yet?'

'That I plan to keep the baby? No. I will, next chance I get.'

'Then maybe we should celebrate.'

Jen was right. It was something to celebrate. And well past time she did exactly that. 'Yes. Let's. Tonight. I'll ring Lizzie and get her and Mitch over. We should all go out.'

'That's good. Now, while Dylan and I go and collect Suzi from school, you can google some of the things in those birth plans. Then we can talk about them. There's plenty of time to get it all together.' Jen jumped up and hugged Kayla. 'I'm so happy for you.'

Googling the things mentioned in the birth plan was enlightening, but a bit disturbing. Mention of forceps and suction and stitches made her cringe. Best leave that sort of thing for when Jen was with her. In the meantime, she found herself opening a few of her internet bookmarks. Of course, all the sites were to do with weddings. Wedding venues. Wedding cakes. Wedding dresses. She paused on a dress site. She didn't like anything shown. This dress showed too much flesh. This one had an ugly seam down the front and another had too much ruching on the hips. The neckline was nice but would look far better on an A-line dress. She switched to her email and found some photos of the dress she had reconstructed after the red wine spill. It compared well to those on the designer sites, especially considering she'd had very little time to do it. She felt rather proud of that. Her mother had taught her to sew as a child, and it pleased Kayla to think she'd finally put that skill to such good use. Mum would be proud of her.

She reached for the recently rediscovered sketchbook. Those drawings had been done a long time ago. Her dress design ideas had been put aside in the face of long hours organising venues and catering and flowers and bands, not to mention the bridal parties. Maybe this might be a good chance to start again.

She started drawing, her hand moving across the page with increasing confidence. She could see in her mind how that train would look. How a few sequins would highlight a bride's waist. She continued sketching for a while, then her hand stilled. If she was going to do this, she needed another notebook. Some coloured pencils maybe. Fabric samples. She should have bought those before she left the city. But online shopping would do.

By the time Jen returned, Kayla had given her credit card enough exercise for the day. She was still trying to avoid thinking about a birth plan. Lizzie and Mitch arrived a short time later and were equally overjoyed to hear Kayla's decision to keep the baby.

'You know we're here to support you all the way,' Lizzie said as she gave Kayla an enthusiastic hug.

Kayla was startled to see a glint of a tear in Lizzie's eye. 'Enough of this mushy stuff,' she said firmly. 'I have more than enough to contend with from my hormones without you all adding to it. We should head into Scone now and have a family dinner to celebrate. My shout.'

'You don't have to do that, you know,' Mitch said.

'I know. But I want to, while I still can.'

'Let's go to the Gateway,' Jen said with a sideways glance at Kayla. 'The kids like Connor. And Kay, I'm sure you want to thank him for helping out at the wedding last week.'

Kayla wasn't so sure. A tiny corner of her heart leaped at the thought of seeing Connor again and she did want to say thanks. But mostly her face began to heat at the thought of speaking to him after her actions the evening of the wedding. What do you say to someone you'd thrown yourself at while you were cleaning a wine-stained carpet? Kayla had no idea, but she did know that she was probably going to get it wrong.

CHAPTER
21

An old Harley Hog sounds like no other motorbike in the world. Connor recognised the engine note instantly, even though he couldn't see the bike that was pulling up outside the Gateway. The sound was enough to remind him of how it felt to be roaring through the darkness on a Harley, a woman behind him with her arms around his waist, and the gang following behind. When he was nineteen and just out of jail, it had felt pretty good. The good feeling hadn't lasted though. He had ended up losing the bike, the girl and the gang and going back to jail. The only thing he was thankful for about that time was that while he had stolen and lied and brawled, he had never hurt anyone. No, there was a second thing he was thankful for—that he had come to his senses and left that life far behind.

He watched the door, waiting for the biker to enter. If the man was anything like Connor had been when he rode a Harley, he wasn't welcome here. He was trying to shed his past, but it wasn't that easy. He would try harder. His new start here was going well and he didn't want echoes of the past coming back to spoil it for him.

A figure appeared in the doorway, unbuckling a full-face helmet. Connor stiffened. The biker pulled off her helmet and waved to a family sitting at a table to the side the bar. They waved back and she nodded to Connor as she went to join them.

He shouldn't have felt relief, but he did. He also felt a bit foolish. After all, there was no rule that anyone riding a Harley was a gang member. Or a man.

In a very short time, Thursdays had become family night at the Gateway. Tonight there were four groups who were obviously families seated in the lounge. The drinks consumption was lower tonight than on Friday nights, but Connor didn't mind. They served more food and even though the profit margin was lower, Connor liked the atmosphere in his pub.

His pub. That sounded pretty good.

A few years ago, he would never have thought he would ever say those words. That he would ever own anything. Or have done anything to feel good about. He allowed himself a few moments of pride.

The kitchen door swung open as Emily, the new barmaid, emerged carrying two plates of food. As the door swung to, Connor heard an unexpected sound—singing from the kitchen. A nice melodic baritone singing a country song. Hayden. The boy had a good voice. Not only that, his ex-con chef seemed happy cooking in a small-town pub. Imagine that. A couple of years ago, Connor had struggled to find a job—now he was an employer. Connor had a suspicion that Hayden had started chatting Emily up, but as long as he treated the girl with respect, Connor had no problem with that. He'd never subscribed to the idea that workmates shouldn't get involved. No-one had control over who their heart chose.

He looked up as another family group came trooping through his door and felt his own heart skip a beat.

Kayla laughed at something Jen said as they crossed the room. This was a very different Kayla to the one he'd seen last Saturday. During the wedding, she had been wearing a simple black dress that showed her figure to perfection, with black heels and stockings that made her look professional, but oh so sexy. That night, in the bride's room, a T-shirt-wearing Kayla had been soft and eager and sexy as hell as his fingers stroked her wet skin. This Kayla was wearing jeans and boots and a casual shirt. Her face was free of make-up. She looked relaxed and happy and was still so sexy he couldn't take his eyes off her.

She looked up and saw him watching her. Even from behind the bar, he could see her face redden, which only served to make her even sexier.

What was with him? He was as red blooded as any bloke, but he wasn't one to ogle a woman in a pub. Even if she had made a move on him a few nights before. Those must be some pretty powerful pheromones oozing across the room to catch him like this.

He stayed firmly in his place as the small group walked over to the bar.

'Hi, Connor.' Dylan was the first to speak. 'We came for dinner.'

'Did you? Well, let me see. I guess we can fit you in. See that nice lady over there?' He gestured at Emily, who had just delivered some drinks to a table. 'Why don't you go and tell her that, as you are my special friend, she should give you the very best table we have.'

'Okay. Come on, Mum.' Dylan led his mother across the room and the rest of the group followed, except, as Connor had hoped, Kayla. She stayed at the bar, looking down at her hands resting on the bar towel, close enough to touch his.

'Hi.'

'Hi.'

Look at us, Connor thought, *standing here tongue tied like two kids who've shared a first kiss behind the school bicycle shed.*

'About the other—'

'I wanted—'

They stopped and Connor shook his head with a grin. 'You first.' He waited while Kayla took a moment to gather her thoughts.

'I want to say, I'm sorry about the other night. That's not the sort of person I am. I don't normally grab a man I barely know and … well, you know. I don't know what came over me. Anyway, I'm sorry and it won't happen again.' She let out a deep breath and Connor could see the relief on her face. He was disappointed by that.

'You know, I was going to say the same thing, but when it comes right down to it, I'm not sorry and I like to think that maybe it will happen again.'

She blinked at him. 'You're—'

'What man would be sorry to have a beautiful woman demonstrate that she fancied him? You made me feel good. And I hope I made you feel good as well.' He paused to give her time to cut him dead. If she did, he would accept it.

She didn't. Her lovely mouth dropped open a little in surprise and—did he see a hint of pleasure in her eyes?

'I don't know how to answer that.' Her voice was soft and she looked incredibly vulnerable. It was not what he had expected.

'You don't have to answer. Not really. I just wanted you to know how I felt.'

'I think I'll go and join the others now.' Kayla turned quickly away.

As she sat down, there were whispers between Kayla and the others, and a couple of glances were cast his way. He could see Mitch's frown. Until those few moments of vulnerability, Connor wouldn't have thought Kayla needed looking after. He was glad she had family. Even if the look on Mitch's face seemed to be disapproval.

As he turned back to his work, Connor very much wanted to know what had been said.

★★★

'I told you, it was nothing,' Kayla tried again. 'Just checking on the wine invoice from the wedding last week.'

'Really?' Jen's face was a mask of disbelief. 'Wine invoice?'

'Yes. Now, can we change the subject?'

'Connor seems a nice guy,' Jen said. 'The kids like him. They're usually pretty good judges of character.'

Dylan and Suzi were huddled together over a tablet, playing a game and not listening to the conversation around them.

Kayla glanced at the bar, where Connor was talking to a customer. He was nice. And he was ... hot. She felt herself starting to blush again. Of all the things she had and had not expected of this pregnancy, getting lustful over a barman from the wrong side of the tracks was not one of them. Still, the morning sickness had faded, so this would too. She needed to avoid him until then.

'You should go out with him.' Jen was obviously not going to let this drop.

'What? No!'

'Why not? He's good looking and it's pretty obvious he likes you.'

'And I'm—' she lowered her voice even more, '—pregnant. So drop it.'

'All right.' Everything about Jen's face said she wasn't going to.

'I'm starving.' Lizzie took the lead in her usual fashion. 'Let's order some food.'

All through the meal, Jen's words echoed in Kayla's head. When-ever Connor approached their table, she was careful not to meet his eye. But a few times, when she thought he wouldn't notice, she couldn't stop herself watching him as he moved around the bar. He had a pleasant, easy way with people. Most of the customers called him by name and appeared to be regulars. Certainly, the pub had a good feel about it. People seemed comfortable here. But, nice as that was, Kayla was not interested in Connor, no matter what her hormones seemed to think.

***

That was something she had to tell herself again the very next day.

She was fighting to turn a supermarket trolley with a wonky wheel. Instead of going down the narrow aisle of groceries, where it was supposed to, the heavily laden trolley suddenly veered to the right and collided with another.

'Sorry. This thing has a mind of its own.' Kayla pulled the offend-ing trolley out of the way before looking up, straight into a pair of laughing brown eyes.

'Hi, Kayla. Do you need a hand with that?'

Don't blush. Just don't blush like a teenager. It didn't matter how firmly she told herself not to, she could feel the colour rushing to her cheeks.

'Sorry, Connor. Wonky wheel.'

'No worries. It happens to us all.'

Not to him. She was sure of that. He was strong enough to control the worst of supermarket trolleys. Look at the muscles in his arms … *No, don't.* The glow in her cheeks went up another notch.

'That trolley looks pretty heavy.' Grinning, he reached into her trolley and picked up one of several jars of pickles. 'Are you stocking up for another wedding? I'd be happy to reach an arrangement on the wine again. Very happy to.'

She wasn't about to tell him that she'd been walking down the supermarket aisle past the pickles when she'd been overcome by a craving for the wretched things and started pulling them from the shelves.

'I'm stocking up on a few things.' That would also explain the jars of mustard. If he noticed the baked beans, she'd say those were for the kids. At least the apples were normal. As for the peanut butter … Kayla stopped right there. What was she thinking? She didn't have to explain the contents of her shopping trolley to anyone.

Another trolley rounded the corner and came to a stop.

'Well, fancy seeing you two here.'

It was the woman from the post office. Kayla was struggling to remember her name, but she was a known gossip.

'It's this trolley,' Kayla hastened to say. 'We had a mid-aisle collision.'

'Of course. They should fix the wheels on these things. Shocking really. Anyway, I'm in a bit of a rush. Have a good day.'

The woman carried on, but Kayla had a good view of the smirk on her face.

'That's just what I need.'

'What is?'

She hadn't meant to say the words out loud. 'She's a dreadful gossip, that woman.' Kayla kept her voice down. 'She is going to put one and one together and come up with fifteen. By the end of the day, the whole town will be talking about us.'

Connor's laugh was deep and throaty and her hormones went into overdrive. Again.

'I know. I think she was telling the town I'd bought the pub before I even signed the contract. I tell you what, as they're going

to be talking anyway, do you want to give them something to talk
about?'

'What?'

'Sorry. That came out all wrong. Let me try again. Are you a
Charlie Chaplin fan?'

'Charlie Chaplin? Now I am confused.'

'There's a small pop-up movie festival of sorts in the church hall
next week. It's a fundraiser for a youth group I do some work with.
We're featuring Charlie Chaplin. I was hoping you might come.
With me.'

'You work with a youth group?' That was a surprise.

'When there's not much for the teenagers to do, they get into
trouble. I know that all too well, so I like to help when I can. So,
what do you say? Is it a date?'

A date? That was a very bad idea in her present condition. 'Yes.'

'Great. Wednesday is a double feature. It starts at six. How about
I pick you up about five-thirty? We could grab a bite afterwards.'

'Sure.' Kayla started backing away. 'Sorry, I have to run. I have
to get back.'

'Didn't mean to hold you up. Where do I find you on Wednesday?'

'At Willowbrook.'

'You'll be working.'

'No. I live there. I thought you knew.'

'No. Jen told me she did. For now, at least.'

Kayla hesitated. Now was as good a time as any to set the record
straight. 'I guess the town gossip omitted to tell you one thing.
Lizzie and I own Willowbrook.'

His jaw dropped. 'No. No-one told me. And I didn't make the
connection.'

'I always assume everyone knows. It's been in the family for a long
time. We almost lost it a while back, but it's doing all right now.'

'Of course you own it. The horses and the weddings in the same place. You and your sister. It makes perfect sense.'

'Anyway, as I said, I have to dash. See you on Wednesday. Bye.'

Connor said nothing and made no move to stop her as she turned her trolley and almost raced to the checkout. She had to get out of here before she did something else as stupid as saying yes to a date. Never mind. She'd find an excuse and ring him during the week to cancel.

CHAPTER
22

Wednesday was a long time coming.

In the joint, time had passed slowly, especially for the angry and impatient young man Connor had once been. Days had seemed like weeks, and the end of his sentence a lifetime away. But that was nothing compared to the time it took for half-past five on Wednesday evening to arrive. He was busy enough. The pub opened and shut. He did his accounts, ordered stock and served customers, while in his head, all he heard was the agonisingly slow ticking of a clock. He hadn't felt this excited about a date since— Well, since ever.

Somehow he survived until five o'clock on Wednesday, at which time he was standing in his room above the pub. Still damp from the shower and wearing nothing but a towel around his hips, he opened the wardrobe, looking for a pair of jeans that wasn't faded and a shirt that looked like he had at least attempted to iron it. Kayla had seemed to find him attractive, if that was the word for what had happened between them, in his waiter's outfit. He could only hope she might react in a similar fashion to a pair of blue jeans and a casual shirt.

Fighting back his own reaction to the thought of him and Kayla on the carpet, her hands on his flesh and his on hers, Connor got dressed. But as he did, he looked around the room. He'd turned one of the old guest rooms into a usable, if not exactly homely, space. There was a bed and a chair and a desk. A small TV was mounted on the wall. He wasn't planning to take overnight guests at the pub for a while yet and hadn't given any thought to improving the guest accommodation. Even if he wanted to, he didn't have the money. But if what he was hoping for was to happen with Kayla, there was no way he could bring her here. An old guest room with fading paint and secondhand furniture stained by previous occupants was no place for Kayla. Just like him, it wasn't good enough for her.

Still, she had agreed to this date.

He clung to that thought for the time it took to drive his newly washed ute to Willowbrook. As he negotiated the long driveway, he could see lights on at the house. House? Mansion, more like it. The aging stones gleamed under the lights, which had obviously been designed by someone who knew how to make a lovely building look even better than it was. What was he thinking? Someone like him with the woman who owned this? He should turn the car around now and drive away before someone got hurt. And that someone would probably be him.

He kept driving.

He pulled up near the curving stone steps that led to the main entrance to the house rather than continuing around to the kitchen door. Tonight, he wasn't working, even though he might feel more at home using the tradesmen's entrance. He sat in the car for a few moments, fighting back the demons telling him the sensible thing to do was to drive away. Then the front door opened and Dylan appeared on the veranda, waving.

It was too late now for the demons and their sensible voices.

Connor got out of the car and walked up the stairs. The front door was open, letting the mild evening air flow into the house.

He put his head through the door. 'Anyone home?'

Jen peered out from the kitchen. 'Hi, Connor. Kayla's working … again. She's in the ballroom. Get her and drag her away to have some fun.'

Working? That left him a bit crestfallen. He'd hoped she would be as excited and nervous about this date as he was. But perhaps there was another urgent wedding to arrange.

With Dylan following, he opened the polished wooden doors that led to the ballroom and smiled. Two of the big tables had been pushed together and were covered with white fabric. Kayla was tugging at the fabric, waving a huge pair of scissors and cursing under her breath.

'I think it's dead,' he said. 'You can put the weapon away.'

She glanced up at him and her face broke into a smile that lit the whole room.

'Connor. Hi. I've been trying to beat this muslin into submission.' She put the scissors down and brushed some cotton fibres from her clothes.

'Have you got another wedding coming up?'

Kayla shook her head. 'I'm actually trying my hand at designing wedding gowns. Here's the new one. What do you think?' She waved her hand at a dressmaker's dummy that was draped in fabric.

Connor walked over for a closer look. He was no expert, but it didn't look like any wedding dress he'd ever seen. The material was dull and off-white and there wasn't a sequin to be seen. 'Um. I don't know anything about dresses, but I always think of wedding dresses as shiny. And it's not.'

'It's a muslin test,' Kayla told him. 'This is what it's actually going to look like.' She handed him an artist's sketchpad.

The drawing was good. It showed a woman wearing a wedding dress and with just a few lines conveyed an aura of femininity and elegance. He looked from the drawing to the creased fabric draped over the dummy. He didn't see it, but he was a man.

'If it turns out as well as the one at the last wedding, it'll be beautiful.'

'Thanks.' Kayla took the pad from him and put it down. 'I was going to ask if you wanted a drink or something?'

'No, thanks. I should get to the hall early, being an organiser and all that. If you're ready.'

'Of course.' Kayla reached for a handbag that was lying on one corner of the table.

As they walked towards the front door, Kayla propelled Dylan in the direction of the kitchen and called out, 'Jen, I'm off now. I'll see you later.'

When they arrived at the hall, people were already starting to gather for the film night. Connor leaped out of the car, meaning to open her door, but Kayla was too fast for him and was already greeting people she knew among the twenty or so streaming through the doors.

'Hi, Connor. Who's that?'

He had barely stepped into the hall when the boys who were the focus of this group surrounded him. Their eyes were on Kayla.

'Is that your date?'

'She's hot.'

'Enough.' Connor held up a hand. 'Anyone would think you lot had never seen a woman before.'

'Not one that looks like that!'

Connor shook his head. These were good kids really. Or could be, given half a chance. And they probably hadn't ever met anyone like Kayla before. He was hardly going to disagree with them about the way she looked. But he didn't like the things they were saying or the way they were looking at Kayla. At his date.

At that moment, she left her friends and joined him.

'This is Miss Lawson,' he told the boys.

'You're the wedding lady.' One of the older boys brashly held out his hand. 'I'm John.'

'Hello, John.' Kayla shook his hand. 'Are you planning to get married soon?'

'Um. No.' The teenager blushed furiously.

'Okay. Why don't you take a seat, guys,' Connor told them. 'The film will be starting soon.'

He led Kayla to a seat slightly away from the boys. He knew what they'd be whispering to each other and he didn't want to hear it. Even more, he didn't want Kayla to hear it. He also didn't care when he spotted the town gossip looking their way. He was on a date with Kayla and nothing was going to disturb that. They settled into two of the folding chairs that had been set up in orderly rows.

The lights dimmed and for a moment Connor found himself wishing he was back in the city of his youth, in the cinema he'd frequented as a teenager with his friends. He'd made out with any number of girls in the darkness there. He was ashamed now to think of how he had taken their agreement for granted. But that didn't for one moment stop him wishing he had the same opportunity now with Kayla.

The projector mounted on the ceiling above them added its own degree of fuzziness to a film already old and grainy and not terribly

clear. The black and white images jerked and people strode into
shot, looking more like puppets than real people. But when the man
in the top hat waddled onto the screen, jauntily swinging a cane,
Kayla laughed. It was a simple vibrant sound that seemed to dance
in the air, and Connor realised he was happier with that sound than
with any of the movie theatre encounters in his past.

★★★

Jen listened at the door of the kids' room. She could hear Dylan's
voice. He was in deep conversation with his toys. There was no
sound of Suzi, which meant she was either wearing headphones
as she played some silly game on her tablet or maybe listening to
music while she did her homework. Jen hoped it was the latter but
guessed it would probably be the former. Either way, it meant she
had a little more peace and quiet. Being a single mum was hard—
more so when you weren't used to it. Not that she blamed Brad, not
really … well, maybe a bit.

She turned away from the door and headed downstairs, trying to
fight a sudden wave of anger aimed squarely at her husband. Brad
wasn't a bad man, but he'd been an idiot to let himself get caught
up in that stupid scheme. She's had her doubts right from the start,
but did he listen? Oh no. This was his big chance to make some
good money for the family. It was too good an opportunity to turn
down. Too good to be true.

At least he'd been right about that.

And now look where they were. Their home was gone. Savings
too. She and the kids were reduced to living on the charity of their
family. Not even their family; the charity of her brother's wife and
her sister. Not that Jen wasn't grateful. She had no idea what would
have happened to her and the kids if they hadn't been able to come
to Willowbrook.

It wasn't fair. She and the kids had done nothing wrong, and yet they were paying for it.

Not as much as Brad was paying.

She pushed the voice into a dark corner of her mind. She would admit that later. She would be reasonable and forgiving later. Right now, she was angry and self-pitying and in no mood at all to be accepting or forgiving.

She was also, she had to admit, a little bit jealous of Kayla. Her friend was out on a date with a nice man. She would be enjoying all those wonderful moments that come at the start of a new relationship. The locking of eyes. The first time holding hands, strong fingers curving around yours. The first kiss. Jen remembered each of those moments of her first date with Brad. How wonderful it had been. She'd known even then that he was the man for her and nothing that had happened since had made her regret that decision. Not even this.

She went into the kitchen to start making dinner for herself and the kids, glad of these few minutes alone. Her mind still elsewhere, she opened the fridge doors and started pulling things out. Then she turned on the small TV fixed to the wall near the pantry. The face of the newsreader appeared on the screen.

She was opening the cutlery drawer, searching for a knife to peel potatoes, when the words the presenter was saying seeped through into her consciousness.

' ... in the early hours of this morning at the Arthur Corrie Remand Centre at Wacol, outside Brisbane.'

In her rush to grab the remote control and turn the sound up, the implements fell from her fingers. She barely registered the sound of them hitting the floor.

'Prison officials say most of the inmates remain in their cells. A few are being held in the prison dining room, as fire crews remain in the building. The fires, we are told, are now under control but several inmates are being treated by ambulances on the scene.'

The presenter was replaced by images showing a cell block from above. The ground around the building was littered with rubbish, some of it black and charred.

'These images, taken earlier this evening, show contents pushed from the cells through broken windows.'

Jen gasped as, on the screen, a man's arms appeared through the bars of a window and began waving. A thin plume of smoke drifted skywards from the same window. As the smoke became thicker, the man's arms disappeared, the broken window now illuminated by a glow from inside. The flashing lights of the nearby ambulances painted an eerie pattern on the prison walls. Jen could see people running towards the fire.

Brad was somewhere in that burning building. Or was he one of the injured inmates being treated in an ambulance? That might even be him reaching through those bars as the fire burned.

The vision ended and newsreader was back. 'We will have more on that breaking story as information comes to hand. Now, to other news, and today the prime minister ...'

Jen flicked the sound off with one hand as she grabbed for her phone with the other. She found the number she needed and hit the call button. It took forever for the ringtone to sound, and even longer before it was answered. Then she heard the lawyer's voice and rushed to cut him off.

'It's Jen Harrison. I just saw the news and—' She realised she was speaking to voicemail. She waited impatiently to leave her message. 'Find out about Brad and call me. As soon as you can.'

She had ended the call and was staring at the TV in the hope of a news update when she heard a noise in the hall. She flicked off the TV as Suzi and Dylan walked in.

'What's for dinner, Mum?'

For a moment she didn't think she would be able to answer. As she struggled, the eager look on her daughter's face started to fade.

'Mum? Is everything all right? Is it Daddy?'

'Everything's fine, honey. Don't you worry.' Jen pushed her fear away and turned her attention to her children. 'Now, who's going to help me cook dinner?'

CHAPTER
23

'How did you become a Charlie Chaplin fan?' The movie night had ended and, after escaping Kayla's crowd of young admirers, they were walking towards the main street and dinner.

'When I was in juvie, one of the other kids' dad was a fan,' Connor answered without thinking. 'The kid was so homesick that whenever we got computer time, he'd watch something online so he could talk to his dad about it when he visited. I sort of got hooked then.' His voice trailed off. This wasn't what he wanted to talk to Kayla about. But then again, if they were to have a relationship, and he hoped they would, she needed to know.

'How old were you?'

'Fifteen. The first time.'

'Oh.'

'Fifteen and stupid. It took me a long time to learn, but I did eventually.'

He waited for her to ask more. Ask how long he'd spent behind locked doors. And for what. He waited for her to freeze on him as so many other people had. Family. Friends. Landlords. Potential employers.

'That must have been tough.'

'It was. But I learned a lot.'

'Including to like silent films.'

'Including that.'

As they stepped around a lamp post, Connor's hand brushed Kayla's. She didn't move away so he reached out and gently closed his fingers around hers. She tensed, but only for a second, then her hand relaxed in his and their fingers entwined as if they had been made for each other. It felt good. More than that, it made him feel good. If Kayla didn't think he was worthless, then maybe he wasn't.

'Did you know that Charlie Chaplin died on Christmas Day?'

'No. How sad. It seems the wrong way to say goodbye to someone who made so many people laugh.'

They walked on in silence. It felt so good to hold her hand and enjoy the night air and the feel of the town that Connor was coming to think of as his home.

At last, they stopped walking and Connor looked around. They had walked the full length of the street and were now outside the Gateway. The lights were on and through the window he could see a good number of people, including families, in the front bar.

'Do you want to go in?' Kayla asked.

'No. Not tonight. Tonight is a night off. I don't get that many and I'm enjoying it. It seems I walked right past all the restaurants without even noticing. I'll blame you for that.' He smiled at her and was absurdly pleased when she returned the smile. 'Let's go back the way we came and find somewhere nice to eat.'

The restaurant they chose was the right mix of casual atmosphere and good food. When the waiter brought the wine list,

Kayla declined and asked for sparkling water. 'But you go ahead,' she urged Connor.

He ordered the same. There was nothing wine or beer could add to his enjoyment of the evening. Their table was in a quiet, almost hidden corner, and if that meant the service was a little slow, Connor didn't mind in the least. He would have happily sat there all night, listening to Kayla talk about growing up on a horse stud. When she spoke about the accident that took her parents when she was a kid, the sadness in her voice was tempered by a deep and very real love.

'I'm sorry about your parents. That must have been hard.'

'It was. But mostly I remember the good times, and there were so many of them. What about you?'

'Not so many good times in my family. Mostly my father wasn't there. My mother worked long hours. When she came home, she was too tired to be much of a mother. She kept a roof over our heads and while we didn't have any luxuries, there was food on the table, most of the time. But I was an angry and arrogant teenager. I didn't understand that she was doing her best. There were times I hated her and told her so. I'm ashamed of that now.' The familiar ache returned. 'Eventually, I think it was all too much for her. She stopped trying to be a good mother to me. She went looking for some kind of escape and died of a drug overdose while I was inside. I'll never shake the guilt of that.'

'Oh, Connor. That must have been so hard for you. But it wasn't your fault.'

'Maybe not directly. But I can't help feeling that if I hadn't been such a troublesome kid, if I hadn't made her life so difficult, she wouldn't have started using. And maybe if I hadn't been inside, I could have stopped her. She might still be here.'

Kayla reached across the table and laid her hand over the four fingers with the prison tattoo. The one that said 'love'.

'I needed someone—somewhere—to make me feel wanted. That's where the bikie gang came in. They felt like my family. But ... Well, you know the story. It's a pretty common one. To be accepted I went further and further into that lifestyle. There were drugs and fighting. Stealing just to get approval from my "brothers". I didn't see what I was doing. Where that path was taking me. Not until I got there and was looking at three bare walls and steel bars.

'I guess that must be hard to understand. I imagine the closest you have ever come to committing a crime would be speeding in that lovely red Datsun of yours.'

Kayla laughed. 'You'd be surprised.'

'I actually would. Come on, confess.'

'When I was little, I loved Kewpie dolls—the ones you get at shows. I always wanted the one I couldn't have, of course. The kind you had to win in sideshow alley or that were a bit more money than I had to spend. One year, Lizzie and Mitch and Jen and I played hooky from school ...'

'No!' Connor feigned shock and was rewarded with a withering look.

'We slipped through a hole in the fence into the showgrounds when they were still setting up. I saw a doll. She was perfect and I wanted her more than anything else on earth. So I grabbed her and ran. One of the workers saw and chased me. He tripped over something and fell, so I got away, but for a while I was terrified. I thought he was dead. I was so relieved when I found out he wasn't—and so guilty—that I threw the doll away. Thus ended my life of crime.'

She smiled at him, but beneath it, Connor sensed the frightened little girl she had once been. He took her hand in his.

'And since then, you have been perfect.' He meant it as a joke and was shocked to see her flinch a little, see some of the light leave her eyes.

'No. Not perfect.' The whisper held a sadness that tore at him.

'None of us are.' His voice was as soft as hers. Their eyes met and his heart did a crazy backflip. Neither of them was perfect, but from where he was sitting, Kayla was pretty close.

The waiter arrived with their meals and the conversation veered into safer territory. When they walked back to Connor's car, holding hands seemed the most natural thing in the world.

★★★

Kayla was lost in her thoughts as Connor drove her home. Why had she told him that story? In all these years, she'd never told anyone; not even Jen knew the whole truth. Kayla had never told her about throwing the doll in the creek because she couldn't bear to look at it any more. She moved a hand to unobtrusively caress her stomach. When would she tell him this secret? And what would his reaction be?

As they approached the turn-off to Willowbrook, a motorbike roared past them at high speed. A second later, they saw flashing blue lights—a police car in hot pursuit. She glanced sideways and saw Connor's face highlighted. His expression was taut, as were the hands that gripped the wheel. The past that had marked him so clearly had also made him strong and compassionate. But maybe that's why she felt so safe with him.

Connor had relaxed again by the time they saw Willowbrook glowing softly against the sky. Kayla understood now how easy her life had been compared to his. She'd had two parents who loved her and always had time for her, while he had been forced to seek that belonging among strangers. He had no doubt been a thief, a brawler and maybe even a bully. He'd done bad things. His life had never been perfect, yet he'd lifted himself out of it. She was ashamed of the way she'd judged him when they first met. What right did she have to judge anyone?

'Would you like a cup of coffee or something before you head back?' She held her breath until he replied.

'Yes. Thank you.'

She risked a glance at him and for a long moment, their eyes locked. She felt it then, the same urge that had overcome her on the wine-stained carpet in the bride's room. He felt it too—she could see in his eyes. She didn't know if that was how this night was to end, but she was open to it. Maybe a night with Connor would help wash away some of the bad memories of that night all those months ago. And she supposed if it didn't happen now, it wasn't going to. Her pregnancy would start to show soon, and what man would want her then? Not even Connor was that kind.

They held hands as they walked up the stone steps and Kayla couldn't help but see all the brides she had sent up the same steps, hand in hand with their husbands. She hoped they had been as happy as she was at this moment.

When she opened the front door, instead of the silence she had expected, Kayla heard sobbing.

'Jen? Jen?' She darted into the kitchen and found Jen sitting at the bench, her face in her hands. The sound of the television was a loud counterpoint to her crying.

Kayla crossed the room and wrapped her arms around her friend. Jen clutched her as a drowning woman would grab a life raft.

'Jen. What's wrong? How can I help?' Annoyed by the insistent sounds of voices on the screen, Kayla reached for the TV remote to turn it off.

'No!' Jen grabbed the device out of her hand. 'Leave it on. I have to find out what happened.'

Puzzled, Kayla glanced at the screen. It was a news broadcast, and the presenter was talking about some political row involving the US President.

'Jen, I don't understand.'

'There's a riot. In Queensland. At the prison where Brad is. They're saying it's on fire. And there are ambulances.' She lifted her head to look at the TV. 'I can't turn it off in case there's more news.'

Connor stepped from the doorway, where he had been standing, into the kitchen. 'Where are the kids?'

'They're in bed. Asleep, I hope. I don't want them to see this.'

He nodded and pulled his phone from his pocket. It took Kayla a moment to realise he was checking for news. On the TV, music was playing as the news broadcast ended.

'They're saying the fire is out now,' Connor said.

'Who? Where?' Jen looked around wildly for her own phone.

Connor put his phone in his pocket and moved closer to her. 'Jen, it's going to be all right. Things like this ... they're never as bad as the media makes them sound. There were riots when I was inside. Most of us weren't involved or affected in any way.'

'You told me he'd be all right. That he wouldn't be in danger there. But look ...'

Kayla was taken aback. When had Jen and Connor talked about Brad? Then she realised that didn't matter. Helping Jen was all that mattered right now.

'He's probably not in danger. The guards will have the trouble-makers locked down separate from everyone else. It will be noisy and a bit confusing for Brad, but if he's not involved, he should be safe.'

'He wouldn't be involved in this sort of violence. He's not like that.'

'That's good then.' Connor's voice was calm and confident. Kayla could see Jen taking comfort from him.

'I've been trying to ring his lawyer, but I get no answer.'

'If the lawyer has several clients on remand, he'll be trying to find out what's happening and they probably won't be telling him yet. I'm sure he'll call you if he has any news.'

'You mean he'll call if anything has happened to Brad.'

Connor had his phone out again. 'Jen, I know a few people in the system. I can make a couple of calls. They might know something the media doesn't. And hopefully they'll have a more balanced picture.'

'Oh, please. Thank you, Connor.'

With a nod, he backed out of the room, already scrolling down his phone list.

Kayla felt powerless. How could she help? She fetched a glass of water and placed it on the bench near Jen's hand, all the while knowing that was nothing. She found the TV remote and turned it off. They would get more up-to-date news from the internet.

The silence stretched on. Jen kept looking at her phone and Kayla watched her do it.

'I need to call Mitch,' Jen said at last.

'Are you sure? Aren't he and Lizzie away with the show horses?'

'They are, but that doesn't make a difference.'

'It might be better to wait until you know what's happening. I mean, they can't do anything to help. And you'll only make them worry. They might even decide to cancel the show and come home.'

'I want to talk to my brother. And he would want to be here. Why on earth shouldn't I call him?'

'Well, you know—'

'Know what? For God's sake, Kayla. You are so cold. Everything has to be perfect for you, doesn't it? Don't let the cracks show. Well, life isn't perfect. The cracks do show. We all need to lean on someone. Even you, with the baby coming. You've leaned on me and Lizzie and Mitch. You're even using Connor now to pretend everything is the same as it used to be. But it's not. You're pregnant even if you didn't want to be. We've all got things we wish hadn't happened. So don't tell me that I can't call my brother when I need him.'

A strangled sound from the doorway caused them both to look over. Connor had returned, phone in his hand. He was staring open mouthed at Kayla, his face a mask of shock.

Kayla made as if to go to him, but his eyes narrowed and his face hardened. She stopped.

Realising what she had done, Jen half slid from her stool. 'Oh God, I'm sorry, Kay. I didn't mean … Connor—'

Connor waved her protest aside. 'It's fine, Jen. It's nothing to do with me. I have good news for you. I talked to a parole officer I know who moved to Queensland and works a lot at the Arthur Gorrie Centre. He says the fire is out. The situation is under control and all the inmates are safely locked down. No-one was seriously hurt.'

'But the ambulances—'

'Standard policy when something like this happens. There are a few minor injuries, but no-one has been taken to hospital. Brad will be all right.'

Jen's body sagged. 'Thank you.' She got to her feet and crossed the room to hug Connor. As he comforted Jen, he looked past her to Kayla. She understood the shock on his face, but the look in his eyes was something entirely different. Could it be disappointment?

As Jen released Connor, her phone began to ring. She hurried over to it. 'The lawyer,' she said as she picked it up.

Connor backed out of the kitchen, presumably to give her privacy. Kayla followed him for a different reason.

'Connor—'

'I should be going now, Kayla. I hope everything works out fine for Jen and Brad. If I hear anything else, I'll pass it on.'

'Thank you. I'm sorry I didn't tell you—'

'No. No need to be sorry at all. Why should you tell me? It's your personal business, nothing to do with me. Goodnight.' He left before she could say another word, the front door shutting firmly behind him.

Kayla wished Jen hadn't said what she'd said, but she was right. The fault was Kayla's. If she was thinking of starting something with Connor, he had to know. Well, that at least was dealt with. Although judging from the look on his face, that something was over now before it had even begun.

She heard the sound of an engine roaring to life and a too-speedy departure down the driveway.

***

Connor paused at the Willowbrook gate. A left turn would take him back to the highway where he would face another choice. He could return to Scone, to his pub and the new life he was building for himself. A turn in the other direction could take him south, to where Sydney called. In the city he might find some way to fill the hollowness inside his gut. Among the bright lights he could find old friends from the days when booze and women and aggression filled the empty places in his soul. In all his days with the gang and all his troubles with the police, he had never felt like this; as if the solid earth beneath his feet had crumbled away, leaving him to fall into emptiness.

A right turn out of the driveway would take him away from the highway. Away from people, into the west. He could drive and drive and try to decide how he felt about what he'd learned. He could find a quiet place where he could look at the stars and try to forget. Try to put out of his mind the thought of Kayla with some-one else. The thought that she might still be with him or might go back to him for the sake of the child. He couldn't get in the way of Kayla reuniting with the father of her child. Connor knew what it was like to grow up in a broken family. He couldn't subject a child to that.

And even if he and Kayla got together despite this, was he ready to be a father? What sort of father would he be, with his prison record and the telltale tattoos on his fingers? He was no role model for a child.

He turned right, the car headlights lighting the way into the hills. He drove for hours, his mind racing. He knew what he wanted, but was what he wanted the right thing for Kayla and her baby?

The sun was just peeking over the hills when he finally drove back into Scone. The main street was deserted as he parked his ute behind the pub. He'd made his decision—the only decision he could make. But he didn't like it.

CHAPTER
24

Just as the bride spoke the most important words of the ceremony, Kayla's stomach fluttered, a bit like the nerves she'd felt at her very first wedding. But she had no cause for nerves. Everything was going just fine. Surely her morning sickness wasn't back? Not this far into her second trimester. Not at three o'clock in the afternoon and, most importantly, not in the middle of the first Willowbrook wedding of the spring season. She took a deep breath and the churning in her mid-section seemed to ease. Under the floral bower, the bride and groom were wrapped around each other, kissing with great enthusiasm. Their family and friends were cheering and flower petals were being gaily tossed into the air. Everything was exactly as she had planned it.

Kayla nodded in satisfaction, but her stomach squirmed again. That sudden movement. It didn't hurt and wasn't nausea but felt like—

She slid one hand down the front of her smart but simple black dress, which this morning had seemed far too tight in both the waist and the chest. She stopped as it rested on the bulge that even she could no longer deny.

'Was that you?' She whispered the words so softly she barely heard herself. Could the baby hear her now? Did she—or he— know when Kayla spoke? She waited for another movement, but there was nothing.

The bride and groom almost danced past her, heading into the homestead for their reception. Kayla should get there ahead of them, to make sure everything was perfect. But how could she, when the pregnancy that she had accepted intellectually had suddenly become very real?

She looked wildly around for Jen. Jen would tell her if this was normal. If everything was okay with the baby. Jen would tell her what to do. Of course Jen was nowhere to be seen. She was upstairs with the kids, keeping them out of the way.

The bride and groom had disappeared through the doorway and the rest of the wedding party was following. That was Kayla's cue. She didn't have time to stand here wondering about herself. She moved around the side of the building to the kitchen entrance. The kitchen hummed with activity, but she missed the controlled chaos that occurred whenever Lachie catered her weddings. He hadn't been available, but his replacement was efficient and the food looked wonderful. Maybe it was a good thing Lachie wasn't here. Underneath all that bluster he was a smart and thoughtful man and a good friend. She had never been able to hide things from him, and she doubted she could hide what was happening now. His sharp eyes would have it out of her in a second.

She left the kitchen to check the ballroom, where wine waiters were handing out glasses of champagne. They were moving quietly and efficiently around the room, and Kayla almost managed not to think of Connor and the last Willowbrook wedding. That was weeks ago now, but she hadn't forgotten one bit of what had happened or how it had felt. And she hadn't stopped wanting it to happen again.

She hadn't heard from him since he'd found out about the pregnancy, almost a fortnight ago. And she hadn't had the courage to contact him either. She guessed she should put that down as 'one of those things' and forget about him. She had more than enough on her plate now that the wedding season was back.

Photos on the grand staircase were next on the agenda. She quickly slipped inside the bride's room which was, as she'd hoped, deserted. It was a mess and Kayla began collecting empty champagne glasses. She picked up a discarded robe from the cream carpet. The place where the red wine had spilled at the last wedding wasn't visible; the carpet cleaners had done a great job. Or maybe it was because she'd poured white wine on it almost immediately. Then cleaned it as soon as possible.

The door opened and two figures ducked into the room, almost slamming the door behind them as they became caught up in a passionate kiss.

'Umm ...' Kayla coughed and the bride and groom sprang apart. 'Sorry.'

They laughed, sharing a look of such happiness that a lump caught in Kayla's throat.

'This wedding has been perfect,' the bride gushed. 'Thank you.' She darted over and gave Kayla a hug.

'You're welcome.' Kayla carefully extricated herself. 'Now, are you ready for the reception?'

The arrival of Mr and Mrs Hooper brought rousing cheers as the newlyweds bounced into the ballroom. Kayla went back into the kitchen to check on the canapes.

By eight thirty, she was exhausted. She crept quietly up the stairs and sat at the top, where she could still hear the wedding and swing into action if she was needed. Then she took off her shoes and rubbed her swollen feet.

Jen sat down next to her. 'You look like you've had enough.'

'I am so tired. I shouldn't be. I should be still down there keeping an eye on things.'

'Kay, this is what being pregnant is like. You are going to get increasingly tired as your body starts giving more and more to the baby. You need to give yourself a break.'

'I felt the baby move this afternoon.' Despite her weariness, a smile spread across Kayla's face.

'It's about that time. How did it feel?'

'I don't know. Strange. It's suddenly become properly real. I'm having a baby.' Kayla shook her head as her eyes became suspiciously damp. It felt good when Jen laughed gently and hugged her.

'Yes. Yes, you are.'

'But it's just the start of the new wedding season. I've told Pascale I'll only be doing Willowbrook weddings, and there isn't one booked every weekend. But even so, I'm not sure if I'm up to it.' Kayla gave herself up to self-pity for all of a minute before the light bulb flashed on. 'Jen, will you help? I mean officially help. As my assistant. Paid, of course. You can take some of the load off me and some extra cash might help you.'

'But I know nothing about organising weddings.'

'A lot of it is just solid common sense and attention to detail. You'll be working here, so that makes it easier with the kids. What do you think?'

Jen blinked a couple of times but didn't answer.

'Please. At least think about it. I can't keep up the pace. We can help each other.'

'It sounds ideal, but I'm not so sure I have what it takes. I know nothing about fine wines, or catering, or dresses. I couldn't do what you did to fix that dress after the red wine disaster.'

'You won't have to. I'll still be here. As for everything else, you'll pick it up as you go along. You were always the smart one, Jen. You got better grades than I did most of the time. You'll be as good as me at this, if not better. After looking after two kids on your own, organising a celebrity wedding will be a piece of cake.'

There was a crash from somewhere on the lower floor of the house. Kayla got to her feet.

'That's my cue. Please tell me you'll at least think about the job.'

Kayla's heart sank as Jen shook her head.

'I don't have to think about it,' she said. 'I'm still not sure I'm the right person for the job, but I've been looking everywhere for some sort of work and have found nothing. This would be perfect in so many ways. If you're sure you want me, I'll take it.'

Kayla felt like cheering. 'You'll be great. Thank you.' She felt a lot less tired as she slipped her shoes back on and made her way downstairs.

***

When Brad called two days later, Jen couldn't wait to tell him about her new job.

'I'm pleased for you.' But Brad didn't sound too pleased. Or even very interested. His voice was flat and dull. It had been ever since the riot.

'It'll really help with the money side of things.' Jen did her best to sound upbeat. 'I think I'll enjoy working with Kayla. And it's all from home, so that makes it easy with the kids.'

'That's good.'

'Brad, honey, what is it? How can I help?'

'It's nothing, Jen. There's nothing you can do except look after the kids and keep them safe.'

'Of course.'

'I have to go now. I think there might be some sort of hearing next week. I'm not sure what it's all about, but I'll tell you as soon as I know.'

'That's good. We've been waiting for so long.'

'Yeah.'

Jen bit back a sob as they said their goodbyes. This man on the phone was so different from the Brad she had fallen in love with. He had changed so much in the time since the prison riot and fire, which he still refused to talk about. She could only hope that when this nightmare was over, she'd get her beloved husband back again.

She ducked into the bathroom to wash her face and comb her hair. Confident her distress wasn't showing on her face, she went in search of Kayla.

'All right,' she said, 'the kids are settled. Maybe it's time you started briefing me on this job.'

'Don't you want to know how much you're getting paid first?' Kayla grinned. 'I've talked to Pascale and it's all sorted.'

Of course she did and was pleasantly surprised with the figure Kayla mentioned. She would have done it for much less, though any money at all was a blessing.

'But before we get started on the weddings,' Kayla said, 'I need you to help me get this done.' She indicated the papers that were spread over the desk and the blank form on her computer.

'The birth plan? Are you still fiddling with that? You've got time, but at some point you have to settle down and do it.'

'I know, but it's hard. I don't understand some of the questions and googling did more harm than good. And those videos … No. I need you. You've been through this, Jen, help me. Please.'

'I will. But first, forget all those papers and questions and tell me, what do you want this experience to be like?'

'I don't know.'

'You do. You just haven't put it into words. Now that the baby is moving, it's time to try to get your emotions in order. And when you've done that, the birth plan will be easy enough.'

'My emotions?'

Jen took her friend's hand. 'How do you honestly feel about this baby?'

Kayla opened her mouth to speak, then closed it again. Jen could see the thoughtfulness in her eyes.

'Let's start with an easy one,' she offered. 'Are you certain that having this baby is the right thing to do?'

'Yes.' Kayla sounded certain.

'And that keeping it is right too?'

'Yes. I don't think I could give away a child.'

'Your child.'

'Yes. My child.' Kayla's hand moved to stroke her stomach. 'But, Jen, I'm afraid I won't love the baby when it's born.'

'That's not unusual. Some expectant mothers feel like that. But you will love her, or him.'

'How can you be so sure?'

'Because I am. Kayla, you'll love this baby with all your heart. I know you will. And you'll be a great mother.'

'I hope so.' Kayla looked down. 'I want to be a good mother to you.'

'You know the baby can probably hear you?'

Kayla looked shocked. 'Hear me?'

'Yes. Babies can hear in the womb. So talk to her. She won't understand the words, but she'll come to recognise your voice.'

'Hello. I guess I'm your mum.'

Jen watched Kayla's face as she talked to her baby. She would be fine. Jen was a lot more certain of that than she was of her own future.

'All right, now tell me what sort of experience you want this birth to be.'

'I want it to be calm. And easy. For me and for the baby. And safe. In a hospital. Definitely in a hospital. A big one, with lots of doctors and nurses in case something goes wrong.'

'All right. That's a start,' said Jen, biting back the urge to say nothing about pushing a person out of your body was easy. 'Hospital it is then.'

After a lot more questions and a few dives into Google, the birth plan was ready. Kayla hit print. As they read through the document, it occurred to Jen that Kayla had gone about this in exactly the same way she ran her business. This plan was for a perfect birth. Nothing had been left to chance. Perhaps she should tell Kayla that babies didn't read birth plans and very few births reflect such meticulous planning. But her friend looked so reassured by what they'd done, Jen didn't have the heart to contradict her. She'd come face to face with reality soon enough.

CHAPTER
25

The car pulling up in front of the house was red. Very red. Brighter red and more expensive than Kayla's beloved Datsun. Kayla watched the driver get out. She was blonde and thin and equally expensive. She was mostly dressed in red, but what could have looked tacky or overdone on anyone else didn't on this woman. The clothes were of obvious quality and the woman knew how to wear them. She was exactly the sort of high-end client Willowbrook Weddings catered to.

'You're Kayla?' The woman held out a well-manicured hand. 'Hi. I'm Hailey. I was here for Brittany's wedding, but I don't think we met.'

Brittany? Kayla cast her mind back.

'I love this place so much. That's why we've booked it for our wedding next year.'

That was a surprise. When Hailey had emailed to set up this meeting, Kayla had assumed it was to look at Willowbrook with a view to possibly booking it in the future.

'Sorry, I didn't realise the booking was already made.'

'Of course. I booked early to make sure I could get the date. Brittany's wedding was perfect. Exactly what I want.'

'Thank you. And you're here today to talk about ...'

'Not the wedding itself. My dress.'

'Your dress?'

'Yes, I saw what you did when Brittany had wine spilled all over hers.'

Ah, that Brittany. Kayla had caught up at last.

'I really liked that idea of the high-low with the overskirt. And I can't find something like that anywhere. When I made the booking, Pascale said you might design something for me.'

This was exactly the sort of opportunity Kayla had been hoping for, but still it came as a bit of a surprise. She gave silent thanks to Pascale. 'Why don't you come inside and we can talk about it.'

When the woman was sitting comfortably at one of the big tables in the ballroom, Kayla fetched her sketchbooks and a few fabric samples. And some glossy magazines. Over coffee, they discussed waistlines and hemlines and sequins and the colour red.

'I love red, you see,' Hailey explained. 'In case you hadn't noticed.'

Kayla smiled. 'I had.'

'My mother won't hear of a red wedding dress, much as I would like one.'

'Mothers can be quite traditional like that.'

'But I am insisting on red boots. I already have them. They are exactly the same ones I was wearing when I met Nathan. Look, aren't they divine?' Hailey pulled out her phone to show Kayla a photo of fire-engine red ankle boots with a killer heel.

'They are quite something.' Kayla kept her tone neutral.

'I want to show them off, so I can't have a full-length gown. But Mum says ...' Hailey sighed heavily.

Kayla knew that sigh well. She'd heard it many times before. 'Let's see …' She pulled her sketchbook closer and flicked past the designs she'd already drawn. None of those would suit. She found a blank page, reached for her pencil and started sketching. 'You could have something like this to show off your figure. It would be the reception dress, so I can put a slit in here. On the other side too, if you wanted. Just to show off the boots. And your great legs too. Then, I can make an overskirt like this, which should keep your mother happy, but if the tulle here is only a couple of layers, you'll still get some boot glimpses …'

'Yes! That! Exactly that!' The bride was literally bouncing up and down in her seat.

'And if you like—' Kayla reached for a red pencil, '—I can trim the waistband of the overskirt with diamantes and weave in some red ones, only a few, to match the shoes.'

'And when I take the overskirt off?'

'I'll make you a belt, diamante on red satin. With a long tie to fall down the back of the dress. I could even, if you wanted me to, add some diamantes, just subtly, to the boots, to tone everything through.'

'Perfect.' Tears sparkled in the bride's eyes. She sniffed a couple of times then asked the all-important question. 'What's this going to cost?'

Kayla's mind raced. She knew a lot about weddings and a fair amount about wedding gowns. She had done some preliminary costings on fabric and trimmings, but Hailey was her first actual customer. This was the first time she'd been asked to put a price on her own work. Bespoke gowns from top designers began at around twenty thousand dollars. She couldn't ask that much. But this was supposed to be a business. She mentioned a figure.

Hailey didn't even blink. 'That seems fine.'

Kayla glanced at her watch. It was well after four o'clock. This consultation had taken a lot longer than she'd planned and she had an errand to run. 'How about I get some fabrics, do some detailed drawings and get in touch in a couple of weeks?'

Hailey left in a flurry of smiles.

After waving her off, Kayla went back inside the house to grab her bag and a printout of her birth plan. She could still make it if she hurried.

The clinic didn't seem as strange to her now as it had on her first visit.

'Good afternoon, Ms Lawson,' the receptionist greeted her.

'Please, call me Kayla.'

'Of course. How are you feeling?'

'I'm well, thanks.'

'I didn't have you down for an appointment today.'

'No. I wanted to drop this off. The midwife has been nagging me about it.' She handed over the sheaf of papers.

The receptionist looked at it and nodded in an understanding way. From a nearby chair, Kayla heard someone mutter about nagging. She looked at the woman and they both smiled. For the first time, Kayla felt a connection to the other women waiting on those orange chairs. As she left, she paused to say hello to a couple she recognised from previous visits. A small child peered at Kayla from her mother's lap. Kayla smiled and the little girl smiled back.

Kayla's steps were light as she walked back to her car. She pulled out of the clinic carpark and turned in the direction of the main street. She hadn't consciously thought about it, but she found herself driving past the Gateway. On impulse, she pulled into a parking space and turned the engine off. She would have to face Connor some time and now was as good a time as any. It wasn't as if she'd actually lied to him, she just hadn't told him. And it wasn't as if they were a couple. They'd been to the movies and had dinner, but that wasn't exactly dating. And that one moment after the wedding … that was a hormone-induced thing. Nice as it had been—and it had been very nice indeed—it wouldn't be repeated. No man would want a woman who was carrying someone else's child.

Still, perhaps they could be friends.

There weren't many people in the pub when Kayla walked in. She couldn't see Connor, but a young barmaid was stacking bottles of wine on the shelves.

'Can I get you anything?'

'Lemonade, lime and bitters please.' Kayla waited until the woman served her the drink. 'I don't suppose Connor is around.'

'He's in the office. Why don't you grab a seat and I'll see if he's free.' Something about the way the girl spoke suggested she wasn't entirely sure her boss would want to see Kayla.

Settling at a table in a corner as far from other people as she could get, Kayla saw the barmaid come back into the bar and serve another couple of drinks. No sign of Connor though. She shouldn't be surprised. She'd finish this drink quickly and go. Obviously coming here had been a mistake.

She was about to get to her feet when he came through the door at the back of the bar. His eyes searched the room and when they found her, he nodded with a little half-smile. Her heart did a crazy backflip.

'I'm glad you came,' he said as he slid into the chair opposite her. 'I wanted to go and see you, but I wasn't sure …'

'Sure of what?'

'If I'd be welcome.'

'Why would you not be welcome?'

'You obviously didn't want me to know about the baby. And now I do.'

'I wasn't keeping it a secret just from you. Only Jen and my family know.'

'Anyway, it's none of my business.'

'Connor. I'm sorry.'

'That's fine. I understand.'

'I'm not sure I do.'

'Well, the baby has a father somewhere.'

'The father is not a part of this.'

'Maybe he should be. It's his baby.'

Kayla frowned. 'That really is none of your business.'

'I'm sorry, but as a kid who grew up without a father, I know how hard it is. I care for you, Kayla, but I'm not going to stand in the way of your child having a proper family.'

'That's not—' She was interrupted by a loud noise from the doorway as a group of people entered the pub. The sun was behind them and Kayla had trouble seeing their faces.

But apparently Connor didn't. He froze.

'Where's my man!' A loud voice, rough and possibly already drunk, floated across the room. A big man in a leather jacket with a chain around his waist turned slowly in the middle of the room. When he saw who he was looking for, he dropped a motorcycle helmet onto a nearby table. 'Connor. Brother. So this is where you've been hiding.'

'Kayla, I'm sorry, but I think it would be a good idea if you left now.' Connor got to his feet and walked across the room, hiding Kayla from the man.

'Connor. Baby.'

The squeal was deafening. Kayla only caught a glimpse of the woman who flung herself at Connor. High heels, tight jeans and the arms that were now wrapped around his neck sported a lot of jewellery and bright red fingernails.

There was no way Kayla could leave without walking past the group. Her hand flew to her stomach and its visible bump as her protective instincts flared. She looked around and the barmaid caught her eye. With a movement of her head, the girl indicated the door that led to the back of the pub and Connor's office. Kayla quickly and quietly got to her feet. She stepped smartly across the room, hoping no-one would notice, and was out the door in seconds.

CHAPTER
26

Connor felt a surge of relief as Kayla vanished through the doorway. He carefully untangled the arms around his neck and gently pushed the dark-haired woman away.

'Hello, Molly.'

'Hi, baby.'

Before he could stop her, Molly grabbed him and kissed him on the lips. Hard.

Over the cheering that action prompted, Connor heard a familiar voice.

'You see, Molly? I told you we'd find your knight in shining armour for you.'

Connor pushed Molly away a second time and faced the bearded man in the leather jacket.

'Blue.' His voice was cold and unemotional.

'Hey, brother. How's it hanging?'

'I didn't expect to see you up here. It's a bit far from your normal patch, isn't it?'

'Molly was missing you so I thought we'd come up and see if we could find you.'

'How did you know I was here?'

'You know how it is. I heard a rumour. And here you are. Let's drink to our reunion.' Blue moved towards the bar. The rest of the group followed, except for Molly, who was clinging to Connor's arm like a drowning woman.

From behind the bar, Emily caught Connor's eye. He gave her the smallest nod. He didn't want Blue and his mates in the Gateway and he certainly didn't want Molly climbing all over him. But to refuse them a drink might provoke the sort of incident he was trying to avoid. He'd take it slowly and hope he could get his former friends out of the pub without a fuss.

'Nice setup here,' Blue said to Connor as the drinks were poured. 'Nice town. Nice folks. Nice tips too, I'll bet. Maybe skim a bit off the top for yourself that the boss doesn't know about.'

Connor shrugged. He could feel his old self looking over his shoulder. He wasn't that person any more, but maybe the person he used to be could help him now.

Emily finished pouring beers. Molly had asked for wine and once that was poured, Emily hovered, holding the payment machine.

'What do you think, Connor? Maybe you should buy your mates a drink for old times' sake?' The challenge in Blue's face was clear.

'It's on the house,' he said.

'On the house. That's good of you. Are you sure the boss won't mind?'

Connor didn't reply and Blue's face tightened.

'There is no boss, is there? You're the boss.'

There was no point denying it.

Emily put the card machine back on the counter and opened the door into the kitchen.

'Oh, no, sweetheart.' Blue gave a nod to one of his gang, who stepped up to Emily and took her arm. 'I think you should stay here with us. The more, the merrier, if we're going to have a party.' He gave her a leering grin.

Connor fought down the urge to slam his fist into Blue's face. He gave Emily what he hoped was a reassuring look. She was probably wondering about Hayden. Connor hoped he hadn't arrived at work yet. The boy was on parole and didn't need something like this to screw everything up for him. The bikie released Emily and she took up her usual position behind the bar, looking frightened. Connor hoped she understood that he would not let anyone harm her. Not without a fight.

'So, looks like it's true. You have gone straight. Seeing as how you own such a nice place, we might stay for a while. What do you think, Molly? We could stay tonight if you wanted to.'

'Oh, yes. Connor, that would be so nice. It'd be just like old times.' She rubbed against Connor and he almost recoiled. He couldn't understand what he'd once seen in her. Compared to Kayla—

A movement across the room caught his eye. A middle-aged couple who had been drinking quietly were leaving—not quite running out the door, but obviously keen to get away. Connor couldn't blame them. The atmosphere in the pub was thickening and rapidly becoming unpleasant. After all the hard work he'd put into this place, Blue and his gang were going to wreck it. He wasn't going to let that happen. Whatever it took. His hands curled into fists.

Blue laughed and took another swig of his beer, emptying the glass. 'How about another?'

'You got your bikes outside?'

'Of course.'

'Then I think maybe, instead of another drink, you should get on those bikes and head back to Sydney.'

Blue drew himself up to his full height. He was a good few centimetres taller than Connor. Broader too. And the tattoo on his face gave him an even more menacing air. 'Are you throwing your old mates out of the bar? Too good for us now, are you?'

Connor forced his fists to unclench. He would not confront Blue. 'No. I'm just saying it's a long ride and there's lots of cops on the highway. You don't want to get caught by an RBT.'

'Who cares? I might just have to serve myself.' Blue stepped towards the bar, but Connor blocked his way.

'I said, I think it's time you left.'

Blue's mates joined him and Connor found himself facing a wall of men. He knew the looks on their faces and the tension in their bodies. They were begging for a fight. He'd been like that once. Been the leader of a gang a lot like this one. And Blue, one of its members. Had Blue learned this from him? He hoped not. He'd never been a fighter, tried to avoid the gang wars if he could. Sure, he had used his fists when he had to, but he'd never been the first to turn to violence. He could still take pride in that one small thing. Blue, however, had always been a bully and a fighter. Jail had changed Connor, but obviously not the man standing in front of him.

'Look, Blue—'

Before he could finish the sentence, the door from the kitchen swung open and Hayden came through. 'Everything all right in here, boss?'

'Sure, no problems. Just go back to work.' He had to try, but he didn't believe it would work.

'I wasn't doing nothing much,' Hayden said. 'Happy to help here if you need me.'

'And who's this?' Blue studied Hayden, who was already wearing his chef's apron. 'Are you the cook, kid? That's a good idea; why don't you rustle up some grub for me and my mates?

Steaks would be good.' Around him, the others didn't even bother to agree. Everyone already knew that whatever happened next was not going to involve food.

Connor sidled towards the bar, where Hayden was standing close to Emily. 'Look, Blue—'

He saw the swing coming and pulled back. Blue's fist barely grazed his chin. He'd always been slow.

Connor raised his fists, instinct and experience taking over. Beside him, Hayden did the same. Blue's mates stepped forward, pushing back their sleeves. Connor knew this wasn't going to end well but there was nothing he could do to stop it.

Someone took a swing at Hayden. It connected and Hayden staggered backwards, crashing into the bar. Connor heard the shattering of falling glasses as Emily squealed.

Blue took another swing at him. Once more, Connor saw it coming and ducked under it. Then he lunged forward, driving his shoulder into Blue's stomach. They fell. He landed on top of Blue and heard the wind forced out of his adversary's lungs.

In a flash, Connor was on his feet. He spun to face the other three men approaching him. One thing prison taught a man was to know when he was in trouble. Connor was about to take a beating and it was going to hurt. Then this place that meant so much to him was going to be trashed. All he could do was try to give as good as he got. He balled his fists again.

★★★

Kayla paused at the turn-off to Willowbrook, waiting for oncoming traffic, listening to her indicator. *Tick, tick, tick.*

Those men walking into Connor's pub had looked like trouble. The woman too, although hers was of a different kind. Kayla had leaped at the chance to slip out the back door and get away. She was pregnant; she wouldn't risk anything that might harm the baby. The oncoming traffic cleared, but Kayla didn't move. *Tick. Tick.* For a few seconds she sat perfectly still in the middle of the highway and thought about the threat emanating from those men in the bar. Then she slammed the Datsun into gear and spun her back wheels into a sliding U-turn.

As she headed back towards town, Kayla fumbled in her bag for her phone, cursing her love for this old car that lacked such modern conveniences as a Bluetooth connection. She ignored the speed limit signs as she turned off the highway into town. Her phone was in her hand and she glanced down as she began to dial. How could she not have done this the moment she left the bar? No-one was going to go into the pub and help Connor, not with the reputation that place had—or used to have. It was up to her.

She listened to the ringtone that seemed to go forever before she heard a voice at the other end. 'You've got to come now. The Gateway Hotel in Scone. Someone's going to get hurt.' She dropped the phone on the spare seat and concentrated on driving.

Forced to slow down as she entered the main street, Kayla's fear continued to grow until she eased the car into a parking place outside the pub. A few metres away, five powerful motorbikes parked in a row told her those men were still here. But of the police there was no sign.

She hesitated for only a second. Despite the current awkwardness between them, Connor was a friend. Maybe more than a friend. She had to find out what was happening.

She placed a hand on her stomach. 'We'll be all right. I won't let anyone hurt you. But I can't leave him.'

Kayla paused near the window. Cautiously, she peered inside and gasped.

Near the bar, two men were holding Hayden as he struggled to free himself. There was blood running down his face. Another had the young barmaid pinned against the bar. The dark-haired woman was sitting on the bar, waving her arms in the air and yelling, although Kayla couldn't understand the words. Two figures wrestled on the floor in front of the bar. As Kayla watched, the gang leader heaved himself to his feet and swung a leg in a violent kick. On the floor, Connor grunted in pain.

Kayla cried out and the bearded man looked up. He gave Connor another contemptuous kick and turned towards the open door. Kayla ducked back into the shadows just as a police car pulled up outside the Gateway. Two uniformed men got out and marched into the bar. From her hiding place, Kayla heard a loud crash and a firm voice.

'That's enough!'

Silence settled on the room. Kayla approached the door and looked inside. She saw Connor slowly getting to his feet, his face twisted with pain.

'I thought you said we wouldn't need to do this any more,' the sergeant said to Connor. 'I am very disappointed.'

'Sorry.'

'It's all right, officer,' the gang leader said as he fought to bring his breathing under control. 'It was only a momentary misunderstanding between me and Connor here. We're old mates. Isn't that right, Connor?'

Connor didn't reply to that. He looked at Hayden. 'Are you all right?'

Hayden nodded as he ran a hand over his lip to wipe away the blood.

Unable to stop herself, Kayla stepped into the bar.

Connor saw her. 'You shouldn't be here.'

'I had to come back. I was …' Her voice tailed off. What could she say? That she was frightened for him?

'Was it you who rang us?' the sergeant asked.

'Yes. I'd seen them come in and I thought there might be trouble.'

As she spoke, the roar of a car engine and flashing lights outside the pub heralded the arrival of another police car. Two more officers came into the pub and started handcuffing the gang, starting with the leader.

'I'll need you to come to Murrurundi Police Station and give a statement. Tomorrow will do,' the sergeant said. 'Your name is?'

'Kayla. Kayla Lawson.' She almost whispered the words. Blue was taking a lot of interest in the conversation.

'You should go home now and leave this to us. This lot will be cooling their heels in our cells tonight.' The sergeant turned to Connor. 'And as for you, it probably wouldn't hurt to get yourself checked out.'

'I've had worse,' Connor mumbled.

'I imagine you have. But get yourself checked out anyway. Both of you,' he added as Hayden picked up a chair that had been knocked over in the melee.

'I need to get this place straightened out,' Connor said.

'Your call.'

Kayla watched the gang being led away. As he passed, the leader looked at her. She almost recoiled at the anger in his eyes and breathed a sigh of relief when the pub was empty again except for Connor, Hayden, Emily and her.

'Hayden. Emily. Are you all right?' Connor asked.

Hayden reassured his boss that he was fine, while Emily reached behind the counter for a cloth. She held it under a tap for a few seconds before going to Hayden to dab at the blood running down his face from a wound on his forehead.

'I think you're going to need a couple of stitches in that,' Connor said. 'Emily, can you get him to the hospital?'

'No, I'll stay and help straighten things up.' Hayden pushed the barmaid's helping hand away.

'No, you won't.' Emily's voice was firm. 'I'm taking you to get that looked at. In the car. Now.'

Kayla had to smile at the strength in the girl's voice. She was a tiny thing, but there was some steel under there.

'Yes, go. And thank you. Both of you,' Connor said.

'If you're sure …'

'Of course. Go on.'

They left, and Connor slowly moved his shoulders and torso. Watching him, Kayla could see how much it hurt. He came closer to her and took her hand in his.

'Thank you. If you hadn't called the police, things might have got a bit nasty.'

'Might have?' She held his hand tightly. Couldn't seem to let it go. 'What can I do? I can drive you to the hospital.'

'I don't need to go to hospital.'

'Are you sure?' He wasn't visibly bleeding, but Kayla could see the pain in his eyes.

'I'm sure. I've had worse than this before. And some of it with the same bloke. Why don't you go home, Kayla? This has been a terrible experience for you too. In fact, maybe I should drive you home.'

'You will do no such thing. You're not in a fit state to drive. I'm fine, but I'm happy to stay and help clean up if you want me to.'

'No. I'll close for the evening and sort this out. By morning, all will be as good as new.' He winced as he moved an arm to indicate the mess in the bar. He was lying and they both knew it. It'd take more than a night for his bruises to heal. And probably much longer than that for Kayla to forget the fear that had engulfed her when she saw him lying on the floor at the mercy of the bikie gang.

CHAPTER
27

When Connor dragged himself downstairs into the bar the next morning, he ached in every part of his body. The bruises on his ribs were impressive, but he expected they would get worse before they got better. He glanced at the clock on the wall. It was almost ten o'clock. Laura would be here soon. Hayden wasn't expected for another hour yet. He wouldn't be early. He hadn't taken as much of a beating as his boss, but he'd still be feeling it.

The room looked as it should. All signs of last night's incident had been cleared away before Connor had collapsed onto his bed. He was not going to let this one setback get in the way of his plans. He would make a success of this venture and nothing from his past, not even his old gang, was going to stop him. At the dot of ten o'clock, he opened the doors for business as he did every morning.

The first thing he noticed was that only one motorcycle remained parked outside the pub. He must have been dead to the world if the gang had picked up their bikes this morning without waking him. He was about to check the front of the pub for new damage when he spotted the sergeant leaning against the police car parked across the street.

'I've seen the other guy.' Baker followed Connor back into the pub. 'You look like hell compared to him.'

'I've been better.' Connor touched his fingers gently to his bruised and swollen eye. 'It would have been a lot worse if you hadn't shown up. Thanks.'

'Say thanks to Kayla Lawson. She's the one who called us.'

'I will.' Connor went behind the bar and poured a glass of water. He took a deep drink. 'You let them go?'

'I let the others off with a warning. Brought them back here to collect their bikes.'

That explained why there was no further damage to the pub.

'The leader is still cooling his heels in a cell. I wanted to talk to you first. I could charge him with assault.'

It wasn't a question, but the implication was clear. Connor thought carefully for about thirty seconds. 'If you charge him, he'll come looking for payback. Not just against me, but the others as well.' The thought of Kayla being targeted by Blue sent a chill through him.

Baker nodded. 'Seems possible.'

'Then I think I might be happier if you let him off with a warning not to come back.'

'I could do that, if you're sure?'

'I'm sure.'

Baker took a couple of steps away and spoke briefly into his phone. 'The rest of the gang are bringing him back to get his bike. I might stick around until he does.'

'Thanks.'

'I've got to take your statement anyway. I don't suppose there's a cup of coffee anywhere round here?'

'Two coffees coming up.'

They took a seat within sight of the door and the sergeant pulled out his notebook.

'You know this guy, right? Tell me about that.'

Connor talked to the sergeant about his own role as leader of the gang and where that had taken him. 'Blue took over the gang while I was inside. When I got out, Blue had plans I didn't want to be any part of. I walked away.'

'Those plans involved an armed hold-up. A bystander got hurt. In the end, you testified against Blue.'

Connor nodded. 'You checked me out?'

'I check everybody out. It's my town, I look after it. So, tell me about last night.'

As Connor talked, he began to relax. For the first time in as long as he could remember, the presence of a uniform didn't have him on the defensive or ready for confrontation. Baker was on his side this time and that was a whole new experience.

He'd almost finished recounting the events of the evening when they heard the roar of motorcycle engines outside. Connor tensed and began to stand, but the sergeant shook his head. Connor subsided back into the chair. The room darkened slightly as a figure filled the open doorway. At least one of Connor's punches had hit home. Blue had a swollen and split lip and he was staring at Connor with hatred in his eyes.

The sergeant turned in his chair to look at the man in the doorway. Their eyes locked and tense silence settled for a few seconds, until someone behind Blue spoke to him. The gang leader vanished from the doorway and moments later, they heard the sound of motorcycles leaving town.

Baker closed his notebook and put it in his pocket. 'Well, I guess I'm done. Thanks for the coffee.'

'Thank you.' Connor shook the offered hand and watched Baker leave.

He was carrying the dirty cups to the kitchen when Laura burst through the door.

'I heard what happened last night and I just saw those—'

'It's all right. The sarge was here. They've gone now. With any luck that's the last we'll see of them.'

Connor hoped he was right, but he wasn't sure. Even so, the damage was already done. If Laura had heard about the fight, so would most of the town. So much for building the Gateway's reputation as a safe, friendly, family pub.

Laura stepped closer to examine his face. 'You look awful, boss. Why don't you get out of here before you start scaring people. It's quiet. Hayden will be in soon. We can handle today.'

'After last night, I doubt we'll be overflowing with customers.' The words left a bitter taste in his mouth.

'Don't you believe it. People around here have got to know you. They like what you're trying to do. And this town always supports its own.'

Its own. That sounded good. His spirits lifted a little. It was tempting to take some time.

'Go on. Get out of here.'

Connor decided that Laura was right. And he knew exactly where he should go. 'I'll have my phone. Call if you need me.'

'I won't. Off you go, and say thank you to her from me too.'

★★★

'Kayla, did you hear me? I asked about transport to and from the airport for the fly in, fly out weddings.'

Kayla blinked and frowned. Across the table, Jen was looking at her with a concerned expression. 'Sorry, Jen. I was miles away.'

'I know you were. Are you all right? That must have been pretty scary last night.' Kayla had told Jen briefly about the incident at the pub and her part in it.

'I'm fine.' Kayla waved a dismissive hand. 'It's not me ...'

'You're worried about Connor.'

'Oh, Jen. That guy was beating him and kicking him. He could have been badly hurt.'

'You did the right thing. You called the police. There was nothing more you could have done.'

Jen was right, but Kayla knew she could have called earlier. When she thought of what had happened to Connor in those minutes she'd delayed, she shuddered.

'That was a pretty horrible thing for you to go through too. Do you want to talk about it?'

'I was scared.' The words erupted from the deepest part of her being. 'Really scared.'

'Of course you were. You could have been hurt.'

'No. Not for me. For the baby.' Kayla choked back a tear and stroked her small bump gently. 'I had no right to put the baby in danger by going back there.'

'You did what you thought was right. And it turned out okay in the end. You saved Connor. Who knows where that situation could have ended up.'

'I guess.'

'Why don't you go and talk to him? That might make you feel better.'

'I can't.'

'Why not?'

Kayla gave up any pretence of working. 'I can't risk it. What if those bikies come back some time and I'm with Connor? I didn't plan for this baby. I didn't want a baby. But now, I want nothing more. I can't risk her for anything.' The last words were almost a cry of anguish.

Jen leaped to her feet, came around the table and embraced Kayla, who leaned into her friend and let go of her icy control for a few blessed moments. 'Don't you ever worry, Jen? When Brad comes back, don't you worry that his past will come with him?'

'Of course I do, but we'll deal with it the way we have always dealt with everything else. It's what a partnership is all about.'

Kayla took a deep breath and straightened her back. 'You always were stronger than me.'

'No. You just have a different kind of strength.'

If Jen was right, she would need all that strength now. 'I have to stop seeing him. For the baby's sake. It's not as if there was any chance of something permanent between us.' Saying it out loud like that was almost enough to make her believe it.

'Why not?'

'How could I ask him to be a father to another man's baby?'

'You might not have to ask.' With a tilt of her head, Jen indicated the open window.

Kayla recognised the car pulling up outside. She brushed the tears off her face.

'You look fine,' Jen told her. 'A lot better than he does, I'll bet.' She went to open the door for their visitor.

Kayla gasped when Connor walked into the room. 'Your face …'

'I wish I could say the other guy looks worse.' Connor's mouth twisted into a wry smile.

'Sit down.' Jen waved him at a chair. 'What can I get you? Coffee? Raw steak for that eye?'

'Coffee would be great.' Connor lowered himself gingerly into a chair.

'Are you sure you're all right?' Kayla asked. 'Have you been to the doctor to get checked out?'

'No. But I'm fine. A bit battered and bruised but I'll be as good as gold in a week, maybe two.'

Kayla wasn't convinced.

Jen put a mug of coffee in front of Connor and then left, saying something about the kids that Kayla didn't really hear. Her entire being was focussed on the man sitting across the table from her as she gathered courage to speak.

'I'm sorry,' she said. 'If I'd only called the cops as soon as I got out of the bar, they would have got there earlier and you … you …'

'No.' Connor winced as he reached across the table to take her hand. 'You saved me. And I thought I was supposed to be the knight in shining armour.'

It wasn't much of a joke and she didn't laugh.

'They'd have done the same to Hayden when they finished with me, before trashing my place. And the cops probably wouldn't have found out until next day, by which time they would have been long gone.'

'But they've been arrested, right? They'll go to jail.'

Connor shook his head. 'They've been let off with a warning.'

'What! How could they do that?'

'Because I wanted them to.'

That shocked Kayla to the core. 'Why? Why on earth would you want them let off?'

He squeezed her hand gently. 'Because Blue would have ended up back inside. And as soon as he got out, he'd come for me. I could live with that, but I'm pretty sure he knows you called the cops. So he would come back for you too. I cannot live with that.'

'Won't he come back anyway?' Her voice quivered with uncertainty.

'Maybe. Maybe not. But just in case …'

He withdrew his hand. Kayla felt almost bereft as the warmth of his touch faded.

'Kayla, we can't see each other any more. If Blue comes back and knows that we are—that you mean something to me, he'll come after you. I can't have that happen. You have that baby to protect.'

As he echoed her own words back at her, Kayla realised that wasn't what she wanted.

'But—'

'Look at what he did, Kayla. I've had worse. I can take it. But I will not put you at risk because of me. And besides … The baby. The father. I know you said he's not in the picture, but maybe he should be. Could be. I grew up in a home without a father. I wouldn't want that for any child. I won't be responsible for breaking up a family.'

'We're not a family. And don't you think that's my decision to make—not yours?'

'Of course it is. But if I'm not around, you might make a different decision. It's better this way.' He stood up, leaving the coffee untouched on the table. 'I'm your friend, Kayla. But that's all it can be. Call on me any time you need a wine for a wedding. Come to the pub for a meal with the family. I'm always here.' He paused as if there was something more to say.

Kayla looked at his handsome face. There was so much she wanted to say, but what use was any of it? They had both decided on this course.

'I'm truly sorry.' Connor walked out the door.

As she watched him leave, it occurred to Kayla that Connor would be a far better father to her baby than any other man she'd ever known.

CHAPTER
28

Seven weeks was not long to learn how to organise a high-end wedding, and at the same time, make one happen. Especially not one that was tucked in so close to Christmas. But that was all the time Jen had been given, and looking around her now, she felt a twinge of pride. She'd done all right for this first wedding that had fallen completely on her shoulders. When she'd started working as Kayla's assistant, she had expected them to work together. But since the day of the brawl at the pub and Connor's last visit to Willowbrook, Kayla had lost interest in the business. Apart from answering Jen's questions, she hadn't been involved in any of the organisation for this wedding. Pascale and the girls in the Sydney office had helped, of course, but if this wedding was a success, all the credit would be Jen's. That felt good.

The wedding preparations had also kept her mind away from the trial that never came for Brad in Queensland. It was far better to think of the life she was building for herself and her kids than consider the fact that he was becoming ever more distant on their phone calls. She was building a life that could continue without Brad if it had to.

'Will Santa be at the wedding, Mummy?'

Jen looked down at Dylan and ruffled his hair. 'I'm not sure, sweetie. It depends on whether the bride and groom invited him to come.'

'When I get married, I'm going to invite Santa!'

'Then I'm sure he will come. Now, can you go back upstairs and play for a while? I have work to do.'

'Okay.' Dylan headed up the stairs, allowing Jen to turn her attention back to the ballroom where the cleaners were giving a final polish to the gleaming wood of the dance floor.

'That looks good,' Jen told the team. 'Now we need the tables laid out. Here's the plan.' She held out a piece of paper.

'Yes, Mrs Harrison. We'll get right on it.'

Oh, but that sounded good. Jen restrained herself from running her hands down her neat black dress. It was perfect already. She knew that because it was one of Kayla's: a business outfit she didn't use any more.

Not only had Jen learned a lot about weddings over the past few weeks, she'd discovered something unexpected about herself. She loved being a wedding planner. Those jobs she'd had after school had been just that—jobs. Until now, being a full-time mother was the only thing she'd ever wanted to do. This job, however, had the makings of a career, and that was exciting. While Jen knew she was only helping temporarily until Brad was free again and they could start over, deep inside, she wanted it to continue. Kayla was nearly eight months pregnant. She was getting bigger by the day. Once the baby was born, she would want to go back to work, but Jen was hoping she'd still need an assistant.

Or maybe Kayla wouldn't want her old job back. She too had found a new passion, plunging headlong into wedding dress designing. What had begun as an enjoyable sideline had rapidly turned into something much more. Boxes of fabric were arriving on their doorstep on a regular basis and Kayla had found a local seamstress to turn sketches into sample dresses. The story of Kayla's inventive solution to the red wine dress crisis had spread and customers were almost queuing for consultations.

Jen left the ballroom and made her way to the groom's retreat, which Kayla had been using as a workroom. She opened the door, expecting to find Kayla deep in white lace and tulle as she worked on her latest design. Instead, her friend was sitting on the floor, clutching her stomach and panting.

'Kay?' Jen was at her side in seconds.

'It hurts,' Kayla said, her eyes wide with fear. 'Something's wrong, Jen. There's something wrong with my baby.'

'What happened?'

'Cramps in my stomach. It can't be a contraction. It's too early.'

'How many?'

'Just one. It went on and on.'

Jen knew how slowly time moved during a contraction. 'How long ago?'

'A few minutes. What's happening?'

'It's probably just Braxton Hicks—false contractions. We talked about those. Just your body starting to think about what's ahead.'

'But what if it's not? What if something's wrong?'

'Your last scan was fine, wasn't it?'

'Yes, but—'

'All right. Now let's get you on to the couch.' Jen took Kayla's arms and slowly helped her to her feet then got her seated. 'There, now relax.'

'Relax?' The word was almost a shout.

Jen chuckled. The colour was returning to Kayla's face already. 'At least sit still and don't panic.'

'But shouldn't I get to the hospital?'

'Let's not rush it. I'll get you some juice.'

By the time Jen returned from the kitchen, Kayla was more composed. She had made herself comfortable on the couch and took the glass of juice eagerly.

'Nothing else?'

'No.'

'That's good. Have you had any spotting?'

'A tiny bit, occasionally. But the midwife said it wasn't anything to worry about.'

'That's also good. You should check again when you feel like moving. Just to be sure there hasn't been any today.'

Kayla nodded. She moved on the couch tentatively, her hand pressed to her bulging stomach. 'It didn't really hurt. It just felt … strange. Tight. And I worry about the baby.'

'Why don't you call the clinic? Just to ease your own mind.'

Kayla's conversation with the clinic didn't last long, but she looked happier when she put the phone down.

'They said the same thing. Braxton Hicks. But they had a slot tomorrow so they said to come in. If there's any concern, they can do another scan.'

'That's good. How do you feel now?'

'Better. Thanks, Jen.'

On her feet at last, Kayla stretched, one hand at the small of her back. In her T-shirt and maternity pants with her hair caught back in a ponytail, she looked nothing like the Kayla that Jen had seen that first night in the hallway outside this very room.

Kayla cupped her hands under her growing bulge. 'Are you all right in there? Sorry about the bumpy ride. Maybe you'll grow up to be a rodeo rider.' The look on her face told Jen everything she needed to know. Kayla was very much in love with her baby. Despite that, there were shadows in her eyes at times. Had been ever since Connor had walked out of their kitchen door the day after the fight at the Gateway.

'Sorry, but I'll have to move you out. The wedding crew need to get in here to set up. I'll get someone to help you carry stuff to your office.'

Jen watched Kayla organise the removal of her things. All the fear was gone from her eyes. She looked fine.

'I'm going into town. I have some errands to run. If you're feeling up to it, why don't you come? You might enjoy getting out of the house. We could have a nice lunch.'

Kayla and Connor may have given up, but Jen hadn't.

'Well ...'

Dylan came into the room. 'Are we going to town, Mummy? Can we visit with Connor again?'

Kayla's face closed down in a heartbeat. 'I better stay here and rest. Just in case this is more serious than we thought. You guys go and have a nice time.'

'Are you sure? It's only a lunch. Or we could go somewhere else?'

'No. Look at me. I'm a mess and it's too hot to bother getting cleaned up. You both go. And say ... say hi to Connor for me.' Kayla quickly gathered her last few bits and pieces and left the room with a strained smile.

***

Connor was writing today's lunch specials on a blackboard when Jen walked in. His eyes slid past her, looking for someone else coming in the door. There was only Dylan. He hid his disappointment and, when Dylan called his name and ran to the bar, Connor swept the boy up in his arms. He spun him in a circle before putting him down for a fist bump.

'Hi, Dylan. Hi, Jen.'

'Hi, Connor. We were hoping for some lunch.'

'Well, you've come to the right place. Dylan, do you remember which is your special table?'

'That one.' The boy pointed.

'That's right. Lead the way.'

'You're busy,' Jen said as she nodded a greeting to a couple of regulars.

'Yes. Business is good despite … you know.'

After the beating, Connor had taken a few weeks to heal fully, at least physically. He still looked over his shoulder whenever he heard the roar of a motorcycle engine. Back when he'd ridden with Blue, he'd known barmen to keep a cricket bat under the bar. He would not do that, but he would protect what he was building. And he would protect the people he cared about.

'Kayla's tummy is big now,' Dylan announced as he sat down. 'She's going to have a baby. It will be my cousin. I've never had a cousin before.'

'Cousins are good things to have.' Connor kept his voice light, but he could feel the tearing inside that had not healed in the weeks since that night.

'Aunt Kayla is getting a very big tummy. But she's very happy about your cousin.' Jen sat down opposite her son, but Connor felt the words were directed at him.

'I hope it's a boy cousin.'

'We don't know yet, do we? We have to be patient.' Jen looked straight at Connor. 'Patience is a good thing, but sometimes we have to work, rather than wait, for the things we want.'

It wasn't a very subtle message, and Connor almost winced.

'What can I get you? I can do a special Dylan-sized version of most things.'

'That!' Dylan pointed to an advertising poster that showed an icy cold glass of Bundy and Coke.

Connor winked at the boy. 'I can do a special Dylan version of that. What do you think?'

'Yes.'

'Yes, what?' Jen said automatically.

'Yes, please, Connor.'

'Coming up. Jen?'

'The same please.'

'You can't have the same,' Dylan piped up. 'It's my special drink.'

Connor crouched down in front of Dylan. 'Do you love your mum?' He waited until the boy nodded. 'When you love someone, you try to give them what they want most. Understand?'

Although the message wasn't actually for him, Dylan nodded. 'You can have one of my special drinks, Mummy.'

'Thank you, darling.'

Connor took an order for sandwiches and fetched the drinks. He was kept busy serving right up until the moment it looked like Jen was ready to leave. He stopped by her table again.

'It was good to see you, Dylan.' He ruffled the boy's hair.

'You know you don't need an excuse to drop by,' Jen said.

'I know.' He watched as Dylan trotted over to say goodbye to Laura, who was by now firmly wrapped around his little finger. 'But it's better this way.'

'I hear you say that, I hear Kayla say that, but I don't believe either of you.'

Keeping a close eye on Dylan's whereabouts, Connor asked after Brad.

'We'd hoped he might be home for Christmas, but I doubt it. He says the trial date is soon, but he hasn't given me anything concrete. Neither has the lawyer.'

'These things can take an annoying amount of time, but that doesn't mean the end result is going to be bad. Hang in there.'

'I do.' Jen gave a wry smile. 'What else is there? Come on, Dylan, we've got things to do. We promised Auntie Kayla we'd buy some Christmas decorations for the house. Do you want to help me choose?'

'Santa's coming,' Dylan announced to the world in general as he returned to his mother's side.

Connor thought a lot about that conversation over the next few days, but each time he shook away the glimmer of hope. He didn't have many memories of Christmas. A few from when he was a child and his mother found the money for a small gift or two and a cake. That was before the boy she was trying so hard to raise turned away and found a new 'family' of street thugs and girls only too willing to share his bed. He had driven his mother to a drug addict's early grave.

When he'd finally come to his senses and left all that behind, he'd learned a few things, including that Christmas was a time for real families.

He didn't deserve to have a family.

CHAPTER
29

As she carefully edged her swollen body into the driver's seat, Kayla knew she couldn't delay much longer—she had to sell her beloved red sports car. It was a tight squeeze now, and after the baby was born she'd need something far more sensible, a car that would take a baby seat. She needed something with room for a pram. And a nappy bag and toys and all those things a baby needed. And then the baby would grow into a kid. And then there'd be school trips and school friends and sports days and … and … and …

'Stop that.' She had learned that saying the words out loud was enough to halt the panic attack in its tracks. 'You're fine. If you can organise a wedding for a thousand guests you can sort out a new car.' Getting a new car was the least of the things she was going to have to sort out. 'One day at a time,' she muttered as she struggled with the seat belt.

Jen slid easily into the car, which did nothing for Kayla's mood. 'That's it. The kids are with Lizzie. Let's go.' As she buckled up, she added, 'Are you sure you don't want to take my car? It's not as nice, but there's a lot more space.'

Kayla almost growled at her. Instead, she started the car and drove out onto the main road, turning towards Scone.

'You know, you probably should start thinking about a new car,' Jen said.

'I know that.'

'All right. I was just saying, you've only got a few weeks to go now.'

'I know that too.'

'You're in a bad mood. I get it. I'll sit here quietly until we get to the clinic.'

Silence reigned until Kayla pulled into the clinic carpark. She turned off the engine and ran her hand over her face. 'I'm sorry, Jen. I don't know what's gotten into me.'

'It's fine. You're pregnant. And then there's the situation with Connor.'

'There is no situation with Connor.'

'You can keep saying that, but not even you believe it.'

Kayla started to struggle out of the car then collapsed back into her seat. 'Okay. I wish things were different. But wishing isn't going to make it happen. I wished I wasn't pregnant and look where that got me.'

Jen placed a gentle hand on her arm. 'Do you still wish you weren't pregnant?'

Kayla was slightly horrified at the thought. 'No. Oh, no. I am actually looking forward to it now.' She grinned as she took another firm grip on the door. 'I'm especially looking forward to this bit being over. And also buying a bigger car.' She heaved herself out of the vehicle.

Inside the clinic, they were quickly shown into an examination room. It almost took longer for Kayla to lift herself onto the table.

'Are you sure I'm not having twins?' she asked Doctor Woods. 'Or maybe a baby elephant.'

The doctor chuckled. 'You weren't last time we checked. Shall we have another look?'

The ultrasound gel was cold on the stretched skin of Kayla's stomach, but she'd barely registered that when the image appeared on the screen. It was grey and fuzzy but it was clearly …

'That's my baby.'

'It is.'

She'd seen the shape at her last scan, but this time, this time it really did look like a baby. That slightly fuzzy grey shape was going to be a person. With fingers and toes and hopes and dreams and everything. She could even see those fingers now. It was wondrous.

'Do you want to know if it's a boy or a girl?'

'I … I …' She struggled to gather her thoughts. Did she? She didn't know. 'Jen, did you know in advance?'

'No. We wanted it to be a surprise.'

Kayla laid a hand on her bump, ignoring the sticky jelly. *Hello there. Are you a boy or a girl? Do I want to know?* She felt a twinge as the baby moved slightly.

'I don't want to know,' she decided.

'Of course, that's fine. Some people like to know so they know what colours to paint the nursery or what colour baby clothes to buy.'

'This baby is not going to be dressed in pink or blue. And not just pastels. I want them to have a rainbow of colours in their world.'

Beside her, Jen grinned. 'That sounds like you.'

'Well, everything looks fine. The baby is a little small, but not enough to be worried about,' the doctor said.

'Should I be doing anything different?' Kayla asked. 'Eating more to help the baby grow. Or—'

'No. No. Don't worry. A smaller baby just means an easier birth. You will likely feel some more of those Braxton Hicks contractions. They won't hurt … well, not much. They're entirely normal, so don't worry or panic. If you see any significant spotting, come back immediately, but I don't have any reason to think there's anything amiss.'

Kayla turned to her best friend. 'I'm not so scared any more.'

'Good.' Jen smiled. 'When we're done, let's go buy some things for the baby. You really haven't got much yet. I would like to get my soon-to-be niece or nephew a present.'

***

'Boss, if you don't do it, I will.' Laura stood in front of Connor's desk, hands on her hips.

He looked up from his laptop screen. 'I'll do it. I haven't had time yet.'

'You do know which day is Christmas Day?'

'What? Of course I do. December twenty-fifth.'

'Well, look back down at the screen. See the clock in the corner? What date does it say this is?'

To appease her, Connor looked down. 'Oh.'

'Oh, indeed. Every other place in town has been dripping with tinsel and shiny glass balls for weeks. If you don't get some decorations up, we're going to be losing customers. And we're not so busy that we can afford to do that.'

She was right. Since the visit from Blue and his gang, custom had dropped. Not a lot, certainly not as much as Connor had expected.

But the Gateway didn't have leeway to lose any more. It was the one argument that was guaranteed to convince him.

He shut the lid of his laptop. 'All right. I'll do it now. Look after the place while I'm gone.'

'I always do.' Laura pulled a folded sheet of paper out of the pocket of her jeans and offered it to him.

'What's this?'

'A shopping list.'

He unfolded it. *Christmas Tree. Tinsel. Door wreath. Lights.* Those he expected. But the last two lines …

'Christmas cake for staff party? We're not having a staff party.'

'Yes, we are.'

'Which I guess explains the last item.' *Gifts for staff.*

Laura nodded, then her serious face broke into a grin. 'You don't have to, you know, but we've got a lot to celebrate. *You've* got a lot to celebrate. You've turned this place around. You should be proud.'

'Thank you. But don't go expecting some expensive present just because you're the best barmaid in town.'

'Of course not.' She grinned widely and left him.

Getting Christmas decorations wasn't quite as easy as he had expected. Stocks in the local shops were low. He was told, more than once, that he would have had a better selection if he'd done this a few weeks ago. His unspoken reply was that, a few weeks ago, the decorations wouldn't have been on special and seventy dollars seemed a lot to pay for a fake tree, even if it did come with its own fairy lights. But soon the tree was safely in place in the back of his ute and a couple of boxes of coloured tinsel, glass balls and other shiny things cluttered his spare seat. He went in search of a large gold star, without which, Laura had told him, he was not to return.

He finally spotted one in the window of the Red Cross Shop. And that wasn't the only thing he found there. When he went inside, he saw a slightly battered secondhand acoustic guitar hanging on a wall. Maybe Hayden would appreciate that. Connor could remember the kid saying he used to play. And he was always singing or listening to music. It wasn't cheap, but it certainly wasn't too much for someone who had stood up with him against Blue and his gang.

He'd have to think some more about what to give Emily and Laura. The last gift he'd bought for a woman was something cheap and flashy for Molly a long time ago. Before his last stint inside. He'd have to do better now.

As he paid for the guitar and star, he wondered how long it had been since he'd last bought anyone a Christmas present. Or any present at all. Could a person get out of the habit of giving gifts? He seemed to have. This year he would be giving three gifts, which was three more than he would have thought twelve months ago.

Outside the shop the sound of a woman's laughter floated towards him, driving all thought of his errands out of his head. His traitorous heart skipped.

Ahead of him, at a crowded coffee shop Kayla and Jen were sitting at one of the outdoor tables. Kayla was laughing and the low table between them was littered with shopping bags. Jen was holding some item of clothing up for Kayla's inspection. It was small and purple with what could have been a dinosaur on the front of it. The penny dropped. Clothing for a baby. Kayla's belly was so much bigger than when he'd last seen her. Not only that, she looked so much happier. He'd never believed all that stuff about pregnant women glowing, but she did. Or was it just that, to him, she glowed all the time?

Should he go over? Say hello? He and Jen had become friends of a sort. He could ask if she had news of Brad. It wasn't as if he was stalking Kayla. They were friends too, or if not friends, they were …

Before he could move, two motorcycles roared down the street. The riders' faces were hidden beneath their helmets, but still, Connor froze.

After a few moments, he convinced himself that the bikes weren't the same ones. Despite that, as the engines faded down the street, Connor turned away from the coffee shop. No. It wasn't safe for Kayla to be around him. Not now. Maybe not for a long, long time, if ever. He would not see her in danger. He would not get in the way of any chance, however small, that her baby might get to know its real father.

He made his way back to the ute, carefully adding the guitar to his Christmas haul. As he started the engine, he wondered how it would feel to go shopping for baby clothes with the woman he loved by his side.

CHAPTER
30

Had he seen her in that coffee shop? And if he had, had he simply walked away? Kayla tugged the piece of pretty pink paper and tore it. Damn! She pulled the wrapping paper off the doll, crumpled it into a ball and threw it into the corner of her office.

'Stop it,' she admonished herself. 'He's all you've been thinking about for the past three days. It's over. It's Christmas Eve tomorrow. You have more important things to think about now.'

She moved uncomfortably on her chair. She looked like a whale. No wonder Connor hadn't even stopped to say hello. What man would want to talk to a woman with swollen ankles and a belly that entered a room two minutes before she did? As for the clothes she was wearing, a cheap jersey dress stretched taut across her belly hardly added to her sex appeal. She looked at the doll. She had spent ages online finding this doll. It was the same kind of Kewpie doll she had so coveted as a child. The same kind of doll she had stolen that day she and Jen and Lizzie and Mitch had sneaked out of school to visit the showground. Stolen at great risk and then thrown away, because its perfection had been spoiled by guilt. Jen had been right to remind her about it. While searching for a gift for Suzi, Kayla had stumbled on this doll. It was a perfect gift for her niece. It was a perfect way for Kayla to acknowledge, accept or even change her memory of that long-ago stolen doll.

Kayla smoothed the pale yellow dress sparkling with sequins. Suzi didn't know the story behind the choice, but she'd love it anyway. At least, Kayla hoped she would. She reached for more of the pink tissue wrapping. She'd removed the doll from its stick. It was impossible to wrap a Bo Peep stick. She'd reattach that after the big present opening. She wrapped the doll carefully and added it to the pile next to her desk. That was it. All done.

She picked up the remains of the wrapping paper to put away, then dropped it back on her desk. Put it away? Where? Her once tidy office was a mess. Apart from the pile of wrapped presents, there were bits of paper and ribbon scattered across the carpet. The second desk she had installed some months ago was covered with piles of white fabric. A couple of cardboard boxes filled with similar fabrics sat in a corner, the closed lid supporting a pile of sketchbooks full of dress designs. The bookcase was hidden behind a corkboard, also covered with designs, pins holding bits of fabric to each one. She was ignoring the boxes of baby clothes and toys and nappies. When she'd started Willowbrook Weddings, this bedroom turned office had been neat, organised and businesslike; a pleasure to work in. But now … This was not what she had planned.

She picked up an armload of presents and left the room. There were no more weddings booked until well into the New Year, so the ballroom had been designated the family Christmas space. Kayla stepped through the doors into a room that was every child's Christmas dream. Mitch had brought them a huge, real pine tree, which sat in the middle of the room, glistening with fairy lights

and shiny baubles, tinsel and fake snow. It was very pretty. There
was already a number of gaily wrapped presents beneath it. Kayla
began adding hers. She made another two trips to the office before
they were all in place. It occurred to her that was more presents
than she'd bought in the last four or five—or six—years combined.
While she and Lizzie had been estranged, she'd bought one present
each Christmas for Pascale. Now her pile included gifts not only
for Lizzie and Mitch, but for Jen and her kids. And while Christmas shopping she had made one important discovery about buying
presents for kids. It's impossible to stop at one.

'You'll find that out next year, I guess.' She stroked her bump.

Jen appeared in the doorway behind her. 'Is there room for a few
more?'

'I think we can squeeze one or two in.' Kayla helped her set her
pile of gifts under the tree. As she did, she noticed one label that
said *Brad*.

'Jen, do you think that's a good idea?' she asked. 'Christmas is
only two days away now. Is there any hope at all that he'll be here?'

'No. He said last week that the court case is close, but he's being
saying that for ages. I wanted to believe he'd be here, but I have to
be realistic. I thought this would at least give him a presence.'

'Will it upset the kids?'

'No. I think forgetting to include him would upset them more.
Make them think he was never coming back. And he is coming
back. Just as soon as this nightmare is over.'

Kayla heard the determination in Jen's voice. She nodded and
made room for Jen's gifts under the tree.

A clatter of footsteps in the hallway heralded the arrival of Lizzie
with Suzi and Dylan in tow. Suzi was carrying her riding helmet.

'Mum, I jumped today. It was a really big jump. Jango was
wonderful.'

'That's great, sweetheart.' Jen looked at Lizzie, who shook her head slightly to assure her that it hadn't been big at all.

'Pressies!' Dylan changed the subject abruptly and scampered towards the tree.

'Not yet, boyo.' Mitch appeared in the doorway, laden with brightly wrapped boxes. 'We open presents on Christmas Day.'

Dylan looked crestfallen.

'I'll tell you what, though, you can help me stack these under the tree.'

By the time they were done, it was a pretty big stack. A lot of presents for six people. And what about next year, Kayla wondered. There would be a new member of this family then. If they were all together for Christmas, that pile would be even larger as her baby got her—or his—first presents. *Her*, Kayla thought. She had decided the baby was a girl. Boy or girl, Kayla already loved her child. But she hoped it was a girl. Another Lawson girl for Willowbrook.

★★★

With cheerful calls of merry Christmas, the last patrons filed out of the Gateway at ten o'clock on the dot on Christmas Eve. Connor closed the doors. Behind the bar, Laura and Emily were loading the dishwasher and wiping down the bar. From the kitchen came the sounds of Hayden engaged in a similar task.

'Enough cleaning for now. Hayden, get out here.'

'Just a minute, boss,' Laura said. 'I'm almost done.'

'You are done.' Connor walked to the counter and took the cleaning cloth out of her hands. 'I'll take it from here.'

'But—'

'No buts.' All three of them had been on duty tonight and he'd needed them. But now it was time to rest. Laura had kids to get home to and he was pretty sure Hayden and Emily had plans too.

But not him. He'd spend Christmas Day cleaning and doing minor repairs to the Gateway.

'Before you go, I want to say thank you. You've all worked hard and without you, I'd never have got this place off the ground.'

'Thank you for the job,' Hayden said. 'It's hard when … well, you know.'

Connor knew only too well. No-one likes to trust an ex-con. Not with a job and not with their— He pushed that thought away.

'To show my thanks—' Connor opened the door leading to his office, '—I have this for you, Hayden.' He lifted out the acoustic guitar.

'Wow.' The young man took it carefully and gently ran his hands over the wood.

'It's only secondhand, but I thought …'

'It's great, boss.' Hayden lifted the strap over his neck and settled the instrument against his body. He strummed then winced. 'All it needs is a good tuning. I haven't played since I went to juvie, but I'll get it back. You see if I don't.'

'I thought of getting you some earplugs, Emily.'

The girl laughed. 'I won't need them. Hayden will be great when he's had some practice.' She looked at her boyfriend with shining eyes. Connor wished he had someone to look at him like that. Not just someone— He again pushed the thought away. Christmas was making him mushy.

'Then I hope this was the right thing.' He handed Emily her gift.

'Gee. Thanks, boss.' The girl unwrapped it and Connor held his breath.

Emily held up two large paperback books. 'Oh, my favourite authors. How did you know?'

'I saw you coming out of the bookshop the other week. I asked the woman there and she knew you. If you've already got them, you can take them back and change them.'

'No. But they're on my list.'

'And there's a book token inside as well, so you can pick a couple more you really do want.'

'Gee, thanks, boss.' Emily gave him a quick peck on the cheek. 'I'll have lots of time to read these while Hayden is practising.'

At last Connor turned to Laura. 'I honestly don't know how to thank you.'

'I know, I am a treasure beyond price,' Laura joked. 'Seriously, it's me who should be thanking you. You've made it so easy to fit my shifts around the kids. I appreciate that.'

'I know how important they are to you. And I know that you do everything for them That's why I got you this.' He held out an envelope.

Laura took it and opened it. The card inside was red and covered with sparkling glitter. But there was another smaller card inside. She lifted it out and read it. 'A spa day? For me?' She blinked a couple of times and Connor's heart sank.

'I hope that's all right. I mean ... you never think of yourself, always of the kids or me. I wanted to treat you to something just for you.' A sudden thought hit him. 'I hope that's not inappropriate for a boss to give.'

'Stop. No. It's wonderful. Thank you.' Laura's eyes were a tad misty as she kissed his cheek. 'It's a wonderful idea and I am going to enjoy it so much.'

Connor's shoulders relaxed a little in relief. 'And if you need someone to babysit the kids when you do it, you know where to find me.'

'So I guess that's it. Merry Christmas.' Connor raised his beer in salute.

'Not quite.' Hayden ducked back into the kitchen and returned a few moments later with a large box. 'I've been worried all day that you might find it, but I guess you didn't have a reason to go digging about in the kitchen cupboards.'

'I know better than to dig around in your kitchen,' Connor said to hide the shock as he took the present. 'I didn't expect … I mean, you've all got better things to do with your money.' He put the box on a table and opened it, then stood staring at the contents for several seconds.

'Don't you like it, boss?' Laura's voice was hesitant. 'We thought that since you've left the city for the bush, you needed one of those.'

'I love it.' Connor removed a dark tan Akubra from the box. He turned it over carefully in his hand before placing it on his head. 'What do you think?'

'Oh, that's so you!' Emily squealed.

Hayden nodded.

'Looks all right, I guess,' Laura teased.

'Thank you.' The words almost caught in his throat.

'Thank you, boss.' Laura hugged him.

The party broke up soon after and Connor finished cleaning the bar, the Akubra still on his head.

He might not have a family to spend the holiday with but he had a home. He had the Gateway and he had a good life. This had been the best Christmas for years.

CHAPTER
31

Connor allowed himself the luxury of sleeping late on Christmas morning. There was no reason to get up. No kids jumping up and down, eager to open presents, and he had long since stopped going to church. He lingered over coffee and toast before heading to the bar. A couple of the tables could use a sand and new varnish. He could get that done today and have them dry and ready to use when he reopened on Boxing Day. He'd work on the footpath to avoid dust in the bar. The streets would be empty today.

He collected his sander and the varnish then flicked on the radio. The awning over the front door of the pub gave him plenty of shade from the sun as he worked steadily for a couple of hours. The music coming through the open door was mostly Christmas carols, but that was all right. His Christmas might be different from most other people's, but today he was in the open air, working with his hands on a project of his own devising. He might once have hoped for more, but when he looked back at his life, this was better than he had ever known. And Kayla was safe and happy with her family. He had done the right thing by her. He was content with that.

He was singing softly to himself, thinking about breaking for a late lunch, when he saw someone walking towards the pub from the direction of the train station. He glanced at his watch. It was about the right time for the daily train from Sydney, if it was running today. But who took a train on Christmas Day? The man was alone and carried a rucksack, but nothing more. He was looking about as if he didn't know where he was or where he should be going.

Connor raised a hand in greeting. 'G'day. Merry Christmas,' he said.

'Hello.'

The man was about Connor's age, unshaven with short hair and clothes that looked like they had been slept in. Perhaps on an overnight train. There was something familiar about the way he kept turning his head as if he was looking for someone—or watching out for someone.

Connor held out a hand. 'Name's Connor Knight.'

The man went to take it but hesitated when he saw the tattoos. It was then that Connor realised what was familiar about him. That way of carrying his head and looking around was the sign of a man who had been inside and recently been released. Connor knew it because he too had once looked that way.

Connor kept his hand extended and finally the man shook it.

'Brad Harrison.'

Of course it was. Connor began to smile. 'You're Jen's husband.' It wasn't a question.

'Yes. Do you know her?'

'Yes. I know her, and the kids. Are they coming to pick you up?'

'No. Can you tell me how to get there? To Willowbrook?'

'You've never been there?'

'No.' He sounded defensive and turned, as if looking for someone else to ask.

'Brad. I'm a friend. Jen and I have talked about where you've been.'

The shock registered on Brad's face almost immediately.

'It's all right. As you've seen, I've been where you were. A lot of people helped me when I got out. I'm happy to do the same. Do you need a lift? I could run you out there.'

'I'll walk, if you can tell me which way to go.' He didn't sound too confident.

'If I gave you a lift, you'd be there for Christmas dinner with your family.'

The look on Brad's face was all the answer Connor needed.

'Give me a couple of minutes to put this stuff inside and lock up. While I do that, if you want some water or coffee, I can offer you that.'

They didn't stay long enough for coffee. Connor took two bottles of water out of the fridge and picked up his car keys. When the pub was securely locked, he led the way to his ute.

'It's about twenty minutes to Willowbrook,' Connor said. 'I guess they're not expecting you.'

'No. I didn't want to get their hopes up. I wasn't sure I would make it.'

'I know they've been missing you. This is going to be the best Christmas present they could have.'

Brad looked down at the hands he clasped in his lap. 'I hope so. I only got out yesterday morning. Been travelling ever since. I didn't even call them as I'd promised I would. And I don't have any proper presents for them.'

Connor heard the unspoken words. He wasn't sure of his welcome. That's how it was when you first got out. Brad would find his way and Connor would help him if he could. He turned off the main road.

'Just a few minutes now.'

Nothing more was said until they turned through the gates onto the Willowbrook drive. At the first glimpse of the house, Brad whistled.

'I know,' Connor said. 'It's impressive. The first time I came here, I felt a bit intimidated. I was a kid from the wrong side of the tracks, in and out of juvie and then jail. I didn't think this was a place for me. But I didn't count on Jen and Kayla and the rest of the family. They're good people. The best. But I guess I don't have to tell you that. They're your family, which means you belong here far more than I do.'

'I'm not sure. I let everyone down. I don't deserve—'

Connor parked the ute and killed the engine. 'Don't sell them short. Or yourself, for that matter. You can and will get past this. I did.'

Brad got out of the car, walked halfway to the house and then stopped. He looked back at Connor but before he could say anything, there was a loud squeal from the direction of the house.

'Daddy!'

A small figure with tinsel wound through her hair hurled herself off the veranda and into her father's arms. Brad made a strangled sound and dropped to his knees, his daughter clutched tight to him.

★★★

Jen froze in the act of carrying a stack of plates from the kitchen to the big table being set for a feast in the ballroom. It couldn't be—could it? She felt rather than saw Dylan fly past her towards the front door, calling for his daddy. She turned slowly, almost afraid to look. Through the open door she could see Connor's ute, with Connor himself standing beside it. And there, in front of the car, her two kids were wrapped in the arms of … their father. Jen started to shake.

'Give me those.' Mitch suddenly arrived at her side and relieved her of her burden.

She didn't even look at him. Her heart was pounding so loudly she was sure it was going to burst out of her chest. That she would die before she walked down those stone stairs to the lawn.

'Brad?'

Her voice was barely a whisper, but he heard her. He stood up, gently disentangling himself from the kids. The tears running down his face matched hers.

'Jen. Oh, God, Jen.'

His arms caught her as she felt her legs give way and he pulled her tight against his chest. She buried her face in his shirt, breathing deep that smell that was so familiar, so beloved and his alone.

After a lifetime, his grip on her loosened and she looked up into his face. It was gaunt and unshaven, but it was Brad's face.

'Jen.' He whispered her name one more time and then he was kissing her. His lips were on her forehead, her cheeks, her eyes and at last her lips. He kissed her as if his life depended on it and she kissed him back because she knew hers did.

Something intruded between them and for a moment she wanted nothing more than to push it away. But it was Dylan, wrapping his arms around Brad's waist. And Suzi too. Brad's arms left Jen long enough to pull their children into the embrace.

After what seemed a long time—but still not enough—the family broke apart.

Jen wiped away her tears. 'What? How?' she asked, almost dreading the answer. If it wasn't all over—if he had to go back again—she
wasn't sure she could stand it. 'Why didn't you call?'

'It happened so fast. I wasn't sure I'd get here today and I didn't
want to disappoint you all.' Brad laid his fingers gently against her
cheek and she tilted her head into his hand. 'I'll tell you everything
later, when it's just you and me. But all that matters is that it's over.
I am here and I'm never going to do anything ever again that might
tear us apart like that.'

He was right. That was all she needed for now. She took his
hand, her fingers entwining with his in the way that was so familiar and so right. 'Well, you got here in time. We're about to serve
Christmas dinner. Kids, go ask Auntie Lizzie to set an extra place—
no, wait. Two extra places.' She turned to Connor. 'Please come in
and celebrate with us.'

Connor shook his head. 'That's very kind, Jen, but no. Thank
you. This is a family occasion. I don't want to intrude.'

'You're not intruding. Is there somewhere else you have to be?'

'No, but …' Connor was actually backing away.

'I won't take no for an answer. So that's it. You're coming to
Christmas lunch.'

CHAPTER

32

This room held so many good memories for Kayla and now it was creating another.

Eight people sat around the food-laden table. The four musketeers of her childhood were together again. Mitch was sitting at the head of the table with Lizzie by his side. Jen's family was reunited too. Brad's arrival had put an added glow on the day. Brad and Jen sat very close together, touching hands or looking at each other every few seconds, as if seeking reassurance that this wasn't some dream. The kids were bouncing out of their skins to tell their father everything that had happened since they'd last sat at a dinner table with him. For Kayla's part, it was the first real Christmas she'd had since she and Lizzie had lost their parents when she was only eleven. For a long time they had been estranged, but that wound had healed. Kayla stroked her bump. Maybe somewhere Sam and Kath Lawson were watching and knew there was another generation coming to Willowbrook.

Jen waved her hand for attention. 'We all unwrapped our presents this morning, but before we start eating, there's one more present. Suzi, will you go and get it please?'

Suzi wriggled out of her chair and darted away, returning a few seconds later carrying a small, brightly wrapped parcel. In her other hand, she held an envelope.

'These are for you, Daddy. We put them under the tree in case you came home. And you did.'

Brad's look of surprise soon gave way to a smile that was as gentle as it was touching. 'Which shall I open first?' he asked his children.

'The present,' they cried in unison.

'All right. The present it is.'

Kayla watched him carefully open the gift, holding it as if it was the most precious thing in the world. And perhaps to him it was. When the last layer of tissue was peeled away, he looked at the wooden frame in his hands and closed his eyes as if to hold back tears.

'Don't you like it, Daddy?' Suzi asked hesitantly.

'I love it, my darling daughter. It's the best gift in the world. Look, everyone.' He held up the framed photograph so they could see it. In the image, Suzi and Dylan were sitting on Jango, smiling happily.

'Mummy took the photo,' Suzi said.

'It's lovely,' Lizzie said.

'The card, Daddy. The card!' Dylan yelled loud enough to make his father wince. Brad opened the envelope. The card was covered in childish drawings of four people in front of a house, a big yellow sun shining above them.

'We made it ourselves. Me and Suzi,' Dylan proudly proclaimed.

'It's the best Christmas card ever. Thank you.'

Kayla caught the sheen of tears in Brad's eyes as she, too, blinked fiercely. Beside her, Connor took a deep breath and cleared his throat.

Mitch got to his feet. 'Right. Now I don't know about all of you, but I'm starving. And look at all this wonderful food Kayla and Jen have made us. We are all very thankful to you both for doing that, because Lizzie is a terrible cook and can barely manage eggs on toast.'

Lizzie punched her husband playfully in the arm as laughter broke out around the table. Mitch picked up a carving knife and fork and began piling expertly sliced turkey onto plates, which Lizzie handed out. 'Connor, would you do the honours with drink, please?' she asked.

'Be happy to.' Connor opened a bottle of white wine with practised ease. He poured glasses for Lizzie and Mitch and Jen, then held the bottle in the air, asking without words if Brad wanted a glass.

'Just a mouthful,' Brad replied. 'It's been a while.'

Connor nodded. Then he reached for the sparkling water for himself and Kayla.

'You're not having a glass of wine?' Kayla asked.

'I thought I'd keep you company,' he said with a look that almost made her shiver.

Conversation was limited by the passing of food and the pouring of thick brown gravy. At last all the plates were full and Mitch held his glass of wine high.

'Here's to us. It's wonderful to have so many around this table. Welcome home, Brad. And welcome too, Connor. To Christmas with family and friends.'

'Family and friends,' the adults said as they raised their glasses. Suzi and Dylan joined the toast with their glasses of juice.

That was the sign for everyone to start eating and for a while there were no sounds but the clatter of cutlery on china and the occasional request to pass the gravy.

If her parents were watching this gathering, Kayla wondered what they would think of the man sitting by her side. She'd been startled by Jen's invitation to Connor and vaguely annoyed when Jen had carefully manoeuvred the seating so he was next to Kayla. Her first thoughts were that he didn't belong at this family gathering, that he was doing that one thing he said he didn't want to do—intruding. But as the time passed, it felt less that way and more like he belonged at their table. More like she wanted him there. She no longer saw the tattoos on his hands as he passed the gravy or ruffled Dylan's hair. All she saw were the scars from the hard work he was doing to start a new life. She remembered the way those hands had stroked her body with passion. She loved his kindness and humour, loved the way his eyes glowed every time he looked at her and the way that made her feel. In his eyes, she wasn't a huge, unattractive pregnant woman; she was more than just a single mother facing a daunting task of raising a child alone. When Connor looked at her, he saw *her*—Kayla—with all her hopes and fears and joys and sorrows. That was what she loved most of all.

He seemed to like the food she'd prepared. He was helping himself to more potato when he saw her watching him and winked broadly. 'This is the best meal I have had in years,' he said softly.

'I can't take all the credit,' she replied in a similar tone. 'Jen is great in the kitchen. I simply followed orders.'

'It wasn't the food I was talking about.'

Kayla gently touched his hand. 'I know what you mean.'

About mid-afternoon, they pushed back from the table, unable to take another bite. Kayla noticed Brad and Jen talking quietly in a corner, but every few minutes, one or other of the kids jumped in to interrupt.

'I've got an idea,' she announced. 'I'll bet we need to walk off some of that dinner. Lizzie, why don't we all go down to the stables to wish Jango merry Christmas? We could introduce him to Connor.'

The kids greeted the plan with enthusiasm. 'You come too, Daddy,' Dylan demanded.

Mitch picked the boy up and sat him on his shoulders. 'I think your dad is tired. He travelled a long way to get here to see you on Christmas Day. And he and your mum need some grown-up time together. So maybe we'll take Connor today and your dad can come down tomorrow.'

'Okay.'

Kayla caught the look of gratitude in Jen's eyes as she herded the rest of the family away.

★★★

Connor had never been to the Willowbrook stables before. For someone born and raised in the city, they should have been interesting. But his attention was solely on the woman walking beside him. The path to the stud buildings was wide and smooth, but he found himself watching the ground and Kayla, in case she stumbled. Not that she was clumsy or awkward. She was just … big. He'd never been around a heavily pregnant woman before and it was slightly terrifying. That part of his hind brain that was all caveman had kicked into gear and he suspected he would have growled at anyone who came too close to her. Or maybe it was those pheromones of hers again.

The kids dragged him into a stable to introduce him to a small, chubby and well-groomed beast named Jango, who was apparently the very bestest pony in the whole world. Connor made appropriate admiring noises and when feeding the horses was suggested as the day's next task, he slipped quietly outside. Kayla had wandered a short distance away and was leaning on a wooden fence. As he came closer, Connor realised she was watching the mares and foals. He joined her, leaning on the fence beside her. They stood in silence, watching the youngsters running around, kicking up their heels with joy, while their ever-patient mothers grazed in apparent unconcern.

'They're about three or four months old,' Kayla said. 'Even when we were kids, this was my favourite thing to do, watching the foals. Lizzie was all about the riding and training and competition, but for me, it was the nursery paddocks.'

'They are entertaining.'

'Did you know that when they are born, they stand up within a few minutes? They fall over a lot but they can walk within a day.'

He did know that, but it seemed to him she wasn't looking for an answer.

'We wean them when they're around six months old. After that, they can look after themselves. Imagine that.' She stroked her baby bump.

'It's going to take your baby a bit longer than that.'

'It is.' She turned to face him for the first time and he saw the fear in her eyes. 'I don't know if I can do this, Connor. It's not months, it's years. Seeing Jen with her kids, I can see how hard it is, and she had Brad to help when they were small. She has him again now. I have no-one. I have to do it all on my own and I'm terrified I'll do something wrong. Hurt my baby in some way.'

Connor held out his hand. She hesitated, then placed hers in it. He curled his fingers gently around hers. 'Did you ever reconsider the father?'

'No. I told you. He's not part of this. He—' Her voice faltered.

'He what?'

'When he found out, he wanted me to get an abortion. Told me he'd pay for half of it. That's when I knew I didn't want him anywhere near my baby.'

Connor fought down the rage that flared inside him. 'Had the two of you been together long?'

'No. It was a stupid one-night stand that I regretted the moment it was over.' She lowered her eyes, almost as if she was expecting some sort of condemnation.

'Kayla, you're human. We've all done things we regret. No-one knows that more than me.'

She looked at him and he saw that those few words had touched the part of Kayla that was, if not ashamed, at least not proud of what she'd done. He could only hope he'd brushed away some of the hurt.

'I know. I may regret that night, but I will never regret my decision to have my baby. I love her so much.'

'Her? You know already?' Connor's mind filled with images of a tiny girl who looked just like Kayla. Who shone with the same brightness. This was the first time he and Kayla had talked since he'd found out she was pregnant. It was also the happiest he'd been since that day.

'I didn't want the doctor to tell me, but I can feel her in my heart. You know, Willowbrook has been in my family for generations.' Kayla pointed out a large tree on top of a hill in one of the nearby paddocks. 'My parents are buried there. And my grandparents. Their parents are buried across the creek, near the old church where Lizzie and Mitch live. The Lawsons are very much a part of this land. I'm looking forward to telling my daughter all about her heritage.'

'If she's anything like her mother, she's going to be incredible.' He meant every word.

'I hope so—hope that I'm incredible, I mean. I'm not so sure.'

'I am.' He gently squeezed the hand he was still holding. 'I was wrong when I walked away from you. And her. I would like to be a part of your lives … if you want me.'

She looked down at her bump and he held his breath, suddenly afraid that she would tell him she had no time for him in a life about to be turned on its head by a baby.

When she looked up, she had tears in her eyes. 'I would like that. Very much.'

He lifted her hand and kissed it. Then he took her face in his hands and kissed away the tears. Then he kissed her mouth and his heart sang as she returned the kiss. He gently put his hands on her shoulders to pull her closer … to feel her body against his. But it didn't go quite the way he wanted it to.

They broke the kiss and looked down. Her baby bump was keeping them well apart. They both began to laugh.

'We need to practise this,' Kayla said. She turned her body and leaned forward to kiss him again, this time with more success.

'You know, I can't fit into my car any more,' Kayla said sadly. 'I know I need something more practical for when the baby comes. But I hate the thought of selling it. And I've left it a bit late.'

'I'll drive you anywhere you need to go. My ute has plenty of room.'

'If I can climb up into it. It's a lot further off the ground than the Datsun. Actually, I've got to sort something out for later this week. I have a dress to take to a bride. I was going to ask Jen if I could borrow her car. But now that Brad's here, I suspect they'll have things they need to do.'

'There's no need, I'll drive you.'

Kayla laughed. 'The last thing a nervous bride wants is some bloke hanging around the house while she's trying on a wedding dress. How about I borrow your car?'

Connor wanted to drive her. He would sit outside in the car all day, but she would have none of that. In the end, he agreed to bring the car around in three days for her to borrow.

'You'll get to take the Datsun back into town. You'll enjoy that.'

He probably would.

The sun was starting to sink so, still holding hands, they turned away from the mares and foals and walked back to the house.

'Have you had a good Christmas?' Kayla asked him.

'Yes. I can't remember when I last did a family Christmas. After my dad left us, Mum was working two jobs. She didn't have a lot of money. And then I drifted into the gangs. Their idea of Christmas mostly involved a lot of alcohol.' And sex, but he didn't want to tell her that. He never wanted to think of those days again.

'It's been a while for me too,' Kayla said, surprising him. 'I'll tell you the story one day, but after our parents died, Lizzie and I didn't do Christmas any more. I was at boarding school, then uni. We were both a bit broken and we weren't getting on very well.'

'What about when you were living in Sydney?'

'Work. Christmas weddings. New Year weddings. There was never time for this.' She stopped walking for a second and stretched up to kiss his cheek. 'And I like this.'

So did he.

'But,' Kayla continued, 'I need to have a serious conversation with my family. There were lots of presents under that tree. And every one of mine had something to do with the baby. That's great and I'll need all those clothes and everything, but a little something just for me as me—not as a mum—that would have been nice.'

'I wasn't expecting to see anyone today. I don't have a present, but this is just for you.' He kissed her again.

★★★

It was well past eleven o'clock by the time Jen managed to convince her sleepy children to go to bed. Kayla was already asleep and Connor had left. Mitch and Lizzie had walked arm in arm back to the creek crossing. Jen carried a sleeping Dylan up the stairs, followed by Brad carrying Suzi, who had been fighting to stay awake for a while now. Their beds had been moved into their small living room. It was a tight fit, but meant Jen and Brad would be alone in their room. Dylan didn't stir as she laid him into his small bed and pulled the sheet over him.

'Daddy, will you still be here when I wake up tomorrow?' Suzi said, her voice heavy with exhaustion.

'Yes, my darling girl. I will still be here tomorrow.'

'Promise?'

'I promise.' Jen heard Brad's voice break and her eyes filled with tears.

'Goodnight. We both love you very much.' The room was already in semi-darkness, lit only by a lamp on the table between the two beds. Jen flicked that off and she and Brad left the room, closing the door behind them.

'Suzi's not afraid of the dark any more?' Brad asked.

'No. She's grown up a lot in these past few months.' Jen paused by the bathroom door, not wanting to look Brad in the face. 'Why don't you go in? I'll be there in a moment.' She ducked through the bathroom door before he could answer.

Alone, she leaned against the door and closed her eyes. She put her shaking hands to her face and tried to calm the fears raging inside her. After several deep breaths, she went to the basin to splash water over her face. Brad was here. It was wonderful and terrifying. He seemed just the same, but different. What if he had changed so much he didn't want her any more? Or maybe she wouldn't want him. After all these months alone, she longed for him, but she was as nervous as she had been the very first time, all those years ago.

She splashed more water on her face and looked at herself in the mirror. She was wearing her favourite dress in celebration of Christmas, but without make-up or having her hair cut, she felt frumpy—worn down by loneliness, fear and frustration. This was Brad; she should have faith in her husband's love. So why did she feel like this? Perhaps it was because they'd had barely any time to talk since his arrival, just a few snatched minutes while her brother distracted the kids. It wasn't quite the reunion she had dreamed of, but Brad was home. That's what really mattered.

She picked up a hairbrush and ran it through her hair. She would trust the love on which her whole life was built.

When she walked into the bedroom, it was empty. She stepped back into the hall and saw that the kids' door was still shut. Deep in her heart, she understood where Brad would be. She went down the grand staircase. The front door was open and she could see someone standing at the top of the steps. She went outside and stood beside him.

'Do you remember when we first met? We used to go down to the park by the creek at night and watch the stars. It seems years since I stood outside and looked at the stars.'

She reached for his hand and entwined her fingers in his. 'I saw the riots on the news. I was so afraid for you.'

'I was afraid too. Not for myself. I was afraid I would never see the kids again. Never see you again. Never get the chance to tell you ...' He turned to face her and she saw the tears in his eyes. 'Never get the chance to say how sorry I am. I was a fool and you and the kids suffered because of it. These past months, I've been so afraid that you … that you wouldn't want me back in your lives.'

'Never think that.' She took both his hands in hers. 'The kids love you. I love you. Of course we want you back in our lives.'

'But—'

'No.' Jen placed a finger against his lips. 'No buts. Whatever we need to do to rebuild our family and our lives, we'll do it. We have friends and family who will help. But most of all, we have each other.'

'I love you, Jen.' His arms went around her to pull her close. Then he was kissing her with relief and love and passion.

And she returned all of those emotions in equal measure, feeling the protective walls she'd built around her heart start to crumble.

It was fairly quiet at the pub so, leaving Laura in charge during the day, Connor set out on a quest. This was the most important gift he had ever bought and he wanted it to be perfect. He spent the first day searching in Tamworth, with its bigger town centre and more varied shops. The museum shop had some interesting things, but nothing was what he was looking for. He spent ages peering through the windows of the jewellery shops, but that wasn't right either. It was too soon; perhaps sometime in the future, if he was a very lucky man. Besides, jewellery was a cliché and he wasn't going to fall into that.

He must have walked up and down the main shopping street three times without success before he had to head back for the evening rush at the Gateway. Next morning, armed with the results of many late-night Google searches, he set out into the countryside to the craft world. He looked at pottery and quilts, paintings and handmade furniture. He even dropped into a wool factory and a plant nursery. But nothing caught his eye and he was running out of time. He had to be at Willowbrook the next morning to give Kayla his car, and he had to give her his present at the same time. If he left it any longer, it would be too late.

He turned back towards Scone feeling desperate and despondent. The sign appeared as he was slowing through Wingen: ANTIQUES. He pulled into a parking place. It would probably be a glorified junk shop, but at this point, he'd try anything. Inside, there was an array of beautifully restored furniture; polished wood gleamed gold in the filtered sunlight coming through the windows. He ran his fingers gently over a sideboard so beautiful, he barely dared to touch it. He flicked the tag over and blinked. This was no cheap second-hand place, but if he had the money, he'd have paid the asking price for such a wonderful piece that exuded history and warmth.

Something smaller perhaps.

Down one wall, shelves and cabinets held a display of china. The flowers and fancy gold trim were pretty enough, but not to his taste. Nor Kayla's either, he imagined. He made his way to the antique jewellery display. There might be something there, something out of the ordinary. He didn't make it that far, his wandering gaze falling instead on something tucked away in the corner of the big room. He carefully eased his way over to it. Like everything else here, it had seen much use but had been brought back to life with care and skill. And it was perfect.

'Can I help you?'

Connor turned to find a woman standing beside him. 'Yes, please. I'd like to take a closer look at that if I may.'

'Of course. Let's move it out where there's a bit more room.'

It took the two of them a few minutes to manoeuvre the piece out from its hiding place.

'It's easy to adjust,' the saleswoman said. 'Like this.' She deftly demonstrated. 'It's 1930s and as you can see, it's been well used.

When we restored it, we left some of the marks in the top there. I think it adds to the appeal, don't you?'

'It's perfect. I'll take it.'

'Wonderful. Of course, it's not inexpensive.'

Connor didn't care. He had found what he wanted for Kayla and now he had seen it, nothing else would do.

It took a bit of effort to get his find onto the back of the ute. Cast iron and wood are heavy. The saleswoman gave him an old blanket to wrap around it to protect the polish.

'Is it for you?' she asked as she handed him the receipt.

'No. It's for a friend.'

'Well, I hope they enjoy it. It's a lovely thing.'

'Thank you.'

Connor drove carefully back to Scone, glancing often in the mirror to check that the bundle had not come to harm. At the pub, he enlisted Hayden's help to bring it inside for the night.

Laura came to look at it. 'That's for Kayla?'

'Yep.' Connor felt a sudden twinge of anxiety. He didn't have much experience when it came to giving gifts to someone who really mattered.

'She'll love it. You're good at this, boss.' Laura slapped his arm gently and went back to work.

***

With Brad's help, Kayla had everything ready. Since Connor had offered the use of his ute, she'd added an extra stop to her errands. She had two boxes of fabrics and designs for her seamstress, as well as the almost completed gown for her bride to try. The bride was the daughter of a winery owner in the Lower Hunter. Kayla would go there first to have the dress fitting, then detour off the highway to deliver the fabric and patterns on her way home.

She wandered back into the kitchen, feeling the baby moving restlessly.

'It's all right, little one. This is the last one, I promise. No more trips or deliveries until you're able to come with me in a car seat. It'll be far more comfortable for both of us. How does that sound?'

As if in agreement, the baby gave a mighty kick.

'Oww.' Kayla bent forward, holding her stomach.

'Kay? Is something wrong?' Jen appeared at her side.

'No. I think she's going to grow up to be a jockey, the way she's kicking.'

'Or one of the Matildas.'

'My daughter is not going to be a football player.'

'She might have something to say about that. And what if it's a boy?'

'Okay. If it's a boy, maybe.'

They were interrupted by the sound of an engine outside.

'That'll be Connor. Great. I can get this done.'

By the time Kayla had the door open, Connor was climbing the stone stairs, lugging something big and sort of square wrapped in an old blanket.

'What on earth is that?'

'A heavy object. Let me in before I drop it.'

Kayla stepped back. Connor walked into the hallway and gently put his heavy object on the carpet.

Kayla frowned. What looked like a cast-iron bracket or stand protruded from the lower edge of the blanket.

Connor straightened and stretched his back. Grinning widely, he made a grand gesture to indicate his load. 'Merry Christmas. Sorry, I didn't wrap it—but I didn't know how.' He didn't look the slightest bit sorry. In fact, he looked absurdly pleased with himself.

Kayla was starting to laugh. 'I'd better have a look then.' She began tugging at the baling twine holding the blanket in place. By now, she had an audience—Brad and the kids had come to see what was going on, joining Jen where she sat on the grand staircase to watch.

'I need some scissors,' Kayla said.

Jen went into the kitchen and returned with the implement.

'Thanks.'

Kayla cut the string in two places and this time when she tugged, it came away. So too did the old blanket, revealing the polished wood underneath. It was scarred and marked and not at all perfect, but it was lovely. She reached out to stroke it.

'What is it?' Dylan asked in a loud whisper.

'It's a table,' Kayla said. 'A very special one. Watch.' Awkwardly, she reached down to loosen the nuts keeping the tabletop vertical. She swung the table down until it was at what she thought was a good angle and tightened it again. 'It's an architect's table. You can set this at any height or angle you want.'

'Why do you want an architect's table, Auntie Kayla?' Suzi asked. 'You're not an architect.'

'Because it's the perfect table for drawing on. Especially when you are drawing wedding dresses and you need lots of room for big sheets of paper.'

Kayla turned to face Connor. He was looking at her with uncertain eyes.

'It's perfect,' she said. Her chin was quivering as she held back her tears. 'Thank you.' She threw her arms around his neck and kissed him. He kissed her back.

They were kissing for the third time, much more slowly than the first two, when Dylan declared loudly, 'Eww. Too much kissing!'

Jen shushed him but Kayla started to laugh.

'All right. I have to go. I've got a long drive in front of me.'

'Are you sure you don't want me—'

'No. But if you help me load this stuff into your car, that would be good.'

With the old blanket and her boxes and bags safely stowed in the back of the ute, Kayla heaved herself into the driver's seat. It wasn't easy, but it was much better than her own car. She listened to Connor's instructions about the gears and handbrake. Not that she needed to; she could drive almost anything with four wheels, but she did like the sound of his voice.

When he'd finished, she dug into her bag and pulled out the keys to the Datsun. 'Here. Enjoy.'

He took them and leaned in the window to kiss her one more time. 'Drive safe. Text me when you're on the way home.'

'I will.'

CHAPTER
34

In her years as a wedding planner, Kayla had met more bridezillas than she cared to remember. And a few mumzillas too. Dadzillas were less common, but they were out there. Kayla had learned to handle them all with tact and grace, but it had been a strain. Today's bride was a welcome change from all that, and her excitement began to restore Kayla's joy in weddings.

The moment Kayla had arrived, the bride had been almost as concerned and excited about Kayla's baby bump as she had been about the dress. She'd pointed out that Kayla should be thinking about a baby shower rather than her wedding dress. Kayla didn't mention that a baby shower had never even crossed her mind. The dress had been a hit. A few minor modifications and the bride would be ready to walk down the aisle. The morning had passed in a gentle, happy way. After a light lunch the bride had insisted Kayla eat, she was heading back to the Upper Hunter again, the dress safe in its protective bag on the seat beside her, along with her notes. Even with the baby coming, she'd have that dress finished in plenty of time for the wedding. She was beginning to think designing wedding dresses would be more than just a thing on the side.

She turned on the radio to find it already tuned to a jazz station. Connor liked jazz? She hadn't known that about him. The thought of him sitting behind the wheel of this car, listening to jazz as he drove made her smile. She flexed her hands on the wheel. She had thought she'd hate driving a big four-wheel drive ute, but she actually kind of liked it. The car was a few years old but had a feeling of strength and solidity about it. A bit like Connor.

'Oh, stop it.'

Stop thinking about Connor every second like some silly school-girl. She had more important things to think about, like the almost complete wedding dress beside her and where her business was going. Jen had shown a real ability for organising weddings. Since she'd come on board, Kayla had stepped further and further back. Not simply because she was pregnant, but because she could see how good Jen was, and how much she still had the enthusiasm and spark that Kayla had lost. For her part, Kayla was becoming more involved in her dress designing business. She hadn't worked with many brides, but every one of them had been thrilled and sung her praises to their friends. She was already working on a website and soon she'd be hiring another seamstress.

Perhaps it was time to step away from Willowbrook Weddings.

Jen and Brad had already been talking about renting a small cottage in town as soon as one of them had a solid job. Kayla could understand their need to have their own home again and Jen could easily do her wedding work from there. In exchange for his evidence against the drug dealers, Brad had faced a lesser charge. When he pleaded guilty, not only was he allowed to walk from the court without jail time, he'd also been given permission to serve out his parole in New South Wales. He had a record, but not a bad one. And Kayla knew Connor would help him find work.

Soon the house would be hers alone again … Well, her and the baby. One of the rooms Jen was using would become a nursery. Kayla would set up the one next to it as her design studio, all organised around that lovely, sloped drawing table. With the adjoining door open, she could keep an eye on the baby as she worked. It wouldn't be like having a full-time job, she could work just the hours she wanted to. Each dress was a single project that brought in a good return. And if she needed some help with the baby, that would be fine.

The future looked bright, especially as it had Connor in it.

She caught her breath as her stomach clenched. Ow. Another false contraction. This one hurt more than the others had. Carefully she pulled over to the side of the road, where she sat and breathed deeply, but the pain was already fading. She waited and waited, but there wasn't another. Braxton Hicks again. They were a little more frequent now, but she'd learned not to worry. It was too early for the baby. She started the car again and pulled back onto the road. Perhaps she should go home.

She drove quite slowly for a few minutes, but the only thing to disturb her was a gentle kick from the baby. She decided to finish the day's errands, then she would be done and could concentrate on herself and the baby. She picked up speed in anticipation.

About ten minutes later, Kayla eased back on the accelerator. She was approaching the turn-off to a narrow, hard-to-spot road. A few miles in from the highway the road became gravel and after that, an even smaller track led to the small cottage where her seamstress lived.

As she flicked on her indicator to turn, Kayla became aware of a group of motorcycles rapidly approaching behind her. The more she slowed for the tight corner, the faster they approached. She took the corner a fraction faster than perhaps she should have in a strange car, but her unease was quenched when the bikes roared on past the turn-off and continued up the highway. She drove more slowly now; this road wasn't good and she was glad there would be little, if any, oncoming traffic.

She'd hardly travelled half a kilometre when she again heard the sound of motorcycles. Looking in the mirror, she saw the same group of bikes closing fast behind her. They had turned and followed her.

Memories of the events in the pub that day began flooding back. Memories of Connor lying on the floor as the gang leader punched and kicked him.

'No. It's not them. It can't be. Why would they be here? Now? After all this time? And why would they be following me?'

This time saying it out loud didn't help her anxiety, because she knew the answers.

She pressed down harder on the accelerator, but knew it was no good. She'd never outrun them in Connor's ute. And besides, where would she go? The only house she knew of on this road was the seamstress's and she wasn't going to lead the bikie gang there. She slowed a little more and edged towards the side of the road. Maybe they were a harmless group of riders on a day out. There was also a place up ahead where the road widened. She might be able to turn around and head back to the highway.

With a sudden roar, two of the bikes passed her, making use of the gap she'd created by moving over. The others stayed behind. She realised she was trapped. They drove over the crest of the next ridge in formation. Kayla closed the window and locked the doors. She reached for her bag and mobile phone. They were descending the other side of the ridge and she watched as the bars on the phone dropped to nothing before she could dial. The two motorcycles in front of her slowed down, weaving from side to side across the road, forcing her to slow down. She revved the engine, trying to get them to move over, but they were having none of it. They seemed to know that, frightened as she was, she wasn't ready to drive over the top of them.

Nor could she turn around. The road was too narrow and the two riders behind were blocking her way. She checked her phone again. If she could only keep going, she'd come to a rise where the signal would cut in again. She looked ahead, but the next ridge seemed an eternity away.

They were moving so slowly now, Kayla only needed one hand on the steering wheel. The other she held across her stomach.

'It's all right, little one. I won't let anyone hurt you.'

But that was a lie. She was out here all alone. If anyone wanted to hurt her or her baby, there was nothing she could do to stop them.

The car was barely moving now. Then it stalled and stopped. Instantly the bikies were off their rides. One leaned on the bonnet of the ute. One was directly behind her. She could go nowhere without running someone over.

When the leader took off his helmet, she recognised him instantly.

Blue sauntered over and knocked on the window. 'Get out of the car.'

'No. Leave me alone. I'm calling the police.' She reached for her phone, hoping against hope she would see bars showing.

'Don't bother. We know there's no signal out here. Now get out of the car.'

She shook her head then screamed as the glass window on the passenger side exploded inwards, sending glass fragments flying. A hand reached through the broken window and opened the door.

A second bikie stood there, leering at her. 'Are you going to get out or am I coming in there after you?'

She unlocked her door and slid slowly out, still clutching her phone. Blue's face curved into a satisfied smile. He lifted her hand and prised open her fingers then tossed the phone into the back of the ute. 'We're here looking for Connor. We followed his truck but you're not him. So now what do we do?'

Hope flared inside her. 'I just borrowed his truck. So if you let me go, I promise I won't tell the police. I won't even tell Connor. I'll say I broke the window.'

'No. That won't do at all. I want Connor to know I broke his window.' Blue stared at her. 'Do you know what, guys? I think we have Connor's bird here. She was the one who brought the pigs last time. And she's got a sprog on the way. Connor's, I'll bet.'

Kayla's heart clenched with fear as she instinctively placed both hands on her bump. *Everything's going to be all right, I promise.* The baby moved and pain flared in Kayla's lower back. She clenched her jaw and forced herself to stay still, silently cursing the false contractions. She couldn't show any weakness in front of these people.

At the back of the ute, a gang member prodded one of the boxes on the tray. 'What's this then?'

'It's fabric. Material and stuff,' Kayla said quickly between teeth clenched against the fear she would not let them see. 'For making dresses.'

The bikie pushed the box away dismissively, then went to look in the cab. 'This looks more interesting.' He dragged the dress bag out.

'That's a dress.' Kayla's heart was in her mouth. 'That's all. A dress.'

'A pretty big dress.' The man started to lower the zip and laughed. 'Hey, Blue. This looks like a wedding dress. Maybe Connor and this one are getting hitched.'

'No. No. It's not mine. I make wedding dresses. It's for someone else. Connor and I aren't getting married.'

'But you are his girlfriend.' Blue stepped closer and leered at her.

'No.' Her voice quivered and the fear inside her grew. 'We're not. And this isn't his baby.'

Blue looked down at her swollen belly.

Kayla began to back away, but Blue moved forward, step matching step, until she was against the side of the car. Without taking his menacing gaze from her face, he leaned into the car and pulled the keys out of the ignition. Then he tossed them into the long grass bordering the road.

'Then what are you doing driving his car? The Connor I know didn't like others to touch his things. His car. His woman.' Blue lifted his hand and slowly stroked her cheek.

Kayla flinched away from his touch as defiance flared in her heart. 'This isn't the Connor you knew. He's changed. He's a better man than you will ever be.'

'Well, well. Listen to her, mates. She's sweet on Connor. And I bet he's got the hots for you too, baby or no baby. So what are we going to do with you now?'

A shaft of pain cut through Kayla. She grunted, clutching her belly, and leaned into the ute for support. These contractions were too close together. That hadn't happened before.

'Woah.' Blue held his hands up and stepped back. 'I didn't touch you.'

Kayla fought to control her breathing. Another anxiety was growing inside her. She couldn't be in real labour. It was too early for that. It must just be the fear and stress caused by the bikies. Whatever it was, she was not going to have this baby by the side of the road.

Blue and his mates took a couple of steps away, casting worried looks at each other.

Kayla gathered her scattered thoughts, thinking their concern might be a way out for her. Perhaps she could convince them she really was in labour. They might take her to hospital. Or at least leave her alone to keep driving. She gave a loud moan and saw the panic on their faces.

Before she could do anything else, her child moved again and warm liquid streamed down her legs.

CHAPTER
35

Connor glanced at his watch and frowned. He thought he would have heard from Kayla by now. Still, wedding dresses were a mystery to him. It might be that such things took longer than a mere male would expect. He busied himself with ordering supplies but found himself checking his watch ever more frequently. When his phone still showed no message from Kayla after what must have been the twentieth check, he got to his feet.

'I'm going to Willowbrook,' he told Laura.

'Okay.'

The little red Datsun was a joy to drive and he could see why Kayla loved it. But it was impractical and she would need something different when the baby came. Connor was no expert on such things, but he thought they had almost another month before that. He could help her find something in that time, but until then it would be a shame not to enjoy the Datsun while he had a chance. He gunned it a little more as he drove out of town.

He had hoped to see his ute parked at Willowbrook, but there was no sign of it. He checked the time again, starting to worry.

The front door opened and Jen emerged. For once, Connor was pleased to see the kids were not with her.

'Have you heard from Kayla?' he asked as he took the stairs two at a time.

'No. I was going to ask you the same thing. I was expecting her back before now.'

'Have you tried to phone her?'

Jen nodded. 'No answer.'

Connor pulled out his phone and tried anyway. He went through to voicemail. 'Kayla, it's Connor. Just wondering when you wanted your car back. Call me.'

Jen looked puzzled at the message.

'I didn't want to say we were worried,' Connor explained.

'I know, but I am worried.'

'Do you have the name of the person she was taking the dress to?'

'I should be able to find it. Come on in and I'll look.'

In Kayla's office, Jen shuffled papers on the desk. 'Here we go. This is the seamstress she uses. Should I give her a call?'

Connor nodded.

Jen reached for the landline.

'Hi, this is Jen Harrison, Kayla Lawson's associate. I was wondering if she's still there?'

Connor watched her face as she frowned, then nodded a couple of times.

'That's fine. I'm sorry for the mix-up. I'm sure Kayla will be in touch soon to sort it out. Bye.' She hung up. When she turned to look at him, Connor saw the very real worry in her face.

'She never showed up there.'

Icy fear began to grip him. 'I shouldn't have let her go alone.'

'Connor, you know as well as I do that no-one "lets" Kayla do anything. You couldn't have stopped her. Let's not panic yet. I'll see if I can find out what time she left the previous stop.'

Jen reached for the phone again. By the time she had finished a quick conversation, she was looking very worried indeed. 'She left there after lunch. She should have been with the seamstress at least an hour ago.'

'I'm going looking for her. Can you give me both addresses?'

Jen scribbled details on a piece of paper. Connor took it and went back to the Datsun.

'Let me know if she calls or turns up,' he said.

He drove most of the way down the driveway, well out of Jen's sight, before stopping and dialling a number.

'Sergeant Baker. Connor Knight. I'm a bit worried about some-one and wanted to ask—have there been any road accidents this morning? Between here and Newcastle?'

'Not that I've heard of. I can check. Who are you looking for?'

Connor told him and waited, his heart in his mouth, until the sergeant spoke again.

'There's nothing in the system. Have you got a reason to think there's something wrong?'

Connor explained the situation. 'I'm setting out now to look for her. She might have broken down.' He desperately hoped those words were true.

'I'll let you know if I hear anything.'

'Thanks.' Connor hesitated, his deepest fears rising to the sur-face. 'I don't suppose … there haven't been any reports of trouble? Bikies?'

The silence at the other end told him the sergeant's thoughts had been moving the same way as his.

'No,' Baker said eventually. 'I'll ask around.'

'Thanks.'

Connor started the car again and kept driving.

A few kilometres outside of town, Connor slowed. Should he keep going towards the last place Kayla had been or turn right towards the place she had never arrived? She had to be somewhere between those two. If she had broken down on the highway, surely someone would have stopped to help. Or she would have called. He turned right. This was the less travelled road and mobile service would be patchy among those ridges. If she'd broken down on this road, she'd be less likely to get help. And that's what it was. She was broken down. He would not allow himself to think of any other option.

Let her be all right. Please let her be all right.

Several minutes later, he saw his ute up ahead, stopped almost in the middle of the road. There was no sign of Kayla. He sped up, then slammed on the brakes when he reached the ute and threw himself out of the driver's seat.

'Kayla? Kayla!'

No answer. He ran to the ute and peered inside the cab. It was empty. The passenger-side window was broken and glass was scattered through the cab, but there was nothing to suggest what had happened to Kayla. He looked wildly around and spotted her phone lying in the tray of the ute, the screen broken.

Frantic, Connor almost screamed her name. 'Kayla!'

His voice echoed into silence. Then he heard a faint voice.

'Connor …'

He darted around to the other side of the car. Kayla was a couple of metres away, half sitting with her back against a tree where a bit of shade gave her some protection against the scorching sun. She clutched her protruding belly with both hands and her tear-stained face was as white as a sheet.

In an instant he was beside her. He dropped to his knees. He wanted to pull her into his arms but was afraid to touch her. 'Kayla. Are you hurt? What happened?'

'Blue … the bikies. They forced me to stop. They said …' The words faded as Kayla grabbed her sides and started breathing heavily.

Rage flashed through Connor. Blue and his friends would pay for this. But not now. Now Kayla needed him.

'Connor.' She grabbed his arm, her fingers digging deep into his flesh. 'Help me.'

'It's all right.' He spoke in a soothing voice. 'They've gone.'

She shook her head wildly, her eyes wide with panic. 'The baby, Connor. The baby's coming.' She hunched forward with a moan.

Only then did he notice that her clothes were stained and wet.

'Okay, Kayla, I'll call for help.'

'No. No. Connor don't leave me.' Her breath was coming in sharp gasps and her fingers dug even deeper as she pulled him back down.

'I need to get my phone. Then I can call an ambulance.'

'There's no signal.' Kayla's deep sobs cut through him like a blade.

How was he supposed to get help? He couldn't leave her, not like this. She was terrified.

'Don't worry, Kayla. I won't leave you. I promise I'll take care of you. Now, I want you to breathe. Long, slow, deep breaths. That's it. Slowly. You'll be fine.'

He knelt next to her, holding one of her hands in his, and tried to think of a way out of this. If he couldn't call for an ambulance, he had to get to a place where he could. But he couldn't leave Kayla. She couldn't go in the tiny passenger space of the Datsun.

'We'll take my car.'

Kayla shook her head. 'They threw the keys away. I looked for them. But I couldn't—'

'Forget it. I have a spare.'

Then she screamed again, her fingers closing on his so tightly it hurt. The reality of her sweaty face and panting hit him hard.

'You're in labour. I have to get you to the hospital.'

'It's too soon,' she cried. 'It's not ready yet. Connor, don't let my baby die.'

Her anguished cry tore him in half. He had to do something. 'Kayla, we need to get you and the baby to hospital, and to do that I have to go to the car. Just wait here a minute. Let go of my hand. I won't be more than a few steps away.'

'Please, don't leave me.'

'I will never leave you. I will always be here for you. But you have to let me go to the car. All right?'

She nodded, her eyes wide with fear.

'I'll only be a few seconds.' He stood up. The need to get Kayla to hospital was the only thing that could drag him from her side. He gave her what he hoped was a reassuring smile and dashed back to his car.

He pulled his spare key from the holder under the rear bumper, but when he looked into the cab, it was littered with broken glass. The big grey garment bag he'd helped Kayla with that morning had been tossed carelessly onto the seat. He could move that and maybe clear away enough of the broken glass to make it safe for Kayla. But even as the thought formed, he knew that wasn't an option. He glanced at where she was lying on the side of the road, her eyes fixed on him like a drowning person on a lifejacket. Her hands cradled her stomach and her legs were stretched wide. She couldn't sit in that seat.

That left the tray.

The blanket that had protected Kayla's drawing table was still there, with the two cardboard boxes of dress fabric they'd loaded that morning. If he could flatten the boxes a bit, she could maybe lie back against them. He swung onto the tray and made the best bed he could, then he lowered the tailgate.

When he returned to Kayla, tears were streaming down her face.

'Kayla, it's going to be fine.'

'No, it's not. It wasn't supposed to be like this.' Her voice was shaking. 'It was going to be in hospital, with music. I've even picked the music. It's such calming music. The baby was going to be born loving Bach. And Jen would be there to meet her. And there'd be doctors standing by. Not here. Not like this. It was supposed to be perfect.'

'This baby doesn't need perfect. This baby has everything he or she needs in you.' He wiped her hair back from her wet face and kissed her forehead. 'I'll carry you to the ute, but it would help if you could stand up.'

She nodded.

'Right.' He held out his hands, trying to keep his voice positive. 'Let's get you on your feet.'

He saw the hesitation in her eyes and wished he could say something to reassure her. But he couldn't. He had no idea if making her stand up would hurt her or the baby. Nothing had ever prepared him for this. All he knew was that he had to get Kayla to a hospital. And this was the only way he knew how. He could only hope it was the right thing to do, because if anything he did harmed her or her baby, he would never forgive himself.

* * *

Kayla placed her hands in Connor's. She trusted him, but she was terrified. This was happening too early. She wasn't ready. The baby wasn't ready. She needed to be in a hospital. That birth plan she and Jen had put together made it very clear. Hospital. A nice, safe, clean hospital with doctors and nurses and all the medical care she or the baby could need. A perfect birth. Not like this. Not on the side of a dirt road. Not in the back of an old ute.

'Ready?'

No, she wanted to scream. She was not ready. Instead she took a deep breath and nodded.

Slowly and carefully, Connor helped her to stand. It hurt. Oh, how it hurt. She whimpered.

'I've got you.' His arm was around her waist, holding her with such gentle strength. 'Now, can you walk to the car, or should I carry you?'

'Walk.' It was barely a whisper.

A few steps seemed like a few miles as she shuffled forward, hands cradling her belly. She made no attempt to stem the tears running down her face. As she reached the car, another contraction hit her and she doubled over with pain, panting to get air into her lungs. Connor's arms were around her, supporting her until the pain lessened and she was able to straighten.

'They're too close together,' she gasped. 'It'll be soon. Help me …' The cry was torn from the deepest recesses of her soul.

'Put your arm around my neck.' Connor guided her. 'I'm going to lift you now. I don't want to hurt you but I have to.'

Still panting, she nodded.

There was a flash of pain and then she was on the back of the ute. Connor leaped up beside her and helped her settle onto the blanket, her back against the rear window of the cab. He slid the boxes of fabric, now battered and squashed, behind her to protect her back. It was not comfortable, but she could survive this if it would get her and her baby to where they needed to be.

Connor gave her hand a squeeze and jumped to the ground. 'I'll drive as slowly and gently as I can,' he told her as he fastened the tailgate.

'Not too slowly.'

Connor got into the driver's seat and started the engine. Kayla braced herself for the pain as the car began to move. Connor did a three-point turn on the narrow road and set off towards the highway.

'Are you all right?' His words were almost carried away on the wind.

Her mind flicked back many years. She and Lizzie were small, riding in the back of a very different ute as their father drove carefully across one of the home paddocks. *Are you all right?* he'd called. *Stay sitting down and hang on.* They'd replied with joy and excitement at this unexpected adventure. In Connor's ute, Kayla smiled at the memory as her fear lifted for a moment.

'I'm okay,' she called, almost but not quite believing it.

CHAPTER
36

Connor thought he heard Kayla yell. He started to slow down.

'No. No. Don't stop. Keep going.' She sounded wild with panic.

He grabbed his phone again. There was still no signal.

Torn between the need to hurry and Kayla's distress, he increased speed a little, eyes alert for potholes.

They crossed one more ridge and this time when he looked at his phone, he had a signal. He dialled triple 0. Relief flooded him when it was answered.

'I need help ...'

When the call was over, he twisted in his seat. 'The hospital is expecting us,' he yelled.

There was no answer. Had she heard him? Was she all right? He couldn't see her. Should he stop and check? But that would only delay them.

'Kayla?'

He heard a muffled sound. That had to be her. The intersection with the highway was ahead. When he turned onto the better road, he increased speed again. Fifteen minutes and they would be there.

He had to slow down when he reached the outskirts of Scone.

'Kayla, we're nearly there. Kayla?' he yelled.

Again there was no answer but by now the hospital was almost in sight. When he saw the white stone gates, he swung into the nearest entrance and drove to a ramp leading into the building. He slammed on the brakes and leaped out.

'Kayla?'

'Connor?' Her voice was weak and fearful. She was lying in the ute, covered with sweat, her hands clasping the blanket beneath her and her legs spread wide. 'She's coming, Connor. She's coming.'

'I'm getting a doctor. Hang on.' He raced up the ramp into the hospital.

'I can't hang on!' Kayla's scream followed him through the doors.

'Help me! Someone help me!' he called.

A woman at a reception desk looked up. 'What is it?'

'In my car. Kayla. She's in labour. The baby's coming.'

'All right.' The woman picked up a phone. Connor looked wildly around. Where were the doctors? The woman on triple 0 had said they would be ready and waiting.

A door at the end of the corridor opened and a nurse appeared. She was pushing a wheelchair. A wheelchair? Kayla needed a bed or a stretcher or something.

'Hurry.' He turned to go back outside.

The nurse put one hand on his arm. 'Sir, you need to calm down now. Right now. You're no good to your wife if you're panicking.'

'She's not—' That didn't matter. Nothing mattered but Kayla and the baby. He took a deep breath and nodded.

'All right? Now, take me to her.'

'My car is outside.'

He heard the nurse's sharp intake of breath as she saw the ute and Kayla in the back. 'Right, love, let's get you out of there.' She turned to Connor and gave him a fierce look. 'You can make yourself useful and help her down.'

Connor lowered the tailgate and stepped onto the tray. Kayla's fingers dug deeply into his flesh as he helped her slide across the tray. He jumped down then gathered her in his arms, placing her as gently as he could in front of the wheelchair. He and the nurse settled Kayla carefully into the seat.

'Now, how many weeks are you?' the nurse asked.

'Thirty-six.'

Connor saw the look of concern flash across the nurse's face, but she hid it quickly. 'A bit early, but that's all right. You're here now and we'll take care of both of you. Let's get you inside.'

Kayla looked less frightened now, but she was still grasping his hand so tightly it hurt. The pain he felt in his hand was nothing compared to the fear and guilt he was barely able to control.

'You.' The nurse turned to Connor. 'Push the chair up that ramp.'

He extracted his hand from Kayla's grasp and did as instructed.

'Right. Now move that car this instant. That's the ambulance bay.'

Kayla grabbed his hand again. 'No, no. He has to stay with me.'

The nurse was having none of it. 'We've got to get you ready to have a baby. He can come back when he's moved that car.'

Connor knelt next to Kayla. 'I'll be back in a minute, I promise. And I'll call Jen so she can come down and be with you. Just like you planned.'

'Yes. Yes. Call Jen. She should be here. But come back; don't you dare leave me.'

'I won't, Kayla. I promise.'

She answered with a throaty scream as she clutched at her belly again.

'I think we need you in the delivery suite.' The nurse pushed the wheelchair down the corridor.

Connor reluctantly turned away and went outside, where a uniformed attendant was examining his car.

'Sorry. She was in labour. I'll move it.'

Connor got behind the wheel and drove away. The hospital carpark was full, so he had to leave the ute on the street. As he walked back, he pulled out his phone and dialled Willowbrook. It clicked through to an answering machine.

'Jen, Brad. It's Connor. I've just taken Kayla to Scone Hospital—'

Before he could finish speaking, the phone was picked up. 'Is she all right?' Jen asked.

'I think so. She went into labour out on the road.' He didn't think it was the right time to say what had caused it.

'It's early.'

'Yes. That's what the nurse said. Jen, is it too early. The baby?'

'I don't know, Connor. It should be fine, but with babies, you never know.'

'She needs you.'

'I'll get there as soon as I can, but in the meantime, you get back in there.'

'But I don't know anything—'

'She needs you, Connor. Go.' The line went silent as she hung up.

Would Jen say that if she knew what had happened? That Blue and his gang were responsible for this? That he, Connor, was responsible? If it wasn't for him, Kayla would never have found herself at the mercy of the bikies. She would never have gone into labour on the side of a road. She could have had that perfect birth she had planned. She deserved better than this.

She deserved better than him.

But he was all she had right now—and she didn't deserve to be alone.

Connor started to run. He burst through the hospital doors into an empty corridor. Where was she? Forcing himself to walk, he set off in the direction the nurse had taken with the wheelchair. He hadn't gone very far when a door swung open at the end of the corridor and he heard a scream.

A nurse he hadn't seen before looked at him. 'Are you Connor?'

'Yes.'

'Take this mask and get in there. The baby is coming fast and your wife needs you.'

He hesitated—he couldn't claim a husband's right. He couldn't even claim a father's right. But surely love was enough?

He heard Kayla scream his name and he put the mask on and followed the nurse.

Kayla lay on a bed at the centre of a swirl of attention. A woman wearing scrubs was seated on a stool at the end of the bed, between Kayla's open legs. Two nurses hovered and the room was full of unknown and terrifying hospital equipment that made Connor's insides clench.

Kayla looked distraught. Her eyes were swollen and tear stained, and her sweat-matted hair clung to her face.

'I'm here, Kayla.' Ignoring everything else in the room, he went to her side and laid a hand on her arm, taking care not to disturb the drip feeding into the back of her hand.

'Connor.' The word ended in a low growl as another contraction hit her.

'Good. You're doing fine,' said the masked person between Kayla's legs. 'You're nearly there. Don't push yet.'

'This is all your fault.' Kayla rounded on Connor. 'Your fault.'

'I'm sorry—'

His apology was interrupted by another contraction. Kayla puffed and panted through it, squeezing Connor's hand as if her life depended on it.

'Don't worry about that,' a nurse whispered in his ear. 'Right now she'd be blaming any man. They all do it. She'll have forgotten she ever said it by tomorrow.'

She might, but Connor wouldn't, because Kayla was right and Connor would never forgive himself.

Connor didn't know how much time passed. The room was a blur of Kayla's pain and screams and his fear for her and for the baby.

After what seemed an eternity, the actions of the staff changed.

'Next time I want you to push. Push as hard as you can. This baby needs to come out now.'

Kayla started to pant and screamed again.

'That's it, push.'

'Push,' echoed another nurse.

Kayla raised herself half off the bed and screamed with an intensity that shook Connor to the core.

'That's it. The baby's here.'

At those words, Kayla collapsed back on the bed. The nurse and the doctor were huddled together over a small, towel-wrapped bundle.

'She's not crying.' Kayla struggled to rise. 'Why isn't she crying? Connor?'

What could he say? He didn't know. A terrible dread clamped around his heart. He couldn't breathe until he heard the weak but clear sound of a baby's cry.

'It's a girl,' the doctor announced. She stepped forward and laid the bundle on Kayla's chest. Connor barely looked at the tiny, red, squalling child. He couldn't take his eyes from Kayla's face.

'You did it. You are amazing,' he said, not knowing if she would care or even hear him.

'I have to take the baby now,' the nurse said.

'No. No. Leave her with me.' Kayla's voice was weak.

'I'm sorry, but we need to look after her for a bit. But she'll only be over there.'

They carried the child away and placed her on a strange-looking table that seemed half crib, half hospital bed. It was surrounded by monitors.

'Connor, she's going to be all right, isn't she? Connor?' Kayla had grasped both his hands and was staring at him with such desperation on her face, his heart tore apart.

'Let the doctor do what she has to do. Everything will be all right, I'm sure of it.'

But he wasn't. Not at all.

'No. No, let me up. I have to go to her.' Kayla started to struggle.

'Kayla, it's fine. Lie still. You need to rest too.' His words had no impact.

The doctor was back. 'The baby is fine. She's a bit small and weak, but breathing all right. We just need to keep an eye on her, that's all. Don't worry. Now, we're not quite finished with you yet.'

Connor was hustled out of the room so they could do what they had to do. Standing outside the door, he heard Kayla begging to see her baby. It felt like someone was tearing into his heart.

He couldn't stand it any longer and walked away. He found Kayla's family in the waiting room.

'It's a girl,' he said as he dropped, shattered, into a chair.

Jen sat beside him. 'It's early, but not too early. What did the doctor say?'

'I think she said the baby would be fine. I—I don't know.'

'And Kayla?' Lizzie asked.

'She's fine. They're just making her comfortable. I think she'll want to see you soon.'

'Wouldn't you rather be there?'

No. He wouldn't. And Kayla wouldn't want him to be there either. After what had happened on that remote road, she probably wouldn't want to have anything to do with him ever again.

'You were supposed to be her birth partner,' Connor told Jen. 'She'll want you there now.'

Mitch held out his hand. 'I'm so glad she was with you. Thanks for taking care of our Kayla.'

Connor couldn't stand it any more. He staggered to his feet.

'I have to go. There's something— Tell her ... Tell her congrats from me. She's amazing and she's going to be a wonderful mother.'

He walked swiftly away before anyone could try to stop him.

CHAPTER
37

Kayla felt as if she had been run over by a bulldozer. She struggled back to wakefulness, aware that almost every part of her body ached. When she opened her eyes, she saw Jen sitting by her bed, her nose buried in a wedding magazine.

'Jen?'

Her friend put the magazine down and smiled. 'Good to see you awake. How do you feel?'

'I really don't know.' Kayla lifted herself carefully into a sitting position against the protest of her tired and overloaded muscles and looked around the room. 'My baby? Where is she? Is she all right?'

'She's fine. The midwife says she's doing very well for an early baby.'

Relief coursed through Kayla. 'Why isn't she here with me? I need to see her.'

'Let me go and find the nurse.' Before she left, Jen stepped to the bedside and hugged her. 'Congratulations. I'm so happy for you.'

Kayla lay in the empty room, fighting back the tears. Her body felt overwhelmed and her emotions did too. Through the window she could see it was night time. Was it still the same day? Had all this happened in just a few hours? Memories were flooding back. She shuddered as she remembered the confrontation with the bikies and that horrible drive to the hospital in the back of Connor's ute. It was all a bit fuzzy, but the only things clear in her mind were the sound of her baby's cry, Connor's face and the sound of his voice. Where was he? He should be here, sharing this with her. If not for him—

The door opened and she looked up eagerly.

'How are we?' the nurse asked.

'I don't know about you,' Kayla snapped, 'but I feel as if I just had a baby and it hurts.'

'Kayla!' Jen's shocked expression was overridden by the nurse's chuckle.

'We get that a lot. I'd be worried if you didn't feel like that.'

'I'm sorry.' Kayla was instantly contrite. 'It's been a hard day. It is still today, isn't it?'

'Yes, it is.'

'I need to see my baby. Where is she?'

'We've been keeping a close eye on her, but she's doing just fine. In fact, she's on her way back here now. Let's get you ready to meet her again.' The nurse helped Kayla into a more comfortable position and passed her a glass of water. 'You were a bit dehydrated when you came in, so make sure you drink plenty of liquids.'

Obediently, Kayla drank some water, but her eyes remained fixed on the door. At last it swung open and another nurse wheeled a covered humidicrib into the room.

'Is something wrong with her? Why is she ...?'

'We've had her in there until you woke up. Once she's fed, she'll stay here, with you, in that.' The nurse indicated an open crib in the corner of the room.

The nurse lifted a tightly wrapped bundle from the humidicrib and carried it to the bed. She placed the baby gently into Kayla's waiting arms.

Kayla didn't try to stop the tears. She held the baby close to her, looking into her tiny face with a feeling of such wonderment. 'Hello. I'm your mum.'

Those few words were all she could manage. The baby opened her eyes. They were a beautiful shade of blue-grey. Kayla knew the world was still a blur for her daughter, but it seemed to her that for a few seconds, her baby looked back at her with the same overwhelming love that she felt. The baby might be early and have had a pretty unconventional entry into the world, but she was perfect in every way.

'She's got my mother's eyes.' It was ridiculous and probably not true. 'I'm going to call you Kathy. After your grandmother. She would love you so much if she was here.'

A sniffle by the bedside dragged Kayla's attention away from her daughter.

Lizzie had walked into the room. 'Mum would love that,' she said as she wiped away her tears.

Kayla nodded. 'Come and meet your niece.'

When Mitch joined their little group, Kathy's family was complete. A corner of Kayla's heart, however, was aching.

Oh, Connor, I wish you were here.

***

It was late when Connor pulled up outside the shabby pub in Sydney's west. He got out of the ute and ran his eye over the line of motorcycles outside. He found the one he was looking for and walked into the pub. He glanced around. It took only a moment to spot Blue and his gang clustered around a pool table.

He walked up to Blue. 'We need to talk.'

For a moment, Connor thought he caught a flash of fear in the man's eyes. And well might he be afraid. If Kayla had been hurt—or worse—right now Connor would be talking with his fists.

'Hi, Connor.' Blue hesitated as if about to say something more—or ask something.

The other gang members moved towards their leader. Several of them were carrying pool cues and didn't look like they were planning to use them in a game.

Connor held up a hand. 'If any of you move, you'll regret it.' He was outnumbered, but the rage simmering inside him was explosive.

'It's all right. Connor and I are old mates,' Blue said. 'We're just going to get a beer. You lot carry on with the game.'

Blue gave his pool cue to one of the others. The rest of his gang took this as a sign they weren't needed—at least, not yet. They returned to their game while still casting glances at Connor and Blue.

'Hey. You two. Take it outside.' The barman nodded at the door, a determined look on his face.

They hesitated for a few seconds, their eyes locked, then Blue turned and led the way into the carpark. In the dim light and without his gang behind him, Blue seemed far less sure of himself. All the confidence and bluster had faded from his face. Perhaps he could sense the fury that had been building inside Connor since the moment he first saw Kayla lying in the dirt beside the road.

'How's your girl?' Blue asked.

'You could have been facing a murder charge.' Connor's hands had curled into tight fists by his side. It took all of his control to keep them there.

'We didn't touch her.'

'You didn't have to. You saw she was pregnant and you left her there. I wouldn't do that to a dog.'

'But she's all right. Isn't she?' The words came out high pitched.

Connor looked at him with disgust. 'Yes, she's all right and so is the baby. You're lucky I came along.'

Blue sagged with relief.

'But there is one thing I want to make very clear.' Connor stepped closer to Blue. 'Kayla is under my protection now. If you come near her, or her child, or her family. If you come within ten kilometres of her, you will answer to me. Do you understand?'

Blue took half a step back. He was bigger than Connor. Just a few weeks ago, he'd beaten Connor in his own pub. But that was before he'd threatened Kayla. Nothing would stop Connor from defending her, and if it meant an assault charge or another stint inside, so be it. Connor hated what he was doing. He hated who he was at this moment, but to protect Kayla, he would do whatever it took. He would become whoever he had to be.

'Okay, mate.' Blue held his hands up, open palms outwards as he backed away another couple of steps. 'Take it easy. There's no need to get physical about this.'

'There is *every* need for you to make me believe you will never go near her again or else the next person walking in your door will be a cop. And I'll be their star witness. The things I could tell them.'

'Fine,' Blue spat. 'You go back to that shitty little country town and that fallen down old pub and your posh girlfriend. I will be happy to never see your ugly face again.' Blue walked away.

Connor watched him go. Was that enough? Could he believe those words? He raised his hand, still curled into a fist. He had been so very close to smashing that fist into Blue's face. He thought he'd changed and become a better man, but he hadn't. He was still that teenager who had broken shop windows to steal a bottle of booze. He was still the gang member who had terrorised barmaids and taunted the police. Kayla and her child deserved better than him. He walked back to his ute, stopping to pull another piece of loose glass from the frame of the broken window. He didn't care about the damage to his car, but as he got behind the wheel, he could still hear her words.

This is your fault.

She was right. He didn't deserve Kayla, but he wasn't sure he could leave her either. And not while the threat of Blue still loomed. He would stay at the Gateway. He'd keep trying to make amends for his previous life. He'd make sure Blue kept his word, and if he was lucky, he might see that baby girl grow up from a distance. She wasn't his daughter and he had no right to be part of her life, but in even those brief moments when he'd seen her tiny face, he'd loved her as if she was his. He would protect her with his life if he had to.

He started the engine for the long journey home.

★★★

Dawn was approaching by the time he was back in Scone. He knew he needed sleep, but the only place he wanted to be was the hospital. He needed to see Kayla and the baby, to reassure himself they were all right. Then he would walk away, just as Kayla wanted him to. People found honesty at extreme moments and he believed she was right. It was his fault the perfect birth she'd planned had been taken from her. So he'd content himself with making sure she was safe and letting her get on with the life she wanted. Let her find her perfect life.

He walked into a hospital not yet beginning to wake up. That's when he realised he had no idea where Kayla and the baby might be. He imagined they'd be in a room somewhere, but he couldn't just walk around looking for her. There was no-one at the front desk, so he went into the waiting room. He'd wait there until a member of staff appeared and then he'd ask them for help. If he could catch a glimpse of Kayla and the baby through a door, that would be enough. It would have to be. Surely not even the toughest matron would deny him that?

★★★

'Sir. Sir. Are you all right?'

Someone was gently shaking Connor's shoulder. He dragged himself back to wakefulness.

A young nurse was looking down at him with a serious face. 'You shouldn't be sleeping here. Are you all right?'

'I'm sorry.' He sat up, his muscles complaining bitterly. He ran his hands over his face. 'I wanted to find out how one of the patients is doing, then I'll leave. I don't want to disturb them.'

'You must know that visitors aren't allowed at this hour.'

'I know. But I want to know if Kayla and the baby are all right. I brought them in yesterday—'

The nurse smiled. 'You must be Connor.'

That was a shock. 'How ...?'

'The whole hospital is talking about how you brought her here in the back of your ute.'

'Oh.'

'She's so lucky you found her. It could have been touch and go for the baby if you hadn't got her here in time.'

He shook his head in denial. The nurse was wrong. They all were. 'Are they all right?'

'Yes. Of course. They're fine.'

His shoulders sagged with relief. 'Thank you. I guess I should go now.'

The nurse hesitated. 'I shouldn't do this, but it's so early, there's no-one here yet. If you promise not to wake either of them, you can take a quick look through the door. Just to set your mind at rest.'

'Thank you.'

He got to his feet and followed the nurse. She stopped outside a room. There was a glass panel in the door. He stepped up to it, saw the crib, the tiny figure inside.

'You can stay here for a couple of minutes, then you have to go. All right?'

Connor nodded, unable to speak. The nurse walked away.

He could barely see the baby. He gently pushed the door open a few inches to get a better look. She looked so tiny. Tiny and infinitely fragile.

'Hello, little girl. I'm so sorry your arrival in this world wasn't how it should have been. That was all my fault,' he whispered. 'I'm glad you and your mum are doing fine. That's all I ever wanted. Your mum is amazing. You're so lucky to have her.'

'And we're lucky to have you.'

The sound of her voice, gentle yet strong, was like soft rain in a desert. He pushed the door open a little more.

Kayla was awake and beckoned him into the room.

'I've called her Kathy, after my mother.'

'That's nice.' He still couldn't look at her. 'Kayla. I am so sorry. If it wasn't for me—'

'If it wasn't for you, I wouldn't be safely here in the hospital with my daughter. That's all I know or care about.'

'They will never come back,' he said. 'I'm sure of that.'

'And if they do, we'll deal with it,' Kayla said.

He thought he heard a new strength in her voice—a mother's strength. She slipped out of bed and gestured for him to come closer. Together, they stood by the crib and the sleeping baby. He almost stopped breathing as Kayla's hand reached for his and their fingers entwined. Then she kissed him on the cheek. In disbelief, he turned to look into her eyes. The love he saw shining there was more than just a mother's love for a child—it was the promise of a whole new world.

Kayla put her hand into the crib and gently stroked the baby's arm with one finger. 'Baby girl, I want you to meet Connor.' After a few seconds, she removed her hand. 'It's your turn now.'

'I—I might hurt her.'

'Connor Knight, you could never hurt her.'

Tentatively, he reached into the crib. Following Kayla's example, he gently stroked the baby's arm with the back of one finger. She was warm and soft. He did it again, and this time his finger brushed the palm of her tiny hand. Small fingers curled around his tattooed finger and stole his heart.

Beside him, Kayla smiled. 'Perfect.'

EPILOGUE

The wedding party had moved into Willowbrook's ballroom and from the sound of things, they were having a good time. Kayla paused on the grand staircase to listen. She hadn't organised this wedding. Jen had done it all and she'd done a great job. In the weeks since Kathy's birth, Jen had completely taken over Willow-brook Weddings. She, Brad and the kids had moved into a cottage on the outskirts of Scone. Brad worked some shifts at the Gateway with Connor but had recently been offered some part-time relief teaching. Connor and Brad had spent a lot of time together and had become friends. Connor never told Kayla what he and Brad talked about, but she had seen how the tension in Brad was slipping away as he took back the life he had lost. The love between Jen and Brad was strong and the kids were thrilled to have their father back. Kayla knew they would all be fine.

Kayla's contribution to this wedding had been the dress, which everyone agreed was a roaring success. It was one of the designs she'd been taking to the seamstress the day Kathy was born. Kayla had shown the dress to the baby this morning, before the bride arrived, and told her the story of her birth. Kathy had smiled and chuckled, not understanding a word. Maybe Kayla would tell her again when she was older. For now, it was enough that Kathy was growing, was strong and healthy despite her early and fraught arrival. Kayla didn't have nightmares about the bikies very much any more. Or about going into labour on the side of the road. And when she did, Connor was there to hold her in the darkness.

Kayla put her arms around the child in the carrier nestled against her chest. They were both rugged up warmly against the first autumn chill. Kathy's knitted bonnet matched her eyes, which were still blue-grey and showed every sign of staying that way. A lock of dark amber hair peeped out from under the wool.

'Shall we go?'

Connor was waiting for them outside the kitchen door, wearing the Akubra he'd worn almost every day since Christmas. As always when she approached him like this, Kayla felt a surge of love and gratitude. How had she ever judged him because of the prison tattoos that still marked his hands? Hands that held Kathy gently and rocked her to sleep? Hands that brought such joy to Kayla when they touched her body? He was the only man she had ever loved. Would ever love.

Another burst of laughter from the wedding guests followed them down the path. They walked past the stables and Kayla raised a hand to Lizzie and Mitch, who were in the exercise yard working a couple of horses. Then Kayla led the way towards the lone tree on top of the hill. They didn't hurry. The sky above was brilliant blue dotted with white clouds and the sunlight streamed down on the paddocks and the homestead.

At the top of the hill, Connor opened the iron gate leading to the little graveyard. The stone grave markers looked a little more worn than last time Kayla had climbed the hill, but the names engraved on them remained clear.

'Mum. Dad. I want you to know. There's another generation of Lawsons for Willowbrook. Meet your granddaughter. Her name is Kathy. After you, Mum.'

Kathy gurgled happily.

'When she's old enough to understand, I will tell her about her biological father. She has a right to know. Maybe she'll want to meet him one day. I'll let her choose. But regardless of that, she will always have two parents who love her.'

A light breeze rustled the tree above them as Kayla turned to face Connor.

'Mum and Dad, this is Connor. He is the best man I've ever known. He's kind and honourable. Smart too. And funny. He had a bad start in life, but he's turned that around. Mum, Dad—I love him. So does Kathy. And he loves Kathy as much as any biological father ever could. If he'll say yes, I'd like him to be part of our family.'

Connor's brow creased, but he said nothing.

'Connor?' Kayla smiled. 'Connor, I'm asking you to marry me. Please say something.'

'But—'

'Are you going to say yes, or do I have to get down on one knee?'

'No. I mean yes. I mean … That's my job.' Connor dropped to one knee and took Kayla's hand. With his free hand, he gently touched the baby's blanket.

'Somewhere in my life, some day I don't remember, I must have done something to make the gods smile on me. I will marry you, Kayla. I will be a father to Kathy. I will protect and love you both until my last breath.'

He kissed her hand.

ACKNOWLEDGEMENTS

Once again I find myself thinking of all those people who help me every day as I pursue this weird and wonderful writing career.

There's my publisher Rachael Donovan and my editor Julia Knapman and all the team at HQ. My agent Julia deserves a medal for putting up with me at times. But there are a lot of others too … fellow writers who understand and are there whenever I need them, especially the Quayistas and the Naughty Kitchen. I love you all so very much.

My husband John—words are not enough to express my love and gratitude for all your support.

And you, dear reader. A book is nothing without a reader. To use the words made famous by Tom Cruise—in this endeavour, you complete me.

Thank you all.

Janet

talk about it

Let's talk about books.

Join the conversation:

f @harlequinaustralia

♪ @hqanz

◉ @harlequinaus

harpercollins.com.au/hq

If you love reading and want to know about our
authors and titles, then let's talk about it.